"And then we get hit. A 20mm punches through the side armor and it's rattling round from wall to wall to wall, and it's taken half my gunner's head off and I've got his blood all over me and I'm ducking and trying to see and not run into anything. There's flame coming in through the view slit and I think we're on fire because my eyebrows smell like they're burning and my goggles are starting to melt, but, in fact, we've only run through a napalm smear that's all but burnt out, but I'm still thanking Jesus that I've got solid tires on the rig.

"Then finally the choppers run out of juice and peel off and the ground troops make their move. They got full-sized tanks, M5s and M7s, and they're pounding on us nearly as bad as the gunships, but at least it gives some of us a chance to run. I mean, those tanks, those sons of bitches, they got muscle but they're slow. That's all I can say, thank God they're slow. That was the only thing that saved our ass."

**Other Car Warriors™ Adventures
published by Tor Books**

*The Square Deal* by David Drake

# BACK FROM HELL

## CAR WARRIORS™ #2

## Mick Farren

A TOM DOHERTY ASSOCIATES BOOK
NEW YORK

Note: If you purchased this book without a cover you should be aware that this book is stolen property. It was reported as "unsold and destroyed" to the publisher, and neither the author nor the publisher has received any payment for this "stripped book."

This is a work of fiction. All the characters and events portrayed in this book are fictitious, and any resemblance to real people or events is purely coincidental.

CAR WARRIORS II: BACK FROM HELL

Copyright © 1999 by Mick Farren

*Car Wars*™ and *Car Warriors*™ are registered trademarks of Steve Jackson Games Incorporated, used under license. All characters in this book are the property of Steve Jackson Games Incorporated.

All rights reserved, including the right to reproduce this book, or portions thereof, in any form.

A Tor Book
Published by Tom Doherty Associates, Inc.
175 Fifth Avenue
New York, N.Y. 10010

Tor Books on the World Wide Web:
http://www.tor.com

Tor® is a registered trademark of Tom Doherty Associates, Inc.

ISBN: 0-812-51991-4

First edition: March 1999

Printed in the United States of America

0 9 8 7 6 5 4 3 2 1

# BACK FROM HELL

## CHAPTER ONE

After the two-hour free-for-all, the arena was littered with the hulks of stalled, damaged, and burned-out vehicles. During some games, the wreckers constantly darted in and out, hauling away the debris, clearing the field of play. Through others, though, the wreckage was allowed to remain where it lay until the end of the session. It was largely a choice of the director. Some went for a clean ring, letting the one-on-one combat speak for itself, but an increasing number favored what was being called the "armageddon look," turning the arena into a cluttered battlefield, a chaos of burning oil, twisted metal, and drifting black smoke.

Like most drivers, Val Paladin loathed the armageddon look and the way that it was becoming the latest fad in TV autoduel. It made skill and experience increasingly irrelevant and introduced too much random chance into a sport that was already pushing the envelope of luck and fatality. Autoduel players took enough risks as it was without factoring in sudden areas of poor visibility and a mess of random obstacles.

Paladin hastily spun the wheel of the Kali as a big

old Colossus cabover loomed out of the smoke, coming round to broadside him. Paladin looked for Turk, but with all the smoke and the crap that dotted the field, he couldn't see his partner's bright orange Desperado anywhere. He cursed the director and spoke quickly into his headset.

"Yo, Turk. Where are you, bro? That kid in the Colossus is dogging my ass again."

Paladin loosed a burst from his ATGs, and the Colossus veered off, looking for a less dangerous target. They'd been having trouble with the new fish in the Colossus all afternoon. He was a pushy kid looking to make a rep for himself by going after the big name featured players, something that went against the unwritten rules of TV autoduel.

Turk's voice crackled in Paladin's helmet. "I can't help you, buddy. I'm over here by the wall but I got nothing to shoot with, I'm tapped out of everything, and my armor's bald."

"So head in. You been out here long enough."

Turk laughed. "Screw that. I'm just ten minutes short of the duration bonus and I need the money. I'm hanging. Just staying clear of the fun'n'games and coasting for the cash."

Paladin smiled to himself. No shame attached itself to a featured player who decided to coast for the cash. That was the way the front office liked it. Paladin and Turk were two of the highest paid drivers at the Pomona Bowl, and they didn't go out of their way to solicit grief. At Pomona, as at the other major autoduel bowls across the country, the featured players were a big deal. They had fan clubs, product endorsements, and deals with toy manufacturers. They weren't supposed to jump into every bit of available heat and get themselves greased for zip. Featured players picked their moves, fast and flashy for the cameras, and got the hell out again. The arena had plenty of eager-beaver newcomers to make up the body count.

Paladin circled the arena, also not looking for trouble. Time would be called on the free-for-all marathon in a matter of minutes, and even though he wasn't on a start-to-finish bonus deal like Turk, it still looked good if you stayed to the end. The kid in the Colossus was at it again, now charging across the width of the arena straight at Petey Lee's brand new Lambard. Paladin switched channels on his com-set to the one that connected the drivers with the control room and was just in time to hear Lee's lazy southern drawl complaining about the kid. "Will someone call off the silly son of a bitch, and tell him to stick to the script? I ain't looking to get myself killed this late in the day."

The field manager's voice came on the net. "Field One to Colossus One. Will you knock that off? You ain't going to make yourself a star by messing with everyone in sight."

Either the kid's radio was out, or he thought that he could buck the field manager. Either way, he kept on going, straight for Lee's Lambard. Lee desperately spun his car out of the way, but the Colossus altered course, seemingly bent on a suicidal impact. In Paladin's helmet, Petey Lee's voice sounded uncharacteristically ruffled. "What's your problem, kid? You got a death wish?"

The question was followed by a short ominous silence and then a shouted exclamation by Lee.

"Holy Jesus!"

His voice was cut off by a burst of static and the boom of an explosion from the other side of the arena as a ball of orange flame went rocketing into the sky. Stunned drivers broke normal radio discipline as they reacted to the two needless deaths.

"Petey's rack blew!"

"What did that idiot kid think he was doing?"

Both units were burning, and Paladin couldn't see how either driver could have come out alive.

"This shit is getting out of hand!"

Moments later, the time tone, indicating that the session was over, came loud and clear through Paladin's headset. It was a few minutes early. The director must have decided to halt the free-for-all before things turned any uglier. Paladin breathed a sigh of relief. "Thank God for that."

He switched back to his closed link with Turk. "Hey bro, let's hang it up and take it in. I need to get good and drunk."

Paladin could imagine Turk grinning as he answered. "A-firm on that, buddy."

Turk was coming around a pile of wreckage, heading for the gate on a line that would take him past the still burning remains of the Colossus and Petey Lee's Lambard. The rocket seemed to come out of nowhere, and as far as Paladin could tell, it must have hit Turk's Desperado in a soft spot where his armor had balded out. Whatever the answer, the Desperado fireballed, right before Paladin's eyes. He couldn't believe what he was seeing. Even in the worst grudge match, it was unthinkable that anyone would go on shooting after time had been called.

"Who the hell fired that thing?"

A second later, his question was answered. A black figure, trailing smoke and with the charred rags of his battle suit flapping around him, staggered from behind the ruined Colossus. Somehow, the fish had survived the wreck, not only bailing out blind side to the cameras, but also taking some kind of shoulder-mounted RL with him. The kid must have been badly burned and crazy with pain, or maybe he was just crazy from the get-go, in the throes of a do-or-die, glory dream. Either way, he'd taken it into his head to lay low in the shadow of the hot wreckage until he saw a suitable target for his RL. Turk had just been in the wrong place at the wrong time, and now Paladin's partner was dead.

With the last of his strength, the kid waved his arms above his head in a gesture of triumph. Cameras were closing on him and he was going for his moment in the spotlight. This fish was truly insane. Fury overwhelmed Paladin. He floored the Kali, heading straight for the kid. The fish didn't even see him coming. He was too busy posing for the cameras, doing some weird spastic victory dance. The front fender of the Kali took him out at the knees; he bounced from the hood, left a smear of blood across the car's Lucite windshield, and was then thrown high in the air.

Paladin didn't even bother to look where the body had landed. He braked the Kali hard, threw off his safety harness, pulled the lines from his helmet, and ran for the burning Desperado. A fire truck was already on the scene and foaming the wreck. A paramedic unit was screaming out of the gate with its sirens blowing. As Paladin came running up, one of the fire crew turned and looked at him.

"You whacked that bastard good. He had it coming, firing after time was called."

Paladin took no notice. "That's my partner in there! We go back years!"

The fireman didn't look particularly concerned. "Figure you're going to have to find a new one."

Paladin knew he wasn't acting rationally but he didn't care. "Get him out of there!"

The fireman didn't seem to be getting the message. He continued to shoot foam at the wreck. "We're doing the best we can, but you gotta face it, Paladin. He's barbecue."

Paladin swung round and grabbed the fireman by the front of his flamesuit.

"You get him out of there!"

A second fireman moved in and took Paladin by the arm. "Come on, man, get a grip. We'll cut him out as soon as we got the wreck cool. The freezer truck's coming, and if his head ain't burned too bad and they can get a brainread, you'll have your partner cloned and back in a couple of weeks."

"I want Turk. I don't want to be partnered by any damned clone."

Paladin's most fervent hope was that he'd never be cloned. He prayed that when his time came, his head would be smeared along a hundred yards of highway, completely unreadable. He'd stood and watched while the firemen had finished foaming down the Desperado and while they'd cut Turk's body from the wreckage and loaded what was left of him into the freezer truck. Gold Cross had a mobile right at the Pomona Bowl that was capable of brain and tissue extraction. From there, the vital brain section and the basic DNA samples would be choppered out in a container of liquid nitrogen to the big Meditech cloning facility in Torrance. If all went according to plan, and some minimum-wage lab assistant didn't screw up the mindread, a few weeks could see a newly cloned Turk in the arena. Here comes the new Turk just like the old Turk.

Only Paladin had never quite bought the idea of cloning. Amalgamated Meditech promoted it as though it was the next best thing to immortality, but Paladin had seen enough clones in his time to know that this claim was somewhere between hype and a damned lie.

Clones were never quite right, always a bit missing, never firing on all cylinders. Val Paladin would never be convinced that they were anything more than a sorry facsimile. They always suffered from those glazed moments of zombie blankout when it seemed as though sections of their memory weren't quite making contact. Paladin had known several men who'd been cloned back to life. Their wives or girlfriends always left them within a matter of months. That had to say something.

As far as Paladin was concerned, whatever creature might come back from Gold Cross, it wouldn't be the Turk that Paladin had known. It wouldn't be the old Turk, just some unsatisfactory replica, strictly for the crowds and TV cameras, walking like Turk and talking like Turk. But Turk—the real Turk—was dead and gone, his spirit departed to wherever the dead went. Or maybe nowhere.

Later that night, sometime after midnight, Val Paladin walked through the rear security area of the Pomona Bowl. The arena floodlights had been turned out, and the spectators had retired to their motels or the tents and RVs on the campground. This backstage area, however, still had a life of its own. Shouts and drunken laughter spilled from the doorway of the Leper Colony, the cantina that catered to the players and crew of the Bowl. It was the same after any arena meet. Shots of Jack Daniels chased down with Himmler Triple-X, loud talk, and games of grabass with the regular pit-bunnies and the new crop of mystery girls who always managed to make it into the rear area at the end of the day's business. Later, fistfights might break out as the air filled with smoke and booze.

Nobody expected anything less. A good deal of drunken craziness went with the territory. One of the major sponsors of the Pomona Bowl was, after all,

Himmler Beer. The idea was even enshrined, with a gladiatorial flourish, in the scrawl over the entrance to the bar. WE WHO ARE ABOUT TO DIE, PARTY!

Very soon the party would degenerate to the final phase of the night, bleary mindless groping in the semi-darkness as the lights of the cantina were progressively dimmed. Faceless sex was the last move of men and women feeling the need to prove to themselves and the world just what big, bad, fearless sons of bitches they really were. Normally Val Paladin would have been right there, drinking and grabbing with the best of them, working as hard as anyone on the desperate morning hangover. This night was different, though. Turk was gone and Paladin wanted to be alone. He owed Turk that much.

Paladin and Turk went back some years. The first rule for duellists was *Never make personal attachments*, but with Turk it had been unavoidable. The short, muscular little man with the shaved head offered unshakable, almost dogged loyalty to anyone whom he considered a friend. They had first crossed paths back in 2037, at the Macon Duel Extravaganza, when both of them had been barnstorming their individual zigzag ways across the country, constantly switching handles, picking up what change they could at unlicensed arenas, faking their way into amateur nights, and playing staged highway fights for dubious promoters and unaffiliated hit-quit TV producers. For a time they'd even worked together as a two-man tag act under the name of the Manson Brothers. Before the old Vigilant station wagon, with the rotating top turret, shook itself to pieces over forty thousand miles of bad road, they'd hired on for a while as convoy guards.

Paladin took a deep breath. No amount of brooding was going to bring Turk back. The only trick was to blot him out of his mind and get on with the business at hand. Maybe that was the key to it all. The fun'n'games had become a business. What had once been a simple, if deadly, matter of man against man, machine against machine—rubber burning, blood pounding, and adrenaline pumping—was now a battle of point shares and residuals. Once he'd been able to revel in the awesome freedom of a killer on the road. Now, despite all the trappings, the money, the fancy clothes, the autographs, and the cheering crowds, his freedom had been bought and paid for by the company. He was working for wages, and according to the code of the old-time roadrunners, that was about as low as a man could go.

The transition hadn't been any sudden change. You took money for one assignment, and then another. The money came in handy. Pretty soon, you were getting used to easy living. Then, one morning, you woke up and found that you were working for the man, and there was no going back.

Another roar of laughter came from the Leper Colony, and Paladin shook his head. All this wasn't what he'd had in mind when he'd headed west out of crippled, riot-torn New Jersey, where he'd been born and raised, thirteen years old and packing with a bike gang. Or when he'd fought for his life in the ruins of Nashville among the survivors of that same gang after they'd run headlong into an armored column of slay-crazy religious fanatics calling themselves the Companions of Blood.

He wasn't proud of a lot of things that he'd done in the wild and woolly past, but at least it had all been on the level. He had never killed anyone who wouldn't have been good and ready to kill him right back, and he'd made it through the madness of the '20s and '30s without any great burden of regrets. Now, here it was

2041. He was twenty-nine years old and not at all sure about the turns his life was taking.

Paladin started walking, heading for the pits where Mac Connolly, his chief mechanic, and a half-dozen pit-monkeys were working through the night to realign the offside front drive linkage. It had started acting up during the final stages of the day's fun'n'games and had to be fixed. He could no way plead car trouble and drop out of tomorrow's line up. The special three-day, midweek event was a big deal, deliberately set up for the West Coast TV ratings sweeps. The featured players were expected to put on a show. These ratings sweeps were crucial in that they provided the numbers on which the advertising rates were based for the next half-year period. The networks would literally stop at nothing to come out on top. On the other hand, he certainly wasn't going out into the deadly madness of the arena with a car that was in anything less than perfect order. He'd be just begging for someone to waste his ass. The only remaining option was for Mac and his boys to sweat it through the night, running on pills if need be, to make sure that everything was 100% by morning.

The Kali sat crouched on the team service bay's hydraulic lift. It was low, sleek, and gleaming, a metallic hunting animal waiting to be loosed on the prey. Connolly was up in the driver's seat, running through the onboard computer functions with a CDU.

As Paladin walked into the service bay, the chief mechanic glanced down at him with an expression of irritation. "And what might you be wanting?"

Connolly saw little reason to be polite to anyone who came uninvited into his domain, particularly one as lowly as the mere driver of what he thought of as his car. It didn't matter what happened in the arena or on the TV screens. In the pits and the service bay, Mac Connolly was the undisputed king and the rest of the mechanics on the team, all highly skilled in their own right, were nothing more than slaves to do his bidding. A boyhood in the mean, murderous streets of twenty-first-century Dublin had left the tall rangy Irishman with an attitude. He'd rather die than kiss ass.

Paladin looked up and shrugged. "Just checking."

Connolly's scowl intensified. "And when did you start checking on me, boyo? Did I ever let you down?"

Paladin grinned. "Not yet."

Connolly scowled. "You should live so long."

"Like I said, just checking."

Connolly completed what he was doing and swung down from the car. He selected a socket wrench and glanced again at Paladin. "So how come you're not boozing and whoring with the rest of the rat pack in the Leper Colony?"

"I didn't feel like it."

"Sorry for ourselves, are we?"

"I said I didn't feel like it."

"So you decided to come over here and waste my time?"

The service crew were grinning at the spectacle of Connolly getting on the ass of the big-time showboat driver.

Paladin ran his hand along the bodywork of the car. "I gotta get drunk every night just to keep you happy?"

Connolly grunted. "Anything that keeps you out of my hair."

Paladin removed his hand from the car. "It's going to be different without the Turk."

Connolly nodded grimly. "Yeah."

The grins of the crew faded. Paladin walked round to the other side of the car. Connolly called after him. "It happens all the time. Life goes on."

Paladin sighed. "Yeah, right."

Connolly ducked down into the inspection pit. "You think Turk would want it this way? You moping around like Kevin Barry's fucking ghost?"

That was the formula. Show no feelings. A man dies and those who survived reminded each other that life went on. Death might be the only solid reality in this world of fun'n'games, but it didn't pay to think about it too much. Tomorrow it could be you. In Paladin's present frame of mind, most everything else seemed like shuck and jive. So little was real except the fact that every day in the arena was potentially your last.

Even the goddamned name Val Paladin was a phony, not even one that he'd invented for himself. It came from some long gone, twentieth-century TV show and had been handed to him when he'd signed the long-term contract with the Pomona Bowl and Skynet TV to become a featured player. It was a package, the name, the car, the black leather, comic book–hero combat suit with the chrome trim. Oh yeah, he'd become a bought-and-paid-for commodity when he'd signed on at Pomona. No doubt about that. The company owned him body and soul.

Paladin reached out and again touched the black bodywork. The paint job was like a mirror. Ten coats, hand rubbed. It was a pity that it had to carry the Himmler Beer "lightning H" logo along with his own chessboard-knight insignia, but nothing was ever perfect. The Kali was the real compensation. It moved and handled like a thoroughbred and had a power surge like nothing he'd ever driven before. Sometimes he thought that it was only the Kali that kept him hanging on at Pomona and continuing to go along with all the featured-player nonsense. Having one's dream car could make up for a lot of shuck and jive.

Even the Kali, though, came with shuck and jive. A production model Kali straight out of the showroom priced out just shy of forty grand. His car, the one that Connolly and his crew were so lovingly working on, must have cost close to a quarter of a million, a promo deal with Imperial Motors. The custom armor alone must have run to some fifty grand. The weapons system, the twin antitank guns, the micromissile launcher, the two left and right big birds, and the FCD under the body were all hard-wired to a Phoenix high-resolution onboard computer and patched to a Roth Look & Lock virtual-response helmet. The Kali all but ran itself. It hardly needed a human in the loop at all, except to die so the crowd could get its jolts.

The Kali was heavily armed, but even that came with its own measure of deception. All the weapons fired in the arena at Pomona used reduced charges. It was a piece of deceit that the drivers willingly went along with. It meant they lived longer. As weaponry became increasingly sophisticated, the expected duration of the average arena duel became shorter and shorter, and it was clear that if nothing was done to minimize the destructive force available to the contestants, arena duelling would become so swift, bloody, and ultimately so costly that it would price itself out of existence. Pomona had been one of the first to quietly adopt the policy of low-yield weapons, and most of the other arenas had followed suit in a matter of months.

Standing in the service bay, Paladin looked like one of Connolly's crew. He'd hung up the leather and chrome combat suit at the end of the day's fun'n'games. Now he was dressed in a set of dark green coveralls with the Imperial Motors logo on the back. He relished the anonymity of the drab coveralls. When he hung up the black and silver superhero suit, he also hung up the Val Paladin persona. It was a relief to have people treat him like what he was for a while rather than what they imagined him to be. Some didn't even recognize him when he took off the Paladin outfit. Certainly, the three Skynet executives walking into the service bay didn't recognize him at all.

Vanna Kreig and the two men in lightweight silk suits flanking her came into the service bay like they owned the whole Pomona Bowl, which, for most practical purposes, they did. Vanna Kreig was Skynet's Executive in Charge of Autoduel Productions. The two men, to judge by their heavyweight builds and scarcely concealed shoulder holsters, had to be her bodyguards.

Despite her elevated status, Kreig made the radical mistake of putting her first question to Mac Connolly, who was now checking the ignition coupling on the starboard launcher.

"You know where I can find Val Paladin?"

Connolly, who didn't give a damn about executive status and had an ultimate contempt for what he called "suits," paused for a moment, nodded, and went back to work. "Yeah."

Her face colored slightly as though, in that moment, her temperature had risen half a point. She arched a perfectly penciled eyebrow. "Would it be too much trouble to tell me?"

Paladin watched with a silent half smile from the shadows on the other side of the car. This was going to be good. Vanna Kreig could walk around the Pomona Bowl as though she was Queen of the World, but, unknowingly, she had entered someone else's kingdom when she came into the service bay. Connolly paused once again. His voice had taken on an impatient edge. "Listen, lady, if you hadn't noticed, I'm kinda busy right now."

Kreig probably hadn't been called "lady" in quite that tone for a very long time. She and her two companions were Hollywood through and through, and highly unaccustomed to taking lip from the help. Kreig was dressed in a black two-piece executive suit that was cut low enough, short enough, and tight enough to suggest exotic delights for any man who could make it through the ice field of her professional attitude. Her flaming red hair was piled on her head in the kind of conical bouffant that was the Hollywood highstyle of the moment, and her makeup seemed to have been applied with the same professional dedication as the Kali's paint job. Right at that moment, the full force of Kreig's ice field was directed straight at Connolly.

"Do you know who I am?"

Connolly remained unimpressed. He set down his circuit tester, turned, and looked her up and down.

"Oh yes, I know who you are. The real question is, do you know who I am? And do you want your star player out on the field tomorrow? Because if you do, I suggest you get the hell out of here and stop wasting my time. This a repair shop, not the information desk."

Paladin noticed that the two goons were looking a little uncomfortable. He decided he'd better do something before they made an issue of the way his chief mechanic was talking to their boss. He stepped into the light.

"You looking for me?"

Vanna Kreig spun round. The bodyguards tensed, ready to go for their weapons. Paladin held up both hands to prove that he was no threat. "What's the matter, don't you recognize me out of the hero drag?"

Vanna Kreig instantly recovered from her surprise. "Is there somewhere we can talk?"

Paladin looked around the service bay. "Here's as good as any place." He grinned at Connolly. "If Mac doesn't mind."

Kreig pursed her lips angrily. "I mean talk privately. I have something to discuss with you."

Paladin shrugged. "We can take a walk."

# CHAPTER TWO

Something was burning over on Bob Hope Drive and wild orange flames danced high into the night sky. It was probably the abandoned Mission Hills Country Club. Iggy Mengele and Billy Dalton, his second in command, stood on the roof of the Palm Springs Ritz Carlton and watched the fire. Iggy Mengele's eyes gleamed and a faint smile played around the corners of his mouth.

Dalton looked inquiringly at Iggy. "You think we should do something about that?"

Iggy grinned and shook his head. "Let it burn. I like a good fire."

This last statement was the absolute truth. Iggy Mengele loved fire. The bigger the better, and best of all when it involved a building of some kind. As a snot-nosed kid of maybe seven or eight, back in Tuscaloosa in the early '20s, in the years before he'd graduated to motorcycles and mayhem, he'd set a lot of fires. With total chaos all around, and the world breaking down in a horror of hunger and violence, it had been all too easy for a small boy to get away with arson. Of course, back in those days, he hadn't been Iggy Mengele. He'd concocted that name for himself when he'd stolen the ancient Harley Sportster and headed north to join the Tennessee cycle packs. The first name of a crazy twentieth-century rock and roller and the last name of a Nazi mass murderer seemed appropriate for a kid who was determined to make his mark on the world.

Fortunately for what was left of the city of Palm Springs, the sprawling resort complex that constituted the Mission Hills Country Club was surrounded by a parched desert that had once been an eighteen-hole golf course. The fire wouldn't spread. Nobody was about to waste water on putting out fires. Not that Iggy, Dalton, or any of the Horde that had now taken over the town gave a damn if the whole place went up in flames. The Horde would simply move on. Out in the deserts that surrounded Los Angeles, water was a lot more important than real estate.

Iggy continued to stare reflectively at the fire. "Ten years ago, they ran me out of here. It was when I was riding with the Losers. We thought we could blitz into town for some fun'n'games, but the local militia thought different. And they had tanks and a couple of helicopter gunships." His smile widened to a wolfish grin. "And now we own the place. All because they couldn't pay the water bill."

It was ironic that a simple thing like water, or rather the lack of it, should have brought about the downfall of one of the most affluent cities in the whole country. Water had always been a problem in Southern California, and as the area grew and developed through the twentieth century, it had become more and more pressing. By the end of the century water was being piped in from as far afield as Colorado and Oregon. This, of course, all stopped when society started breaking down at the turn of the century. Los Angeles itself had been saved by the giant Long Beach desalination plant that came on line in 1995, drawing millions of gallons a day straight from the ocean, but many of the small towns and outlying suburbs were helpless to stop themselves from simply drying up and reverting to barren desert.

The double irony was that Palm Springs had only failed when most other places were already clawing their way back to normality. With more millionaires per square mile than any other place on Earth, it had bought itself out of the worst of the worldwide social dysfunction. It had weathered the oil crisis, the brief nuclear exchanges with the Russians and Chinese, the grain blight, and the breakup of the Union. When law and order had failed in most other places, the citizens of Palm Springs—slogan "PS we love you"—had hired a formidable militia to scare off the marauding gangs. For a while, they kept the water flowing by paying constantly escalating, premium prices.

Even the wealthiest of cities, however, can't keep on paying through the nose forever. By the late '30s, the rich decided to cut their losses and pull out, heading for parts where rain fell from the sky and normality had reestablished itself without the crippling overhead. The summer of 2038 saw the great mass exodus. The rich took off in their armored limos and private aircraft and the poor were left to straggle back along the broken and dangerous Interstate 10 to the already crowded ghettos of South Central L.A. The once elegant streets of Palm Springs were left to the snakes and the lizards and a few tenacious desert rats who took up residence in the abandoned hotels and mansions. Beyond that, its ruins were nothing more than a stopover point for nomadic gangs drifting north from the fighting on the Mexican border.

While Iggy was watching the fire, Dalton had turned and was staring off in the direction of Indian Wells, where the highway ran along the base of the hills, out of town, toward Indio.

"Look at this, chief. There's more of them coming."

Iggy turned and squinted where Dalton was pointing. Diamond points of distant headlights were strung out along the road, moving through the darkness, clearly heading for Palm Springs.

Iggy slowly nodded. "That's another crew coming in for sure."

Dalton spat on the concrete roof of the hotel. "They just keep on coming."

Iggy continued to watch the lights. His face showed an unhealthy excitement. "Hell, let 'em all come. The more the merrier. We're building an army here, an outlaw army that's going to make the solid citizens crap in their drawers when they see us on the move. You know what I'm saying? Too many citizens out there thinking the likes of us are a thing of the past. They got their dole and they got their TVs and they think civilization's come back, Billy boy. Pretty damn soon, though, we're gonna teach them that ain't quite the way it is."

Dalton grinned. "Question is, what's this crew think it's going to find when it gets here? Are they coming in peaceable to join up with the rest of us or are they coming in for fun'n'games?"

"Most everyone's come in peaceable so far. But I guess we better get down and get ready for them, just in case."

When Iggy and Dalton reached the ground floor of the abandoned luxury hotel that the Horde had taken for their headquarters, word was already spreading through the campsite that another crew was coming in. The outlaw camp that, at sunset, had settled in to drink and party the night away was rapidly coming alive. Men and vehicles were on the move.

It was starting to seem as though every outlaw along

the southwest border had heard that something was coming together in Palm Springs. Burly men and hard-bitten women in ill-matched body armor and stained leathers, driving battered and blast-scarred fighting vehicles, were converging on the town as though it were their last hope. In the three weeks since Iggy and his Horde had moved into the ghost city in the desert, no less than five other outlaw gangs had arrived to join them, and they all told the same story. The border was tightening up. Too much of it was being turned into a patchwork of fortified towns and cease-fire zones. On both the Mexican and U.S. sides, from Yuma all the way to El Paso, army units were moving in to clean up the long strips of southern Arizona and New Mexico that had previously been outlaw country. The borders were hardly being tamed, but the stomping grounds of the old-style raiders were definitely contracting. Many who had treated the Southwest Strip as their private domain were being driven north and toward the ocean, into the badlands of the Mojave.

The ruins of Palm Springs had become a focal point, a place to face the moment of truth. The nomad gangs had limited options. The wealth of Las Vegas lay to the north, but with a formidable force of military and police defending it. To the west lay the sprawl of Los Angeles and the Pacific Ocean, the end of America, still fragmented and disorganized but with some heavily entrenched gangs of its own, well armed, toughened by decades of steet warfare, and pathologically jealous of their hard-won turf. If the nomads were going to retain any of their former glory and not just become dried-out desert rats and blow away, they had to take one direction or the other.

These thoughts were very much on Iggy Mengele's mind as he hurried out into the courtyard of the Ritz Carlton. This had once been the place where the wealthiest of Palm Springs' wealthy lounged around the pool and sipped their drinks in the lap of the most ostentatious luxury. A place of billionaires and presidents, where old men paid the bills and glamorous young women wore diamonds and bikinis. That was why Iggy Mengele had chosen the hotel for his headquarters. And that was why he'd watched with delight as the courtyard had been transformed into a nightly barbaric debauch. He saw it as the modern equivalent of the fall of Rome.

A huge bonfire of smashed furniture, dragged from inside the hotel, blazed in the dry bottom of the ornate, Olympic-sized pool, the centerpiece of a nightly revel that had been going on for three weeks now. Dark figures lounged around the fire, drinking, gambling, and shooting the breeze. In the deeper shadows, other dim shapes rolled and tumbled. Just like fighting men all through time, the Horde were more than willing to hang loose, doing nothing but losing themselves in booze and having mindless sex as long as the supplies held out and no one gave the order to move.

As Iggy walked through the smashed doors of the hotel and down to the pool, the men who, less than a half hour before, had lounged or stumbled around, either drunk or getting that way, were now up on their feet and watchful. Weapons were being kept close to hand and, over in the parking lot, engines were roaring into life.

Although Iggy was smaller than a lot of the men around him—a slight, muscular figure in a black leather tuck-and-roll jacket and pants and heavy steel-tipped boots—he moved with such confident authority that they stepped aside. He read that this had been Napoleon's secret. He had also been a small man, but he had conquered the world. Iggy's straight, greasy hair hung down to his waist, and an Indian poncho with a thunderbird design in black and red was thrown over his shoulders. The poncho flapped slightly as he moved, giving him the look of a hunched and determined bird of prey.

Iggy turned as a voice came out of the darkness. "Yo, Iggy, you know what's happening?"

Iggy Mengele wouldn't permit many in the camp to address him as "Yo, Iggy." Fortunately, the scarred and burly man in the stained plastic body armor, now striding through the darkness toward him, was one of the few who could. Wretched Larry had been one of the founders of the Horde and one of the Losers before that. He and Iggy had fought and partied up and down the Southwest Strip together, on and off, for the best part of a decade.

Iggy turned and faced the big man. Other members of the Horde were crowding around to hear his answer. Iggy shrugged. "You know as much as I do, Wretched. There's lights out on the edge of town like some new crew's coming in."

"Many of them?"

"It's hard to tell. Maybe a dozen, maybe more."

Another man spoke. Charlie Fats was fifty pounds overweight and so filthy in his habits that he even disgusted other outlaws, but he was one of the deadliest gunners that Iggy had ever run with. "Coming in quiet or looking for trouble?"

Iggy spread his hands. "It's hard to tell for sure. They didn't seem to be making any effort to hide themselves, so I guess it ain't no sneak attack." He thoughtfully ran his fingers through his long, greasy hair. "All we can do is wait and see."

When Iggy had started calling himself and his twenty-five followers the Horde, it had been little more than a joke, but in the short space of time they'd been camped in Palm Springs the joke had turned serious. Over 150 outlaws and their vehicles were currently gathered in the dry ruins. More were coming in every day, some alone, some in small groups of three or four riders, and some in large crews like the one that was now bearing down on them.

Each time a new crew came into the camp, it generated its own moment of tension. There was no telling until they actually arrived whether their intentions were temporarily peaceful or if they were kamikaze madmen bent on going out in a final blaze of destruction against their own kind. Weirder things happened.

These latest arrivals were generating more tension, however, than any of the previous crews. The other big outfits had come into the camp in daylight, giving those already there a chance to check them out. These guys were coming in by night, and that, in itself, was a cause for concern. In the dark streets below the hotel, vehicles were already moving into prearranged positions along the newcomers' most likely routes into town. Iggy noticed this with some satisfaction. The extended Horde was already starting to take on a certain military cohesion. When a threat was perceived, they went to work more like a team than a mob.

Not that Iggy Mengele was by any means the overall leader of this new enlarged Horde. He was smart enough to know that you didn't become warlord overnight. The individual crews still maintained their own identity, had established their own separate areas in the empty city, and for most of the time, they followed their own leaders. So far, the extended camp was formally being run by a committee of twelve—Iggy and the leaders of the larger crews plus a selection of the heaviest loners.

It wasn't a situation about which Iggy had any illusions. The committee of twelve could disintegrate into throat cutting and back stabbing at any time and without warning. It might work while the outlaws were just marking time, waiting to see what was going to happen next, but when the Horde made a move, the situation would change. One man would inevitably come out on top, and Iggy Mengele was determined to be that man. He knew if he didn't, he would die in the attempt. He had sufficient reputation that anyone else who managed to seize control of the Horde wasn't going to let him live. Iggy wasn't the kind to play the role of the loyal henchman.

Three of the committee of twelve were already coming through the crowd that had gathered by the Ritz Carlton pool. For Iggy, this was a good sign. They were coming to him to talk about the outside threat. It might be just because he and the Horde had been the first ones there and that their camp at the hotel was the best stocked, best organized, and had a commanding view of the city. But they were still unconsciously recognizing that he had authority beyond just leading his own crew.

Heading up the trio was an individual who went by the name of Tod Slaughter. The man had one of the most alarmingly disfigured faces that Iggy had ever seen. Legend claimed that he had been crushed and burned in the fighting outside of Tucson, and afterward had spurned all talk of reconstructive surgery. Slaughter was the headman in a paramilitary outfit of twenty or so vehicles that called themselves the K-90s. Iggy didn't know Slaughter well, but he had a feeling that both the man and his group could be trusted in a tight corner.

The same could not be said for the individual in the red leather zipper suit and bleached, spiked-out hair on Slaughter's right. Iggy had known Johnny Zone, the leader of the wild and totally disorganized Jetboys, for almost as long as he'd been running on the Strip. Zone was anything but trustworthy. He was the kind of road psycho who would shoot you in the back on a whim and then laugh about it. The only way to deal with that kind was to be very careful never to turn your back on them.

Iggy knew nothing about the third man. He was a silent loner called Ramone who had tattoos covering most of his visible skin. Ramone had ridden into the camp seven days before, driving a chopped and channeled sand blower with solid tires and a front-mounted Resnick laser. He had the hard-eyed reserve of a man who doesn't need to boast about his body count. When he spoke, which wasn't often, what he said was usually thought out and to the point. This was what had quickly elevated him to one of the loners' slots on the council of twelve. With so many psychos and hotheads like Johnny Zone, Iggy needed all the men like Ramone and Slaughter around him that he could get.

Slaughter came straight to the point. "We going to let this new bunch ride right on in here?"

Iggy looked at each of the three in turn. "You got a better idea?"

Ramone's eyes were hard. "I don't like it that they come in by night. They could have waited until daylight so we could have a chance to look them over."

Slaughter nodded. "It would have been the right thing to do."

Zone was studying Iggy's face, reading his reactions. "Ramone's right. They shouldn't be coming in in the dark."

Iggy did his best to sound noncommittal. "They may have their reasons."

Zone scowled. "And they may be trying to screw with us."

"So what do you want to do about that?"

Zone's scowl turned into a sneer. "I thought you were the big man round here."

Iggy let the contempt show in his face. This kind of thing was typical of the Jetboy. He'd start a fight even with a potential enemy bearing down on them. Suddenly Billy Dalton was at Iggy's side. In one hand, he was holding a radio phone, but the other hand hovered near the machine pistol holstered on his hip. Dalton didn't trust Johnny Zone any more than Mengele did. Keeping his eyes on Zone, he held out the radio phone to his chief.

"It's the lookout on Monterey Avenue. He's got visual contact."

Iggy took the phone. "Who is this?"

"It's Moose, chief. I can see them right in front of me."

"What we got here, Moose?"

"It's a mixed bunch, chief. There's some light armor, military stuff, a couple of funny cars, nothing too heavy apart from one big old battle truck."

"How many of them?"

"Fourteen, maybe fifteen units, all strung out like a convoy."

"How are they coming? I mean, are they moving like they were expecting trouble or what?"

"They're coming on real slow and cautious, chief, and they look like they're in bad shape."

"How bad?"

"At least three are burning oil and laying smoke, and they all look pretty beat up. I'd say that this bunch have been in some serious fun'n'games."

Iggy nodded. "Get on back here, Moose. I need you with me."

"You got it, chief. Moose out."

Iggy turned to face the others. "I'd say, while they keep coming in slow, we should let them come." He glanced directly at Johnny Zone. "Anyone got a problem with that?"

For a moment, it looked as though Zone were about to say something, but then the Jetboy appeared to change his mind. Iggy made a quick commanding gesture. "Okay, let's saddle up and move out to meet them. We may be letting them come in but that don't mean we can't be careful."

Followed by most of the men and women from the pool, Iggy hurried to the hotel parking lot where the Foxfire Hades was waiting for him, fueled up and loaded for combat. The Hades MK. 3, with its store-bought body design and its mirror-finish, laser-reflective armor, was hardly the typical vehicle for an outlaw from the Strip. It was hardly practical either. The light suspension was anything but all-terrain and, while the computer-linked triple machine-gun system packed a hefty forward punch, it left his ass completely uncovered. He would have prefered to hang onto his old CA trike, but the thing had taken too many hits and finally died on him with a series of bangs and a whimper.

It had been pure luck that the kid had come along in the Hades, otherwise Iggy would have been walking his way out of Casa Grande. He'd pegged the kid as an idiot from the moment he spotted him, and the kid had done nothing to make Iggy revise that first impression. A smart-ass, snot-for-brains highway dueller from some dogpatch town in the midwest boonies, who'd probably made a bit of a name for himself in the local leagues and thought he could rack up a rep on the Strip before it all went away. Dream on.

That had been Iggy's thought as he'd shot the kid. He'd come down to the Southland with his inappropriate car and his totally inappropriate ideas, and he had died a wholly appropriate death. If the kid had even been halfway smart, he'd have never allowed Iggy to fake him out of his car with the old corpse-on-the-highway gag, but he wasn't and he did and that was that. Now Iggy was driving the Hades, satisfied that it was okay for the moment but still looking out for something that would be a little more robust in rough country.

While his men went to their own vehicles, Iggy pulled on his helmet, eased into the driver's seat of the Hades, and snapped into the body harness. He tried the starter and the 200-cid plant snarled to life on the first twist. Maybe the Hades wasn't such a bad car after all. Before he eased it into gear, he hooked the helmet into the Phoenix weapon computer and booted the combat program. Illuminated targets floated like ghosts in front of the faceplate of his helmet, following his every move as he quietly nodded to himself. Everything was good. The trio of Vulcan machine guns were on line.

The Hades moved forward across the Ritz Carlton parking lot. A number of cars were all trying to get out of the lot at the same time, but all the others stopped and gave Iggy the right of way. Iggy grinned to himself. That was another advantage to driving some fancy showboat rig among a gang of dirty, ragtag, quasi-military machines thrown together out of cannibalized wreckage. Despite the dirt that the Hades had picked up along the road to Palm Springs, it still stood out like a pearl among swine.

Iggy turned right onto Palm Canyon Drive and headed east. Behind him, some of the K-90s had blocked off the intersection with Frank Sinatra Drive, setting up a major obstacle should the newcomers decide to try and move into the densest part of the town. Iggy liked the K-90s' style. They always seemed to be in place to cover his back. It was now Iggy's role, along with the men who had fallen in behind him, to go forward and meet the newcomers head on. It wasn't a role that he particularly wanted, but it was expected of a leader.

He drove quickly for about five blocks and then slowed, signaling to the men behind him that he intended to pull up at the intersection with Cook Street. As the Hades came to a stop, Dalton's old camouflaged Security Seven pulled alongside him. Iggy glanced up at the familiar bulk of the truck and saw Charlie Fats grinning down at him from the rear-mounted laser turret. Iggy smiled to himself. He was in good company.

The lights of the newcomers' lead vehicles were now a little over two blocks away. Momentarily, the spots on the armored scout car in the point position illuminated the tall dead sign that still stood in front of the Ramada Inn. Iggy cut in his own brights, flashing them on and off in a slow rhythm. The scout car flashed him back but kept on coming, although the whole column couldn't have been moving at any more than ten miles an hour. While he waited for them to come closer, he ranged the triple Vulcans to synchronize at a point halfway down the next block. Then he picked up the small microphone that was clipped to the dash and turned on the external speaker unit that had been one of his major additions to the Hades.

Iggy waited until the scout car was only yards from his guns' preset target point, then he rapidly flashed his lights and spoke into the mike.

"You will halt!"

Iggy's amplified voice boomed down the ghost-town streets, echoing off buildings. Above him, Charlie Fats closed and dogged the turret of the Security Seven. Charlie Fats wasn't the kind to take chances.

Iggy spoke into the microphone again. "You will halt or we will open fire."

For about five seconds, it looked as though the scout car was going to ignore his warning. Then it rapidly

## Back from Hell    31

blinked its own lights and cut in a red rear flasher. The newcomers were either going to comply or open fire. Iggy tensed and his free hand went to the Vulcans' firing toggle. He could imagine Charlie Fats crouching over the fire controls of his lasers. If the newcomers were intending to make a fight of it, they weren't going to find it easy.

The scout car was now moving almost exactly into his sights. Iggy's hand closed on the firing toggle.

And then the car slowed to a stop. Behind it, the rest of the column halted. Iggy let out a deep breath and let his hand on the toggle relax slightly. His scalp itched and he realized that he was sweating in his helmet.

Once again, he spoke into the mike.

"Remain exactly where you are. I'm moving forward to inspect your vehicles. I will not open fire if you remain exactly where you are. I repeat, I will not fire if you remain exactly where you are."

The echoes of his voice died away and the newcomers made no move. Iggy slipped the Hades into gear and moved forward at scarcely more than walking pace until he was just some fifteen or twenty yards from the point vehicle. Again he halted and waited. This time, however, he didn't have to wait too long. The flap on the armored scout's turret opened and a head emerged, a head wearing an antique leather flying helmet and round rubber goggles. The head was followed by shoulders and arms as a figure in a dirty, olive-drab jumpsuit hauled itself out of the turret, swung over the side armor, and dropped to the street. For a few moments, the figure tried to stand. Then its legs seemed to cave in and it crumpled to the sidewalk.

Iggy was out of the Hades and hurrying toward the body laying beside the scout car. Either the newcomers were trying some very elaborate fakeout or something was seriously wrong, and Iggy didn't believe that it was a fakeout. As he approached at a dead run, the figure tried to sit up. Iggy saw, to his surprise, that it was a young woman. She was in very bad shape. Black rubber from her goggles was ground into the skin around her eyes, and the right side of her olive drabs seemed to be caked with dried blood. She had the blank stare of someone who'd been to hell and back.

When she spoke, her voice was little more than a hoarse croak. "We would've waited until it was light, but I've got people who are in a bad way."

And, with that, she fainted.

## CHAPTER THREE

"Reports have been coming in for a couple of weeks now that the remnants of a number of outlaw gangs have been massing in the ruins of Palm Springs."

It had taken Vanna Kreig some minutes to come to the point. Up to then, she and Val Paladin had walked in silence, following the curve of the arena's perimeter wall. Her two bodyguards trailed a few paces behind, just far enough to create an illusion of privacy. Paladin was well aware that someone like Kreig hadn't come all the way from Hollywood to wish him luck, even though he was one the major stars of Skynet's autoduel programming. The network executive had something more serious on her mind, and the only thing to do was to wait until she came out with it. Now that the moment had come, Paladin was a little puzzled.

"Massing? Them border rats don't have the organization to do anything so complicated as massing. Maybe a bunch of them rode into the ruins to get drunk and party and see what they could find. There's always been rumors that there was treasure in Palm Springs. How some old millionaire stashed his loot intending to come back for it some day."

"Our information is that a large gang is forming."

Paladin continued to be dismissive. "Listen, everyone still talks about the great outlaw gangs, but the truth is that the really big gangs are a thing of the past. The big eastern crews got themselves mauled so badly back in '32 after the Crusaders tried to take Midville that they never recovered. Out here in the west, they've never managed to run packs of more than thirty or so. That's not counting the big urban crews, like the Crips and the Bloods in L.A. But they're different. Some of them go back almost a century."

Vanna Kreig kept on walking with slow precise strides. Paladin was certain that she was leading up to something that she thought was important but he couldn't, for the life of him, imagine what. "You used to be an outlaw, didn't you?"

Paladin half smiled. "It's all in the official biography."

Kreig shot him a don't-try-to-con-me look. "We all know how the official biographies get written. Were you really an outlaw?"

Paladin looked sideways at Kreig. She was so self-assured and sexy in the tightly provocative corporate suit, with one button more than necessary unfastened on her blouse just to draw attention to the high swell of her breasts. She was out to do a number on him and it wasn't just plain old fashioned get-him-into-bed seduction. Someone like her would never, ever come on to someone like him unless she had some hidden motive, but he still couldn't figure what that might be. Her face might be made up to look like a china doll in the popular Tokyo mode, and the flaming hair and the full red lips might make unspoken promises, but her eyes told him a different story. Those promises were just window dressing and they would never be kept. Her eyes were as cold and calculating as a shark's. Under a sultry layer of velvet, Ms. Vanna Kreig was all steel.

Paladin answered guardedly. "*Outlaw*'s kind of a relative term. It usually depends on who's winning and who's losing. You find the winners always claim that they were the good guys. You know what I mean?"

Kreig shook her head. "You rode with some of what were generally accepted to be outlaw gangs though, am I right?"

Paladin grinned. "Sure, I rode with some bad people. It'd be hard not to have. I was out there for more than ten years. Some of them got called outlaws, although back in the glory days . . ." He paused for a measure of effect. "Back in the real glory days, I didn't notice a whole lot of law to be outside of. Most of the time we just made it up as we went along."

Kreig gestured around her to the high walls of the Pomona Bowl, the towering spectator stands, the gleaming machines in the vehicle parks and service bays. "Aren't these the glory days?"

Paladin looked at her sadly. "This is show business, lady. That's what this is."

"No glory?"

"People still get killed, if that's what you mean."

"So you'd prefer to be living in the past?"

Paladin shook his head. "The past's gone. Dead and buried. Like I said, the great outlaw crews are a part of the past. Anyone with half a brain hung it up and came back in years ago. We're all working for wages now."

"But people still get killed."

Paladin's face grew hard. "You just take the pictures, lady. Let us worry about being killed."

Kreig's eyes locked on his. "What would you say if I told you that, right now, there were nearly two hundred outlaw vehicles in Palm Springs?"

Paladin halted. He'd had enough of this. "What's all this about, Ms. Kreig?"

Kreig also halted. "I just wanted your reaction."

The two of them faced each other. "My reaction is that someone's been handing you a load of bull."

"Just suppose the reports were true. What would you do?"

"What would I do?"

"If a small army of outlaws came rolling in, what would you do?"

Paladin laughed. "Do? I don't know. Maybe I'd join them."

"Does the name Iggy Mengele mean anything to you?"

Paladin's face suddenly darkened. "Iggy Mengele?"

Kreig smiled. "I see from your expression that it does."

Paladin took a deep breath. "I crossed paths with a man who called himself Iggy Mengele one time."

"Just crossed paths."

Paladin avoided her eyes. "That's another piece of the past that's buried."

"Maybe it's not."

"What's that supposed to mean?"

A smile played around the corners of Kreig's mouth. She was enjoying this. "Our latest information is that Iggy Mengele's leading this outlaw crew in Palm Springs."

Paladin thought about this for a few moments. "You seem to have a lot of information."

"It's the key to success in this business. Keep one jump ahead."

Paladin scowled. "I'd suggest that you check that information of yours. It's my understanding that Iggy Mengele's been dead these last eighteen months or more."

"Our sources are very reliable."

"It still isn't the way that I heard it."

Kreig's smile broadedned. "But you said you only crossed paths with this Iggy Mengele, so why should it mean anything to you if he was dead or not? Maybe you got it wrong."

Paladin slowly shook his head. "I didn't get it wrong."

She looked sideways at him. "Are you sure about that?"

"Sure as I can be without actually seeing the body."

Kreig seemed to be waiting for Paladin to say something else. He let out a long sigh. "Shall we cut the crap?"

"That seems like a good idea."

Paladin hesitated. He seemed reluctant to speak. "From the way you dropped his name on me, I figure you know that I more than crossed paths with Iggy Mengele."

Kreig had the look of a woman who knows she's won the round. "You want to tell me about it?"

Paladin shrugged. "Why bother if you know it all already?"

"I'd like to hear it from you."

"There ain't really that much to tell. Iggy Mengele killed some friends of mine."

"That's it."

"That's all I care to talk about. Like I said before, it's part of the past. One of the things I put away when I joined this circus and got myself a new name."

"Not if he's in Palm Springs."

"He's not in Palm Springs."

"Is it true that you hunted him all up and down the border after he killed these friends of yours?"

"I went looking for him. As it turned out, someone else got to him first."

"You really don't like to talk about the past, do you, Paladin?"

Paladin looked coldly at her. "I usually leave that to other people. It's always been my belief that dredging it up doesn't do anything to change it, so why bother."

"Sometimes the past dredges itself up."

A nerve in his face twitched. This woman was jerking him around and it was pissing him off. "I though we agreed to cut the crap."

"So?"

"So what is this conversation all about? You didn't come all the way out here just to tell me that some name from my past may not be as dead as I thought he was. I mean, what are you expecting me to do? Saddle up and go charging over there while you follow me with a camera crew? Pictures at eleven?"

Kreig's expression hardened. She was also getting angry. "That's exactly what I don't expect you to do. You've got a contract with Skynet, Paladin, and we expect you to keep to it. You're one of my featured players and I need you in the arena for the next two days."

The two bodyguards had suddenly become watchful. Paladin took a deep breath and did his best to look relaxed. The bodyguards were armed and he wasn't. "So what's the point of all this?"

"The other players in this arena look on you as some kind of leader?"

"I wouldn't say that."

"You're too modest."

"Maybe."

"Whatever you think, that's why I came to you first."

Paladin's face was set. "Keep talking."

"If our information is correct, and there is an outlaw army gathering in Palm Springs, eventually they'll be coming this way."

Paladin considered this. "That's not necessarily true."

"Two hundred men can't stay in Palm Springs for very long. Maybe a month at the outside. There's nothing there for them to live on."

"Why should they come this way?"

"They can't go back the way they came. The military already ran them out of the borders. Their only choice is to go either north or west."

"If I was in their position, I'd probably go north up to Las Vegas and try my luck there."

"Vegas is very well protected."

Paladin sniffed. "So's L.A. They ain't exactly going to be able to go walking in there either."

"Pomona isn't exactly L.A."

Paladin's eyebrows shot up. "Pomona? You think they'll come here?"

She gestured round at the stadium complex. "You have to admit that it'd make an ideal temporary base, at the very least. The place is built like a fortress."

Paladin looked hard up at the woman from Skynet. If it was possible, he now trusted her less than he had when they'd started the conversation. "If you're so worried about it, why don't you just send in the military and clean out the place right now, before this outlaw army can get any bigger? It shouldn't be too hard with air support."

Vanna Kreig laughed. "Skynet may be powerful, Paladin, but we're not that powerful. We can't just 'send in the military,' as you put it."

Paladin's face was a picture of stony disbelief. "You guys can get the military to do whatever you want."

When she didn't answer, he went on. "Or maybe you don't want Palm Springs cleaned out. If there really is an army of outlaws in there, maybe you'd like them to come here. I mean, that'd be some spectacle, wouldn't it? That'd pump the ratings. The last of the outlaws make their final stand. Outlaw barbarians against the autoduel superstars. You telling me you haven't thought about it?"

Vanna Kreig was silent, and Paladin's lip curled in a cruel smile. "You really get the prize, don't you?"

"What's that supposed to mean?"

"I always knew you suits were cold, but this is the big chill."

"You're paranoid."

"Am I?"

Kreig regarded Paladin with contempt. "Next you'll be telling me that I was responsible for this scum being in Palm Springs in the first place."

Paladin nodded. "I might, except I can't quite figure out how even you could pull that off."

Kreig stiffened. Suddenly she was ultraformal. "I've got some other people to talk to before I leave."

Paladin shook his head. "Whatever you've got to do."

He watched Kreig as she walked away. What in hell did she think she was up to? When she walked about ten paces, he called after her. "There is one thing you ought to consider, Ms. Kreig."

Vanna Kreig stopped and turned. "What's that?"

"Iggy Mengele running around loose with two hundred guns at his back isn't show business. It's a goddamned war."

She nodded. "I'll remember that, Paladin."

As soon as she was out of sight, Paladin hurried back to the service bay, where the Kali was still being readied for combat. Connolly looked up as Paladin walked in. "So what did her ladyship want?"

Paladin chuckled. "Well, it wasn't my manly body."

"That's too bad."

"She claims that there's a bunch of outlaws holed up in Palm Springs."

Connolly nodded. "There's been rumors going round about that for a week or more."

Paladin was surprised. "How come I didn't hear about that?"

Connolly grinned. "You were probably too busy signing autographs or posing for pictures. Can't expect the big star to stay in touch with what's going on."

Paladin blinked. "Is it that bad?"

"One of the prices of show business."

"You also hear that Iggy Mengele is supposed to be leading this outlaw band?"

Connolly looked sharply at Paladin. "Iggy Mengele?"

Paladin nodded. "That's what Kreig said."

The chief mechanic slowly straightened up. "Iggy's dead."

"That's what I thought."

"Killed by Ed Brand about a year and a half ago?"

"Right."

Connolly thought about this. "Maybe somebody had him cloned."

This hadn't occured to Paladin. "Cloned? Why the hell should anyone in their right mind want to clone a little monster like Iggy Mengele?"

Connolly wiped his hands on a rag. "I'm just saying it's possible. The why of it is something else entirely."

Paladin suddenly wished that he'd gone and gotten drunk with the other drivers. The night was turning out decidedly strange. "Now there's something to think about, Iggy Mengele—back from hell and with an army behind him."

## CHAPTER FOUR

"After the first half hour, it stopped being a fight and turned into a slaughter."

In the east, the sun was about to come up over the mountains, and the sky was the soft pink of a desert dawn. In Palm Springs the ruins were casting long purple shadows. Aside from a handful of posted lookouts, most of the camp slept. Some had made themselves comfortable in abandoned homes and hotels, but others simply snored where they'd fallen. Stinking in their leathers and body armor, they'd curled up on the cold hard ground, amid the garbage and discarded beer cans, scratching themselves, coughing, and muttering uncomfortably as the chill crept through to their bones.

Around the dying embers of the fire in the Ritz Carlton pool, however, Iggy Mengele and the rest of the council of twelve, along with a half-dozen representatives of the band of newcomers, were wide awake. Hollow-eyed and unshaven, maybe, but paying attention as the newcomers told their tale. As their story unfolded no one on the council spoke or interrupted.

The young woman who'd been in command of the

lead scout car had been doing most of the talking. Her name was Ilsa McCoy. When Iggy had first brought her into the camp and old Doc Christmas had stripped away her bloody coverall and stopped the bleeding, her wounds had turned out to be a lot less severe than they had at first appeared. Doc had done a patch job on her and given her a pain shot. Within the hour, she was sitting with the council, dressed in a pair of oversized borrowed blue jeans and a T-shirt that was almost clean, drinking tequila, and telling how she and her companions had been run out of the border country.

"We've tangled with the army before, you understand? But nothing like this. A half-dozen Piranha gunships had us bracketed, coming in from every side, throwing everything they'd got at us, lasers, napalm, rockets, the whole nine yards. It was like we'd just taken a dive into hell. Dust, black smoke, tracer, gas, the ground's shaking and there's stuff blowing up all over, huge billows of orange flame, and burning gasoline and you can't see ten feet in front of you. The guy running beside me in a Vigilante takes a direct hit from a full MFR rack from about ten feet above him and that big truck is just gone, man. I'm talking vaporized.

"And then we get hit. A 20mm punches through the side armor and it's rattling round from wall to wall, and it's taken half my gunner's head off and I've got his blood all over me and I'm ducking and trying to see and not run into anything. There's flame coming in through the view slit and I think we're on fire because my eyebrows smell like they're burning and my goggles are starting to melt, but, in fact, we've only run through a napalm smear that's all but burnt out, but I'm still thanking Jesus that I've got solid tires on the rig.

"Then finally the choppers run out of juice and peel off and the ground troops make their move. They got full-sized tanks, M5s and M7s, and they're pounding on us nearly as bad as the gunships, but at least it gives some of us a chance to run. I mean, those tanks, those sons of bitches, they got muscle but they're slow. That's all I can say, thank God they're slow. That was the only thing that saved our ass."

Every eye around the fire was on McCoy as she talked. Big bearded men with tattoos and chains, listening and thinking about how long it would be before the army took it into its head to exterminate them. Johnny Zone, however, was looking at McCoy as though he wasn't quite ready to buy her story.

As the girl paused to take a drink, he jabbed a finger in her direction. "What I'd like to know is what you'd all done to piss off the military so bad."

The girl treated Zone to a long, hard look. "That's the whole goddamned *point*. We hadn't done a damn thing to piss nobody off. There was no action anywhere and we hadn't gotten in any fun'n'games or nothing. We'd been camped maybe fifty miles east of Yuma and I'm not kidding, there was nothing going on. You know what I mean? We were running short of everything and starting to get kind of desperate."

A few of the men round the fire were nodding, indicating that they, too, had experienced the hard times on the border.

Ilsa McCoy went on. "Every day more pilgrims were coming into camp and everything began to get to be a problem. Finally we decided to convoy out and head east and see what we could find. Take the 8 as far as Tucson and then head for El Paso. Maybe cross the border into Texas or maybe up to Alamogordo by the nuclear test site . . ."

Iggy popped the top on a can of Himmler Old 500. "How many of you were there at this point?"

Ilsa scowled. "Sixty, maybe seventy vehicles. It was getting to be a big crew."

Charlie Fats belched. "It's the big crews that worry the hell out of them. Them soldier boys don't like to see no big crews mobbing up."

Johnny Zone shaking his head. "You must have done something. That was always the deal with both armies, the Mex and the U.S., we don't screw around with them and they don't screw with us."

Another of the newcomers, a kid called Vinnie, in a Mylarflex flamesuit grunted. "I think someone canceled the rules. They hit us just because we existed and there were a lot of us."

Iggy wanted more details. "How long had you been on the road when they hit you?"

McCoy answered. "Just half a day. They didn't waste any time. First stretch of open country and they came out of nowhere. First thing we knew, the aircav were coming at us, close to ground level. We were all strung out for a couple of miles, just traveling. They went down that convoy killing everyone."

Sam Deuce, the leader of the Gypsy Bandits, one of the last of the old-time, patch-wearing scooter clubs, picked his teeth with a dirty fingernail. "Gotta be the way the game's going. We're a part of the bad old days that most of the citizens just want to forget. A lot of them out there don't want to be reminded of stuff that they did like five, ten, or fifteen years ago."

A loner called Crapshoot nodded. "Civilization's back and we just ain't civilized. They pulled the same shit on the Indians and now they're pulling it on us."

Now a number of the men round the fire were also nodding. Ramone was staring grimly into his beer. "I hear that, Crapshoot. I hear that. The whole goddamned country's changing."

McCoy glanced at Ramone. "That's why we were headed down to Texas. Taking a chance it might be a bit better there."

Charlie Fats spat into the fire. "You woulda lost the bet. Texas ain't no different. Last time I went into Texas, I had Ranger and Border Patrol all over my ass. I heard how they're stringing the West Texas Frontier with all kinds of shit, sensor mines, bouncers, fixed firepoints, infrared remotes. Them Texicans really don't want anyone coming into their republic except by the road, where they can take a good look at them."

Johnny Zone slapped his fist into the palm of his hand. "I ain't going to be treated like some fucking Indian."

Iggy's face was hard. "That's what Geronimo said and look what happened to him."

Johnny Zone glared round at the others. "Maybe it's time for Custer's last stand."

Vinnie scowled at him. "That's what we said until we were half a day down the 8."

Sam Deuce looked questioningly at Ilsa McCoy. "You think these soldier boys are still coming after you?"

Ilsa shook her head. "I don't think so. We scanned behind us pretty good and we didn't see nothing. I figure that they had orders to fuck up as many of us as they could and run the rest out of the border country. I'd swear that they were herding us up this way. Just like goddamned sheep."

Ramone nodded. "That makes sense, but it don't really matter, do it?"

Crapshoot looked at him curiously. "What that's supposed to mean?"

Ramone unhurriedly took out a thin black cigar and stuck it in his mouth. He fished a burning ember out of the fire and lit it. "Seems to me that whether the army's coming after these guys or not ..." He gestured with the ember, indicating the new arrivals. "... doesn't really matter. We're here and there's more of us coming in all the time, and pretty soon we're going to start making someone nervous enough to want to mess with us."

Iggy took a long pull on his beer and looked at Ramone. "You got a point there, boy. Ain't going to be able to stay here much longer, anyway. Supplies are gonna run out on us."

Sam Deuce scowled. "Goddamned beer's going to run out in a couple of days."

Charlie Fats laughed. "Well, that settles it. If the fucking beer's running out, we gotta pull up stakes and move."

Johnny Zone was on his feet. "Move? Doesn't that mean the same as run? Is that the best we can do? Run? We're the goddamned last of the best here, in case you all forgot. If the rest of you want to be run around the country by the stinking army, that's your problem. Me and the Jetboys go where we want. Nobody runs us around."

Iggy didn't even look up at Johnny Zone, and few around the fire noticed how his expression had changed. Billy Dalton only noticed because Billy had seen it before. The muscles in Iggy's face didn't move. It was all in the eyes. They went dead, as though a light had been turned out. He shrugged his shoulders deeper into the poncho with the thunderbird design, as though the dawn chill was getting to him. Nobody noticed that his right hand was now concealed beneath the folds of the blanket.

Iggy crushed his beer can left-handed and tossed it into the embers. "So what do you want to do, Johnny Zone? You and your boys want to wait around here and explain to anyone who comes by about the 'you don't screw with me and I won't screw with you' rule? I don't think some aircav unit is going be listening too hard to what you might say."

"At least we wouldn't be running."

Iggy finally raised his head and looked up at Zone through the haze of heat above the embers of the fire. "You wouldn't be running, Jetboy. You'd be fried and no questions asked, sautéed in napalm, courtesy of the air cavalry."

Zone started around the fire. "What's the matter, Mengele? You lost your nerve?"

Dalton glanced at Iggy. He still hadn't moved and his right hand was still hidden. Billy Dalton had always known that, sooner or later, Iggy was going to clash with one of the leaders of the other crews. Everyone around the fire fell silent. Every eye was on Iggy.

Iggy's vice was cold and calm. "An old-timer once told me to always be sure that I knew the difference between courage and plain pig-ignorant stupidity."

Nerves twitched in Zone's face. "Are you calling me ignorant?"

Iggy gave the slightest nod. "And pig stupid."

The Jetboy's sidearm was an old Smith & Wesson .45 automag, once "the most powerful handgun in the world." It hung in a shoulder holster built into his red leather zipper suit. It looked flashy but was no good for a speed draw. His hand scrabbled toward the gun like a furious spider, but before he could reach the piece, another gun roared. Johnny Zone pitched backward and fell into the dying fire with a crash that sent a universe of sparks spiraling into the air. A wisp of smoke drifted up from a burn hole in Iggy's poncho. He had fired without even bothering to stand up.

Johnny Zone lay sprawled in the glowing coals. His hair burned and his leather suit started to smolder. It was only then that Iggy rose from his crouch.

"Does anyone have a problem with what I just did?"

Iggy reholstered his sidearm, but his hand still hung

dangerously close to it. Two men moved to drag Zone's body out of the fire.

Tod Slaughter, the leader of the K-90s, spoke for everyone. "I guess he had it coming."

Charlie Fats, however, added a qualification. "Could be the Jetboys won't see it that way when they hear you greased their leader."

It only took a matter of minutes for word of Zone's death to reach the Jetboys. With the rest of the camp asleep, the sound of them starting and gunning their motorcycles came clearly through the morning air from twelve blocks away, and everyone around the Ritz Carlton pool was looking at Iggy to see what he would do next.

The Jetboys' bikes were coming up the hill that led to the hotel. Iggy half smiled and shrugged. "I guess I better go see what they've got on their minds."

## CHAPTER FIVE

Putting on the superstar suit always made Paladin feel like he was assuming a whole new personality. First came the flame-retardant long johns, always a clean set waiting for him in the dressing room, spotless white, neatly folded, and with the Himmler lightning logo where the breast pocket would be if the long johns had one. He looked at himself in the dressing room's full-length mirror. The long johns were so crisp and laundered that they made him look like something out of a hospital or a research lab. It had to be the way clones looked when they were first awakened up, clean as a blank slate.

Next came the suit itself, hanging in the closet in all its somewhat ludicrous glory. Leather-finished Kevlar, with shaped plastic contour plates covering his chest, thighs, and arms, plus stainless-steel reinforcements at the knees, shoulders, and elbows, more decorative than functional. The suit wasn't the most practical outfit that Paladin had ever worn. It was hot and heavy and it cut his freedom of movement, but it looked pretty damn cool on TV, and that, after all, was why he was being paid.

He lifted the suit from the hanger and broke open the velex fastening that ran down the back like a false spine. He eased himself into the lower half of the garment, pushing down one foot at a time and hauling it up over his hips. It felt like putting on another skin, one that might have belonged to a rhinoceros. He hooked the sleeves over his wrists and pushed his hands all the way through, and reached behind him and closed the velex fastening. He straightened up and again looked in the long mirror. His own chessboard-knight logo was blazoned across his chest in bright red. All he needed was a bullet helmet and he could be the modern version of the Rocket Man.

He pulled on the heavy-duty gauntlets and carefully flexed his fingers. His time in the dressing room was close to a ritual. If nothing else, concentrating completely on the mechanics of preparation stopped him thinking too hard about the upcoming show. No matter how long a driver had been on the road, no matter how long he'd been a player or how many duels he'd fought, there was always the chance that the next show might be the last. No one was exempt from running up against an opponent who was faster, smarter, or luckier, but thinking about the possibilities was the fastest way to spook yourself. The dressing ritual focused his mind. It forced his nerves into a one-step-at-a-time mode and stopped him dwelling on what might be stacked up in the future.

As he was bending down and closing the snaps on the heavy steel-tipped boots, someone started hammering on the door.

"You decent in there?"

Paladin grunted. The show was rolling already. He

dropped into his professional growl. "I ain't decent but I'm dressed."

The door was pushed open and a skinny red-haired kid in a blue souvenir baseball cap from the Reno-Cannon International Spaceport was pointing a shoulder-mounted Minicam at him, shooting pregame color. Paladin's status as a featured player entitled him to a private dressing room, but that didn't keep the cameras out. Val Paladin assumed his show-time personality as routinely as he'd dressed himself in the combat suit.

Paladin's utility belt with his holstered sidearm hung over the back of a chair. The weapon in the tooled and decorated holster was a custom rebuilt H&K Starmaster, a long-barreled automag with a built-in laser sight. It had pearl grips and his knight symbol inlaid in gold. The gun was another ultraexpensive, top-of-the-line corporate tie-in, just like the Kali.

Under the cold eye of the camera, Paladin picked up the belt, strapped it on, and snapped the holster to the stud on the leg of his suit. Paladin casually drew the pistol, checking that the LEDs read safe and the clip was full. He spun the gun on his finger and dropped it back into the holster. The move was pure corn, right out of a twentieth-century western movie, but the fans ate up that kind of thing. The cameraman was grinning. He knew shtick when he saw it.

Walking tall, with his gleaming black helmet under his arm, trailing its air hose and computer multicables, Paladin emerged from the dressing room out into the general locker room where the rank and file had to change. The kid in the baseball cap, bent over in a half crouch, walked backward in front of him, shooting as he went. The locker room was crowded with players. If the camera hadn't been rolling, Paladin's entrance would have been met with ribald abuse, shouts of "showboat," and worse. The show, however, started right there in the dressing room, and going along with the Skynet script, the other drivers snarled at him with just the trace of apprehension that his star status demanded.

Paladin, going right along with the script, sneered back. He was promoted as one of the bad guys of the game, the black knight of autoduelling, and no one expected him to come on like a good sport. Leave that to the jerks in the red, white, and blue armor.

Bo Rheingold, the background color man on Pomona's team of sportcasters, dapper in white rollneck and navy-blue blazer with a multicolored Skynet insignia on the pocket, was working the pregame locker room with another camera jock. When he spotted Paladin through the crowd, he made straight for him, his cameraman following, and stuck a wand mike under his nose.

"Val Paladin, the man they call the black knight, and who's been described as every other driver's worst nightmare. I expect you're going to get your licks in today, huh?"

Now two cameras were focused in on Paladin, and without a doubt, it was going straight out on the satellite feed. Paladin struck an attitude of understated menace. "I never look for trouble, Bo, you should know that by now."

Another driver, dressed in a scarred and dirty leather coat, with the skull of a longhorn steer painted on the back, was pushing through the crowd, trying to bluff his way into the spotlight. Bull Nails was a second stringer, strictly cannon fodder as far as Paladin was concerned, but he seemed to be making a try at changing all that. He shoved Bo Rheingold roughly to one side and angrily shook his fist in Paladin's face.

"You ain't no nightmare, Val Paladin! To me, you ain't even a bad dream! You ain't nothing to Bull Nails, because I'm going to kill you today. You got my word on that."

The cameras pulled back a little, making Paladin and Nails a two-shot. Someone in the control room was going with the confrontation, sending instructions to the camera jocks through their lightweight headsets.

Paladin looked coldly at Nails. "It's a pity a boy like you, so full of juice and all, should have to die so young."

Paladin gave Nails the hard eyeball, but secretly he was quite amused by the interruption. The second stringer must have some stones on him, because he was taking quite a chance pulling a stunt like this. The front office could act one of two ways. Most of the time, when a player came on as pushy as Nails, they quickly got rid of him, conned him into a suicide setup, and that was that. Now and then, though, they could decide to feature the guy for a few weeks and see how the fans reacted to him. Nails must have decided that it was now or never.

The second stringer continued to play it for all he was worth. He stuck his face into Paladin's and bellowed. "It ain't gonna be me that dies out there today, it's gonna be you, Val Paladin! It's gonna be you!"

Bo Rheingold was giving Nails a hard look that said, "Move back, sucker, because this is real, this is the show." Nails wasn't so pumped-up stupid that he didn't realize that he'd had his moment of glory. If he pushed it any further, the control room would simply switch feed on him and he'd be gone anyway.

Nails backed off and Bo Rheingold was grinning knowingly into the camera. "Seems like we got a bit of grudge building up here, and maybe we're going to have to watch out for these two going head to head in today's arena action."

Paladin didn't like the sound of this. He could just imagine how some clever son of a bitch in the front office had decided that maybe there was some mileage to be milked from the incident and was right now changing the day's script, writing in some piece of fun'n'games between him and this Nails. The last thing that Paladin needed was some smart-ass kid looking to make a name by dogging on his back. Maybe he should just preempt the script and go after the kid, crush him the moment he got into the arena.

Rheingold had the wand mike back in Paladin's face. "Does that kid worry you at all, Paladin? This Bull Nails seems to have something bad going for you."

Bull Nails shouted from the background. "Damn right I got something bad going for him."

Paladin looked into the camera and made a dismissive gesture. "You should know by now, Bo, they come and they go. Mostly I send them where they're going."

Rheingold leered into the camera. "Well, my friends, there you have it. Val Paladin doesn't seem too worried about this new kid Bull Nails, but you never can tell what upsets can come, and what a difference a day really can make."

Rheingold and his camera were gone, but the redhaired kid in the baseball cap seemed to have been assigned to him for the duration. He signaled to him to turn off the camera. "I gotta go and look at the car and have a private talk with Connolly down in the pits. You can pick me up there in about twenty minutes. Okay?"

The cameraman shrugged. "No problem."

Paladin grinned. "This is the real deal, kid. They don't want it going out on the feed."

The kid with the camera nodded. "I got you, I'll catch up with you in a while."

The interior of the Pomona Bowl, the part that the public never saw, housed the TV facilities and the service areas, the drivers' locker rooms, the living quarters, and the big mainframes and effects systems. The various sections were linked by a confusing complex of corridors, passages, stairways, and catwalks. Paladin had been at Pomona long enough to have the internal geography down, but for the first few weeks, he'd wasted a lot of time wandering around lost and puzzled.

He came out of the locker room, walked down two flights of steel stairs, and turned into a curved corridor that followed the outer rim of the Bowl. It was the fastest and most direct route to the pits that would avoid further encounters with the likes of Nails or Rheingold or any more wandering cameras. The curved corridor was where some of the drivers, particularly the Latinos and the Indians, had put up small personal religious shrines. It was a tradition that had been established by the bullfighters in old Spain and carried on by the autoduel players of the twenty-first century. The front office was totally opposed to any hint of that kind of thing getting public. The Skynet suits liked to maintain the fantasy that the players really enjoyed going into the arena and risking their lives to entertain the unemployed burgerbrains out there in TV land. They squashed any suggestion that the drivers and gunners might be frightened or feel the need to pray. Or that they were only doing it because, after three decades of social chaos, they didn't know how to do anything else.

Paladin emerged from one of the outside doors and walked through the rear enclosure to the pits. Overhead, beyond the perimeter wall, an airship was coming in, nosing its way to the mooring tower, bringing a load of day-trippers from Los Angeles. Paladin stood and watched its docking maneuvers for a minute or so before walking on.

As he approached the pits, Paladin saw that the Kali had been rolled out and looked ready to go. This surprised him a little. He hadn't checked the player schedules, but he'd assumed that he wouldn't be going into the arena until well into the afternoon, maybe not even until after sundown, when the floodlights went on and the gags became a good deal more dramatic. Stars weren't usually wasted on the warm-up bouts, but, if Connolly had rolled the car out already, it must mean that he'd heard something different. The crew chief wouldn't leave the Kali sitting out in the sun for half the day.

Paladin quickened his pace. Connolly, who was kneeling down, checking something on one of the Kali's wheels, spotted him coming and stood up. Paladin pointed to the car. "What's happening? Am I going on early or something?"

Connolly seemed worried. "That's what they told me. They said you'd go in quite soon—maybe in an hour or so." He looked questioningly at Paladin. "They didn't say anything to you?"

Paladin shook his head. "Nothing."

He didn't like this at all: a change of script that he wasn't told about and Connolly with a worried expression. A nagging instinct was loudly insisting that something was wrong with this picture.

Connolly scratched his head awkwardly. "Listen, there's this rumor going round . . ."

"What rumor?"

Connolly was uncomfortable. "It's just a rumor, you understand?"

"So tell me."

"You may be getting set up for something."

Paladin took a deep breath. The nagging instinct was now working overtime. Something was definitely wrong with this picture. The cameraman taking shots of him dressing, the incident with Nails. The front-office suits did have a habit of setting up players for some dangerous gag without letting them know anything about it. The official explanation was that it was done to preserve the spontaneity of the game, but the players all knew it was a combination of deskbound contempt and jealousy. The suits liked nothing better than to screw around with the players.

"You got any idea what the gag is?"

That was the crucial question. Sometimes the setup would be a cliffhanger, a near miss that would bring the crowd to its feet, but from which the player would ultimately walk away. Other times, however, the set up would be lethal and there would be no walking away. Every so often, the suits wanted a star among the body count. It was good for credibility and countered the whispers that Skynet arena duelling was fixed. The corporation never missed a chance to score a few points in their running conflict with the AADA or to do anything to offset their reputation for bending the rules any time that it meant increased ratings.

Connolly sadly shook his head. "They're not going to tell me anything. I work for you."

Paladin frowned. "I need to think about this."

Connolly looked unhappy. "Listen, I'm not trying to spook you. Maybe there's nothing to it. You know how these rumors get started. I shouldn't have even told you about it."

Paladin shook his head. "No, you did right telling me. Ignorance only gets you dead."

Connolly nodded, but he still wasn't happy. "So what are you going to do?"

"I don't know yet. There isn't too much I can do, and there's no Turk to watch my ass. I guess I'll just play it as though all deals are off and I'm on my own. It won't be the first time."

A bank of monitor screens was set up on the other side of the enclosure so the players who were waiting for their entry cues could watch the action in the arena. The screens showed the raw images that were coming from the various cameras in and around the field, not just the edited version that went out to the public via satellite. It gave the drivers and gunners a better indication of what was happening all over the arena than the finished programming, which tended to concentrate on only the more spectacular shoot-outs and explosions.

Paladin gestured to the monitors. "I think I'll take a look at how things are shaping up. Maybe it'll give me a clue as to what's going on."

He walked over to where a small group of players was already watching the screens, drinking beer, and joking about the other drivers' plays. For the most part, they had already been into the arena for some of the first bouts of the day. They'd managed to come through unscathed and were now free, short of an emergency, to idle away the rest of the day getting drunk.

Paladin stood a little way off, looking at the multiple screens on his own. His problem was to try to guess what they might be planning in the control room. He wished that he had bothered to check who was directing this show. That might have given some inkling as to what was really going on. If the plan was to kill him off at some point during the day's event, he certainly wasn't going to go quietly. There was a hell of a lot more to life than putting on a show for Skynet and the great unemployed American public.

As far as he could see, nothing unusual was taking place in the arena. On the screen, a duo of ram drivers in Omega 25s were double dogging the crap out of a Firedrake, who, with his loads all shot, only had his flamethrower to hold them at bay. The gunner would swing the turret to target one of the Omegas and it would immediately sheer away, out of range, allowing its partner to come in from the other side and smash into the van with its Durastress ramplate.

This simple cat-and-mouse gag was a pretty standard routine for early in the day, and Paladin wondered if he was merely being paranoid. He'd been in the game long enough to know that all kind of idiot rumors circulated on the morning of a show. For all he knew, the one that Connolly had heard might well have been deliberately started by Bull Nails or some other upstart in an attempt to psych him out. That didn't explain, though, why the director was sending him in early.

Before Paladin could come to any kind of conclusion, however, his thoughts were interrupted by a woman's voice. "Hey, Paladin, how you doing this morning?"

Bambi Starr was a comparative newcomer to Pomona, but in the time that she'd been there, she'd made herself difficult to miss. She had a hard, lean body, full breasts, great legs, and a mass of curly blond hair that framed her face. If she hadn't been a combat driver, she probably could have been an equal hit on one of the TV jiggle shows. Despite his preoccupation, Paladin turned and grinned. What red-blooded autoduel hero wouldn't grin at Bambi Starr? "Looking good there, Bambi."

"A girl's got to get across any way she can."

Paladin nodded. "I seen you getting across in last month's *Duel* magazine. That was some picture spread."

Starr shrugged. "It goes with the territory."

"I wouldn't mind paying that territory a visit."

She pouted. "Thought you were too big-time for the likes of me?"

Paladin's grin broadened. "I could never be too big-time for you."

The story was that someone in the front office had spotted her driving in the pack at Hammer Downs, the big Detroit arena, and had liked what he'd seen. Bambi had been brought out to Pomona on a multiple-option contract to be groomed for possible stardom. She already had a small but loyal fan following, and a full-color 3D poster of her posing almost naked beside her baby-pink Cyclotron trike was selling all across the country.

Here in the players' enclosure, she wasn't much more dressed than on her poster. The leather shorts, ripped red tank top, and cowboy boots left little to Paladin's imagination, except maybe what they might do together if they ever found themselves alone in a quiet place. So far, they'd just flirted over drinks in the Leper Colony, and hadn't even come close to being alone.

This particular flirtation suddenly seemed to be over. Bambi looked Paladin straight in the eye. "Is it true they're gonna try to write you out of the script today?"

Paladin could feel his grin freeze. "Write me out?"

"You know what I'm talking about. Are they gonna try to kill you off?"

## CHAPTER SIX

The Jetboys brought their bikes to a halt some thirty feet from Iggy. They ritually gunned their engines before they let them fall away to an idle, and the gas-burners among them filled the morning air with blue exhaust smoke.

The Jetboys were, beyond a shadow of a doubt, the strangest crew in the camp. They all rode motorcycles, and, indeed, the only other vehicle belonging to the gang was a huge old Amex Commando, the bus-style troop transport that had been used extensively by the Louisiana People's Militia during the Civil War and the War with Texas. LPM insignia still showed through the bus's haphazardly applied psychedelic paint job. In the hands of the Jetboys, it now served as a kind of mobile supply depot, clubhouse, and the site of their famous rolling orgies. To say that they were colorful was an understatement. Charlie Fats had once described them as "street trash from Mars."

Imitating punk rockers of the late twentieth century, the Jetboys had no truck with ideas like concealment or camouflage. Their leathers and body armor ran to shocking pink, flaming red, or vibrant Day-Glo orange and green. Most refused to wear helmets, but the minority who did tended to deck them with feathers and animal horns, and one individual had welded a World War II bayonet to his, with the point sticking straight up. When the Jetboys went into a fight, they charged with all the reckless flash and flamboyance of Hungarian cavalry.

Right at this moment, though, the Jetboys weren't charging. They just stood and waited. The rising sun was in their faces and Iggy noted to his satisfaction that, in their haste, they had given him a slight edge. For almost a minute, they sat perfectly still, astride their machines, just staring with hard blank expressions, and Iggy, for his part, also did nothing. Predicting what the Jetboys might do under any given circumstances was a virtual impossibility. Iggy would let them make the first move.

Iggy had gone to meet the Jetboys on his own, but, to his profound relief, the situation didn't stay that way. Slightly behind him, Dalton and Tod Slaughter also waited, along with Charlie Fats, Wretched Larry, Ramone, and Sam Deuce, to see how the Jetboys might react to the killing of their leader. The rest of the council of twelve and the others from the pool had followed at a distance, uncertain whether they were backing Iggy or merely onlookers. Few of them had any love for Johnny Zone, but none seemed to have disliked him enough to automatically throw in with Iggy against the Jetboys. Two of the newcomers, however, Ilsa McCoy and the kid called Vinnie, were standing in back of Sam Deuce and Ramone, apparently ready to mix it up if needed.

The leadership of the Jetboys seemed to have fallen to a very tall and unnaturally thin individual called Masthead. He'd been riding point when the Jetboys had roared up and now he was the first to dismount. Iggy noticed that his right arm was hanging loose, close to the machine pistol strapped to his thigh. Masthead was wearing black motorcycle goggles, and Iggy would have preferred to see his eyes. Masthead pointed at Iggy. "Iggy Mengele?"

Iggy hitched up his belt and nodded. His own hand was also close to his gun. "That's me."

"Iggy Mengele, there's a story going round how you just shot Johnny Zone."

Iggy pushed back his poncho and nodded. "That's true enough. I shot the sonofabitch."

From the sound of his voice, Masthead was very drunk. He turned and looked at his companions. "Man says he shot Johnny Zone."

A kid in purple armor with hair dyed the color of lime Jell-O, sitting astride a mean-looking Riotmaster, laughed, while the others accepted the news in silence. Masthead turned back to Iggy. "So why'd you shoot him?"

"If I hadn't shot him, he woulda shot me. Simple as that. Besides, he was a pain in the ass."

The Jetboy with the green hair nodded in agreement. "That's the truth. No denying Johnny was a pain in the ass."

The story in the camp was that the Jetboys brewed their own moonshine. Iggy could only suppose that, while Johnny Zone had been attending the council meeting, the others had been sampling the latest batch. Whatever the reason, they were all as drunk as skunks.

Masthead squinted at Iggy. Now his hand was on the butt of the machine pistol. "Johnny Zone was a pain in the ass, right enough, but that don't mean I ain't going to kill you."

Iggy stood absolutely still. "Why would you want to do that if he was such a pain?"

Masthead looked outraged. "Hey, he was our leader. I was his second in command. I gotta kill you, it's a matter of honor."

Masthead was now gripping the butt of the machine pistol. He was definitely drunk. Iggy took a slow step forward. "Honor? What would trash like you know about honor?" A crazy light had come into Iggy's eyes. He seemed to be deliberately trying to provoke the kid. Dicing with death.

Masthead glared. "Honor . . . you son of a bitch. Jetboy honor."

"You're so drunk, I could give you five seconds start and still cut you down before you cleared leather."

Masthead grinned stupidly. "Screw you, Mengele."

Charlie Fats spoke in a low voice. "You better kill him, boss. If he cuts loose with that thing he's liable to empty the whole clip into us innocent bystanders."

Masthead started to blearily tug his weapon from its holster. The world seemed suddenly to go into stopframe. Masthead's gun was clear of its holster, but he didn't fire. Iggy's gun came out in one swift movement and he fired without hesitation. The top of Masthead's scalp, along with a section of his skull, detached itself from the rest of his head and flew upward like a small UFO with hair attached.

The Jetboy with the lime–Jell-O hair moved to lock down the twin fléchette guns on his Riotmaster, but before he could open up, Sam Deuce blew a hole in his chest. As he flipped backward, the Jetboy's face was a white mask of shocked surprise between the green hair and blood spurting from his chest. As Sam recalled it later, "red, white, and green, he looked like some airborne Christmas decoration, or maybe the Italian flag."

Another of the Jetboys brought up a Mossberg Autoload, but a snap shot from Billy Dalton nailed him in the shoulder. He spun around shrieking obscene curses, and the shotgun went flying.

A Jetboy in back of the pack, perhaps not as drunk as the rest, managed to get an MM on line but failed to set a target. The micromissile flashed over everyone's head and sent both participants and spectators scrambling for cover. Only Iggy stayed standing as the missile plowed into the facade of the Ritz Carlton, blowing away a third-floor balcony and sending an avalanche of plaster and masonry cascading down the front of the building.

Iggy scanned the Jetboys, as though wondering who deserved to be shot next. Everyone had a weapon in his hand and everyone was scanning for a target. It was the moment of frozen time that precedes the insane chaos of a mindless bloodbath. All it needed was for someone to make the first move, and instant, unstoppable hell would break out all over. Both sides would start pumping bullets at anything that moved, and when they got through with the craziness, there'd be a lot fewer of them left standing.

One of the Jetboys in a yellow leather jumpsuit was shouting. "Hold it! Hold it!" He had his arms in the air and was coming toward Iggy. "Hold your fire! This ain't something to get killed over. Hell, I never even liked Johnny Zone, goddamn it!"

Iggy all but fired, only restraining himself at the very last moment. He glanced back at the men behind him. "Okay, hold your fire."

The Jetboy with his hands in the air was white-faced. He had been standing next to the one with the lime-green hair when he'd been shot, and his yellow leathers were splattered with blood. He looked appealingly at Iggy. "This shit ain't worth dying for. I mean, we came up here, juiced up and primed to kick ass, but we ain't looking to start a war."

The Jetboys were nodding in agreement. Two of their number were dead and another squatted on the ground groaning and nursing his bleeding shoulder. The survivors obviously seemed to think that honor had been satisfied. Iggy motioned to his men and they lowered their weapons. He looked the Jetboy up and down.

"Seems like we might have a problem here."

The Jetboy still had his hands in the air. He frowned. "A problem?"

"Where do we go from here? How do I know you boys aren't going to wait until my back's turned and then blow me away?"

The Jetboy half lowered his hands. "Damn it, Iggy, we were drunk. We ain't gonna hold no grudge if you don't."

Iggy turned to the men behind him. "Is that okay with you guys?"

The majority indicated that it was okay with them, and the Jetboy lowered his hands completely. "So we can just stick around?"

Iggy holstered his pistol. "You ought to be more careful picking your leaders."

The Jetboy shrugged. "We never wanted any leaders in the first place. That was Johnny Zone's trip."

"Now you see where it got him." Iggy looked down at the body of Masthead. "What about him? What was his trip?"

The Jetboy also looked down at the body. "Masthead? He was just plain crazy."

Iggy grinned. "You got any of that moonshine of yours?"

The Jetboy nodded eagerly. "Sure do."

He hurried back to his bike and returned with an unlabeled bottle of clear liquid and handed it to Iggy. After the first taste, his face creased into a grimace and he gasped. "Hell's teeth, that's raw. You make this stuff?"

The Jetboy grinned. "Sure is powerful."

Iggy took another drink, and after that his voice was hoarse. "Powerful." He held onto the bottle and gestured to the Jetboy again, indicating the bodies of Masthead and the kid with the green hair. "Maybe you ought to get your buddies off of the ground and into it."

The Jetboys busied themselves hauling away the corpses, and Iggy handed the bottle to Dalton. As he did so, Ilsa McCoy was suddenly at his side. "Is it always like this round here?"

Iggy glanced at her and grinned. "No, but it does seem to be getting that way."

Iggy's eyes ran up and down her body. It was hard to tell through the baggy clothes what she might really look like. It might be interesting, at some point in the future, to investigate further. Right then and there, though, he had more important matters to deal with. With the excitement over, the troops were gathering around him.

Tod Slaughter voiced the question that was in everybody's mind. "It's like you asked that kid just now. Where do we go from here?"

# CHAPTER SEVEN

Paladin looked hard at Bambi Starr. "What do you mean, 'kill me off'?"

The two of them stood in the Pomona Bowl's rear enclosure, still watching the monitors. "That's the word around the pits and the Leper Colony."

Paladin took a deep breath. "It is, is it?"

"That's what they're saying."

Paladin glanced up at the monitor screens. The Firedrake in the arena had been hit behind the rear wheels by one of the Omega ramcars and was spinning out of control. The flamethrower went off, spraying a helix of orange fire into empty air but hitting nothing. The second Omega ran under the flames and broadsided the Firedrake, which flipped and rolled. A spark must have ignited the tank that fed the flamethrower, because the camper suddenly exploded in a ball of fire.

Following the explosion, the images came thick and fast. A camera down in the arena, almost certainly carried by a lunatic with a death wish, caught a close up of the Firedrake's driver. He'd been flung clear in the explosion, and was now trying to crawl away with flames streaming from his body armor. He managed a superhuman ten yards before he collapsed and died.

Another camera, this time in the stands, showed burning debris showering down on the two Omegas as they reversed away from the wreck. A third camera picked up the yellow fire trucks speeding from one of the gates, howling through the drifting smoke with their emergency lights flashing and the other vehicles swinging out of their path. It was strictly against the rules—and also very bad form—to shoot at ambulances and fire trucks.

No sooner had the fire trucks started to foam down what was left of the Firedrake than the main feed cut to more action in another part of the field. A Slayer had come up behind a rear-vulnerable McMurphy, and with its greater turn of speed was weaving from side to side, slicing away the larger car's armor with its X-ray laser.

Paladin blinked in surprise. "It's going kind of fast for so early in the day."

Bambi Starr was unconcerned. "The control room's been cramming the pressure since the opening fanfare."

"Who the hell is directing this show?"

"Vanna Kreig."

"Vanna Kreig?"

"Apparently she insisted on personally supervising the day's games."

"Kreig is directing this herself?"

"It's supposed to be a big ratings push."

Paladin looked grimly at the screen. The McMurphy's driver was trying to spin his car out of trouble, but the Slayer stayed glued to his ass.

Bambi Starr glanced around and then quickly leaned close to Paladin. "Smile, there's a camera watching."

The red-haired camera jock in the baseball cap was back and aiming a camera right at the two of them.

Bambi smiled sexily up at Paladin and lightly ran her fingertips over the chessman emblem on his armor.

Paladin peered at the camera out of the corner of his eye. "Why do I get the feeling that he's shooting file material for my obituary?"

"Smile."

"I can't think of too much to smile about."

"I said smile. Whatever else is going on, it's still show time."

It seemed that Bambi would stop at nothing when it came to playing it for the camera. The flat of her hand was now resting on Paladin's chest. She'd struck a pose as though the simple touch was enough to get her excited. She turned her head away from the camera and slyly winked at Paladin.

"I mean, think what this could do for me. If you get killed today, I'll be in all the last tapes of you before you went to die in the arena. I'll be your very last romance."

"That's not funny."

Bambi pressed herself against him. "It wasn't meant to be."

Paladin looked over Bambi's head. The kid in the baseball cap was still rolling tape, moving around the two of them in a wide circle. Paladin growled. "I'd like to punch that kid right in the lens."

"You should be used to this sort of thing by now."

Paladin scowled, then put his arm around Bambi and steered her away from the bank of monitor screens. Bambi went along but looked up at him questioningly. "Where are we going?"

"We're walking over to the pits to take a look at my car."

Bambi pouted. "Romantic."

"Right at this moment, romance is the last thing on my mind."

"That's not usually the effect I have on men."

"I got other things to think about."

Bambi looked up. For the first time, she showed what appeared to be genuine concern. "You're really worried, aren't you?"

Paladin nodded. "Damn right I'm worried."

"You think they're really planning to write you out?"

"I don't know what the hell they're planning. All I know is that too much weird stuff has gone down in the last twenty-four hours for me to be exactly comfortable."

"And you don't have Turk to watch your ass anymore."

Paladin's face hardened. "No, I don't."

Across, on the other side of the enclosure, a Gatling with a purple and lime-green flame–motif paint job was noisily running its mill, warming up before it went into the arena. Bambi now had her back to the kid with the camera, and although she twitched her hips seductively for the lens, her face was serious. "You think what went down with Turk, that guy greasing him with the rocket launcher, you think that was a setup?"

"I don't know what to think. First Turk buys it, then Vanna Kreig comes by to talk to me."

Bambi's lip curled. "I don't trust that bitch."

"You mean she's not the one who picked you out of the pack at Hammer Downs?"

Bambi stared at Paladin in total disbelief. "You think she'd promote someone who looks like me?"

"I thought she'd do anything for a ratings point."

"She's also a woman."

"I noticed that."

"I think having a bunch of guys like you as featured players is more her speed. I was warned to keep an eye out for Ms. Kreig and her games."

"So who's watching over your career?"

Bambi grinned knowingly. "That's my secret."

Paladin glanced back. "That damn kid's still following us."

The kid in the baseball cap was still rolling tape. Bambi disengaged herself from Paladin's arm. "I'll get rid of him."

She turned and walked back toward the cameraman, swaying everything she had. The kid halted but kept shooting. When Bambi was near enough to be in tight close-up, she pouted and ran her tongue over her lips and put on a breathless, sexy voice. "You think maybe we could have a little privacy just now?"

The kid with the camera actually blushed. He shut off the tape and lowered the Minicam. Bambi strolled back to where Paladin was waiting and indicated that they should keep on walking. "You know, I could always watch your ass for you."

Paladin's eyebrows shot up. "Say what?"

"I said I could watch your ass for you."

"That's what I thought you said."

She gestured in the direction of the arena. "I mean out there, in the fun'n'games. I could replace Turk."

"You've got to be kidding."

Now Bambi's face turned hard. "You think I couldn't cut it?"

"You ride a trike. I mean, no disrespect, but we ain't in quite the same division."

All the come-on had gone out of Bambi's attitude. Now she was angry. "You'd be surprised what I can do, buddy."

"I bet I would be, but it's the arena that I'm talking about."

Bambi stopped dead in her tracks. Her fists were clenched and her eyes glittered furiously. "You really don't think I can cut it, do you? You think I'm some dumb bimbo who's just here to add a little tits and ass to the proceedings."

Paladin also stopped. "I didn't say that."

"No, but you thought it."

Paladin held up a hand. "Listen, all I'm thinking about is getting through this day. Maybe tonight, if I'm still walking around, we can talk about it, but right now I'm wondering if this new guy Bull Nails has been set up to pull something."

Bambi grimaced. "Nails is a moron."

"Even a moron can get lucky. Particularly if he's getting help from the director."

"You think little Vanna's up to something?"

Paladin frowned. "I think she's up to something, but I don't know what, and that bothers me."

"So let me cover your back."

"Today?"

"Yeah, today. Nobody would be expecting a move like that."

"You've already done your bit."

"I don't think anyone would stop me going in a second time."

Paladin looked at Bambi carefully. "You really want to do this?"

Bambi nodded. "I think it'd be good for both of us. I get the chance for people to take me seriously as a player and you might just find yourself bailed out of a situation."

They were almost at the pits. Connolly was still fussing over the Kali and he looked up curiously as the two of them approached.

Paladin glanced at Bambi. "The name Iggy Mengele mean anything to you?"

Bambi's face was blank. "No, why?"

Paladin sighed. "No reason."

Bambi and Paladin turning up together was clearly the last thing that Connolly had expected. He wiped his hands on a rag and looked from Paladin to Bambi and back again. "So what's going on here?"

Bambi playfully kissed Paladin on the cheek. "Just getting acquainted."

Connolly grunted. "I hate to break up a brand-new wonderful friendship but we just got the word that he's on standby as of now."

Paladin grinned. "This lady's planning on coming to my rescue if I get into trouble today."

Connolly's expression was noncommital. "Well, you probably need all the help you can get."

Bambi nodded. "That's what I've been telling him."

Connolly pointed across the enclosure. "Maybe you should start now."

Both Paladin and Bambi turned and saw Kreig and her goons coming across the enclosure, heading directly for the group around the Kali. They paused for a moment to let the green and purple Gatling pass on its way out to the gate, and then continued in the same direction. There was something very purposeful about Kreig's walk.

Paladin raised an eyebrow. "What the hell does she want?"

Connolly grimaced. "Maybe she's come by to salute those who are about to die."

Paladin turned and stared balefully at his crew chief. "That ain't funny."

Connolly shrugged. "What is, these days?"

Kreig walked straight up to them. Ignoring both Bambi and Connolly, she smiled briefly at Paladin. "You're all ready to go?"

Paladin glanced at Connolly. "You got a bottle round here somewhere?"

Kreig's smile vanished and was replaced by an expression that could have soured milk. She clearly wasn't accustomed to being ignored by one of her own players. Connolly fished a half liter of J.T.S. Brown out of a toolbox and passed it to Paladin. As Paladin uncapped the whiskey, Kreig looked at him angrily. "Is that a good idea? I don't want you out there drunk."

Bambi glared at Kreig. "From what I heard, you want him out there any way you can get him out there."

Kreig regarded her coldly. "What's that supposed to mean?"

Paladin took a long pull on the bottle and answered the question himself. "There's a rumor going around that today's the day I get written out."

Kreig's eyes narrowed and she rounded on Bambi. "Are you the one who's been feeding him this garbage?"

Now it was Connolly's turn. "The story's all over the players' area and the dressing rooms."

"It's nonsense."

Paladin slowly lowered the bottle. "So what was with the run-in with Bull Nails? Was that part of the setup? And Turk getting greased yesterday?"

Kreig angrily shook her head. "This is crazy. Why the hell should I want to see you killed?"

Bambi's hands were planted firmly on her hips. She leaned aggressively toward Vanna Kreig. "Ratings, maybe? Dramatic death of a duelling superstar."

Vanna Kreig turned with a sneer. "Stay out of this, girlie. Just stick to flashing your tits for the morons."

Connolly quickly moved in front of Bambi before she could slug Kreig. Paladin picked up his helmet from the seat of the Kali. He took another drink from the bottle and regarded the executive coldly. "I heard you were directing this show."

"Only the important sequences."

"So you better get back to the control room, because I'm going in."

Kreig shook her head. "I don't want you in for a half hour yet."

Paladin swung his leg over the side of the car and eased himself down into the driver's seat. "I'm going in now."

"That's ridiculous."

Paladin grinned. "If I'm going to get myself killed, I'll pick the moment."

Kreig took a step forward toward the car as Paladin powered up the Kali's cyber-system and went into his pregame vehicle check. She was shaking her head. "I can't allow it. I decide when you go into the arena. We have a script and a running order."

"So rewrite it, I'm going in."

"You can't do that. You've got a contract."

Paladin hit the starter and powered up the Kali's mill, then he casually let his hands drop to the manual fire control. "So sue me."

Connolly and Bambi were both grinning. Kreig's bodyguards also realized that they were in Paladin's reality, not Kreig's, and moved back. It took her a moment longer to grasp the absurdity of threatening a determined man in a heavily armed car with a lawsuit, particularly one who suspected that he had nothing to lose. Bambi stepped to the side of the car. "I meant what I said earlier ... about going back in if you need me."

Paladin nodded. "I'll remember that."

Kreig seemed to be about to say something, but then apparently she thought better of it. She turned on her heel and stalked off, presumably back to the control room. The bodyguards trailed after her, looking less than happy.

Bambi yelled at Kreig's retreating back. "What's the matter, girlie? The real world too much for you?"

Paladin put on his helmet and patched it to the air supply and the computer. He took a moment to bring the Phoenix on line and set the images in front of his face mask. He pulled down the canopy and spoke into the helmet mike.

"Tell the director that Val Paladin is going to the show."

With that, he shifted the Kali into gear, gave it a little power, and nosed slowly toward gate number four.

## CHAPTER EIGHT

The sound of the firefight between Iggy and the Jetboys had woken the entire camp. The group at the Ritz Carlton had grown from just the council of twelve and a few hangers-on to a sizable crowd who had hurried up there to see what the hell the shooting was all about. Iggy knew that this was his moment. If he was going to grab the undisputed leadership of this entire motley army, the time was right then. The camp was looking for answers, and if he could come up with the right ones, they would follow him anywhere. He also knew, if he fumbled his play, his potential followers would more than likely turn on him and hang him from the nearest high place they could string a rope.

Dalton's truck was parked in the driveway of the hotel and provided the ideal vantage point from which to confront the crowd. Iggy quickly scrambled up onto the roof of the Security Seven and turned to face the mob of armed men and women. For the moment, they were quiet, waiting to see what he might have to say for himself, but he was well aware that they wouldn't stay that way for long. If they didn't like what he offered, it could be all over in a moment. He scanned the assembled faces and took a deep breath.

A biker in the front row yelled up to him. "What's the story, Iggy?"

It was now or never.

"What's the story? I'll tell you what the story is. I just shot Johnny Zone."

Some people grinned, others remained blank faced, just biding their time. So far so good.

"I killed Johnny Zone because he was crazy and he had it coming. It's been squared with the Jetboys and there's no problem there. Unless anyone else has one?"

The focus of attention turned to a group of Jetboys who had just returned from disposing of the bodies. The Jetboys shrugged, indicating that they more or less agreed with Iggy. Johnny Zone probably did have it coming and his death was cool with them. No one else seemed inclined to make an issue of it.

Iggy moved on. "The question that everyone seems to be asking is 'Where do we go from here?'"

Iggy paused to let this sink in. A number of the crowd were nodding. That was exactly what they wanted to know. They were well aware that they couldn't survive in Palm Springs much longer. Too many were living off a town that had been all but stripped bare in the first place. Supplies of everything from food to ammunition, not to mention beer, were almost gone.

"We all know that we gotta move, but what we gotta decide is where we move to, and it seems to me that, when you boil it down, we only have a couple of choices."

Iggy paused again. Nobody spoke. At least he had their attention, and that was half the battle.

"One thing we know for sure is that we can't go back. If we head either south or east, the army's going to be waiting for us with their gunships and their tanks, and I don't think that any of us really want to mix it up with the military right now."

He glanced down to where Ilsa McCoy was standing beside the Security Seven. Her battered crew of newcomers scowled and nodded at the memory.

Iggy raised his voice slightly. "Seems to me that, if we can't go south and we can't go east, that only leaves us two ways to go. Either north or west. And if we do that, we know what's waiting for us."

Iggy gave the assembled outlaws a moment to digest what he was saying. "That's right. Vegas to the north and L.A. to the west, and ain't neither of those going to exactly welcome us."

Some of the faces in the crowd were frowning. So far Iggy wasn't telling them anything they didn't already know.

Tod Slaughter shouted up to him. "We're gonna get creamed if we go to Vegas."

Iggy nodded. "And L.A. ain't gonna be no bed of roses neither."

A biker in the front of the crowd yelled what everyone else was thinking. "So what the hell do we do except break up and go hide."

Iggy lifted a hand, appealing to the assembled men and women. "We ain't gonna break up, are we? Not after we come so far?"

The crowd looked uneasy. Iggy shouted back at them. "I said we ain't going to break up, are we?"

There were some scattered shouts of no, but the outlaws were hardly eating out of his hand.

"We're the last of the best and if we go, that's the end of it. There ain't gonna be no more like us."

A woman with dirty blond hair, just behind Tod Slaughter, shouted back. "You can say that again!"

Iggy allowed himself a grim smile. At least he was

winning one of them over. Then the biker shouted again. "You ain't telling us where we can go."

"There is one place."

"Where's that?"

Iggy played his card. "Pomona!"

"Pomona?"

"Pomona, that's where we can go!"

The crowd looking at each other, puzzled and a little confused. "So what's in frigging Pomona?"

"The Pomona Bowl, the biggest duelling facility this side of Orange County! That's what's in frigging Pomona!"

This got some laughs and smiles, but a lot of the crowd were obviously thinking. The biker in the front row seemed to have become spokesperson for the whole crowd. "So what are you saying? We all go and be TV stars, all two hundred of us?"

"I'm saying we take the Pomona Bowl. We take it by storm and we make it ours. We take it and we use it as a base. It's like a goddamned fortress. Once we're in there nobody would be able to move us, not even the fucking army!"

A murmuring started in the crowd and there were some shouts of "Yeah!" Iggy grinned. "That's right! We'd be kings of the goddamned castle!"

The biker in the front quickly brought things back to earth. "If it's such a fucking fortress, how do we know we can take it?"

"Because we're the best. All they got at Pomona to defend the castle is a bunch of glamour boys and showboats. We'll roll right over them."

Tod Slaughter was frowning. "Some of those showboats are good. Real good."

Iggy nodded, conceding the point. "Yeah, they're good. I'll give you that. But we're better. For a start, they won't be expecting us. The last thing anyone in

Pomona is going to expect is a wolf pack roaring down on them. And they've gotten soft. They've been playing at the fun'n'games while we've been out in the badlands living it for real. Am I right?"

The question drew a ragged cheer and shouts of "Right!" Iggy was warming to this speech making. He raised a hand like an old-time hellfire preacher.

"Most important of all, brothers and sisters, is that we've even got the numbers. The way things stand at the moment, we outnumber them two to one!"

This drew a louder cheer. A majority of the crowd seemed to like the idea. The biker in the front was one of the minority who had yet to be sold. "Some of us old boys were thinking maybe we should head up to the Black Rock Combat Zone up in Nevada. We figured we ought to be able to find a place for ourselves up there."

Some of the men around the biker were nodding. They must have been discussing the idea. Iggy had heard of the Black Rock Combat Zone but didn't have too much idea of what exactly went on there. It was a free-autoduel area, but he suspected that it came with the usual limits and regulations. All he knew was that he didn't want anybody putting forward any alternative ideas, especially ideas that called for individual crews splitting off from the Horde. Fragmentation was something that Iggy had to nip in the bud. If he was going to take Pomona, he was going to need every driver and every gunner that he could get to follow him. If they started going off on their own, the plan would be doomed before it even started.

Iggy made the contempt in his face plain to see. "So you old boys were thinking of heading to Black Rock, were you? That the best idea you can come up with? Become a damned reservation Indian?" He appealed to the rest of the crowd. "Make no mistake about it, that's what you become when you hit Black Rock." A sneer came into his voice. "Black Rock Commercial Combat Zone? Yeah, right. You know what that sounds like to me? It sounds like the civilized citizen's dream. Put all the bad boys on the same piece of stinking real estate way up on the California-Nevada border or any other place that nobody else wants, and fly overhead and point cameras at them, and watch them on television like it was some goddamned wildlife park, and any time it looks like they might be getting together to cause a bit of real trouble, or get into some genuine fun'n'games like in the old days, hey, you got all the troublemakers in one spot, just drop a tactical nuke on 'em and that's the end of the problem, you know what I mean? You hear what I'm saying?"

The biker was shaking his head. "It ain't like that. . . ."

Iggy roared. "It ain't like that? It ain't like that? Sure it's like that! It's like monkeys in the zoo, that's what it's like! It's like having your balls cut off, that's what it's like! I don't want no damned cameras pointed at me. I'm telling you! I'm a free man, not a stinking TV star!"

The crowd was now cheering loudly. The biker and his friends weren't joining in, though. "Ain't there gonna be cameras at Pomona?"

Iggy waved away this question. "Sure there'll be cameras at Pomona, and the very last thing that they'll see will be us coming at them, the Horde, like something straight from hell, rolling over their showboat duel players and taking the arena. After that, the cameras will be ours and we'll use them any way we like."

This didn't manage to raise cheers again, but there was a scattering of applause. Tod Slaughter, seemingly determined not to be carried away by any mass enthusiasm, still had a question.

"Suppose we take the Pomona Bowl . . ."

Iggy interrupted him. "We're taking the Pomona Bowl."

Slaughter didn't intend to be buffaloed by any cheap rabble rousing. "Suppose we take the Pomona Bowl, are we going to be able to hold it? They could send a force out from L.A., or call out the military. We couldn't hold that place if they came in with tanks and air support. We'd be like sitting ducks."

Iggy looked at Tod Slaughter long and hard. If Slaughter opposed him, he was in trouble. His K-90s commanded a lot of respect in the camp, and if they opted out of the attack on Pomona, a good many other crews would follow their lead.

Iggy dropped his voice. "What do you want from me? I mean, what do you *want* from me? You want some kind of absolute guarantee that it'll all pan out okay? Is that how the K-90s fight these days? Only if they have an absolute assurance that they're going to win and nobody's going to get hurt?"

Plainly these words weren't sitting well with Slaughter. His face was dark and angry and he glared at Iggy. "That's not what I'm saying. That's not what I'm saying at all."

"So what are you saying? You ask me where I think we ought to go from here and I lay out a plan. That's all Pomona is, it's a plan. I figure we have a chance of pulling it off. That's all. Nothing else. I'm not saying that we won't have a fight on our hands. I'm not saying that we may not get our hair mussed. I'm not going to lie to you. Some of us will get ourselves killed. That's what happens in a fight." He paused for a moment. "But I thought fighting was what we were all about!" His voice was building. "I thought fighting was what we did best! I thought that fighting was the only way that we were going to carve out a place for ourselves."

He paused again and stared straight at Slaughter. "Or maybe the K-90s have forgotten that. Maybe they've gotten tired. Maybe they just want to go up to Black Rock like a bunch of castrated monkeys...."

With a growl, Tod Slaughter hurled himself toward the truck on which Iggy was standing. "You can't talk to the K-90s like that, Iggy Mengele!" He started to scrabble up the side of the Security Seven, but some of his men grabbed him and held him back.

Iggy held up his hands. "Hold it, hold it! I wasn't insulting the K-90s. I just care about what happens to us, all of us, and I figure, with the situation we're in now, we either hang together or we die alone. Now, I can't promise when we take the Pomona stadium, we're going to be able to hold it. Maybe they will send in troops with tanks and helicopters and we'll find ourselves screwed, but maybe they won't. All I'm saying is that it could be a way out for us. Sure it's a gamble, but you gotta take some risks in life. The way I see it, though, the odds ought to be in our favor. I'm saying that it's good odds the folks in L.A. won't want no trouble. I mean, it's not like we were moving into their town or nothing. All it means to them is that some place in the boonies, way out in the old dead suburbs, had a change of ownership. Why should they care? They'll accept that what's done is done and let it lay. I'm not making any hard and fast promises that it's a sure thing, but I think the odds are good enough to give it a shot." He gestured round at Palm Springs. "I mean, we gotta face facts, we don't have too much to lose."

Tod Slaughter had calmed down considerably and his men had let go of him, but he still looked resentfully up at Iggy. "I hear what you're saying, Iggy Mengele, and I agree with most of it, but that still don't give you the right to stand up there saying the K-90s ain't got no balls."

Iggy dropped down on one knee to get closer to Slaughter. He spread his hands contritely. "Hey, Slaughter, you know I didn't mean that. You know I've got nothing but respect for the K-90s. Hell, there ain't no other crew I'd rather have watching my back. I just get carried away with the moment, you know how that is."

Slaughter slowly nodded. His anger hadn't entirely evaporated, but for the time being, honor seemed to be satisfied. "You gotta watch that, boy. If you're going to lead this mob, you gotta know what you're doing all of the time. A leader don't get carried away."

That was all Iggy wanted. Tod Slaughter had actually acknowledged his leadership. Now all he needed was one final confirmation. He got to his feet again so all the crowd could see and hear, and he looked down at Slaughter. "So the K-90s are going to Pomona?"

Slaughter hesitated for just a couple of seconds before he answered, but when he did, it was exactly what Iggy wanted to hear. "Yeah, the K-90s are going to Pomona."

The crowd broke into wild cheers, and Iggy waved a clenched fist in the air. "So who else is going to Pomona?"

The roar was deafening. Everyone was going to Pomona. Hands reached out to help Iggy down from the truck, and he laughed out loud. He was the leader of maybe the biggest band of motorized outlaws in history. The crowd didn't let Iggy jump down to the ground. Instead, they hoisted him on their shoulders and carried him away. Even as he was acknowledging their cheers, though, he glanced back at Tod Slaughter. He knew in the future that he would always have to watch the leader of the K-90s. The moment of hesitation said it all. Tod Slaughter was an honest man, a stand-up guy, and it was plain that he had definite reservations about

Iggy, and those reservations made him a threat. He was too much like the voice of sanity. The way that Iggy had things planned, sanity was dangerous. He wanted the Horde so crazy that they would do anything he told them without question.

Iggy also noticed that Billy Dalton was looking at him a little strangely. Iggy smiled grimly. When you became the absolute leader, it didn't do to trust anyone all that absolutely, not even the oldest of friends.

## CHAPTER NINE

One whole wall of the front-office reception area of the Pomona Bowl administration building was taken up with a huge aerial photograph of the facility. On seeing this for the first time, one driver, who'd had a few too many drinks along the way, took a step back and whistled out loud. "Sweet Jesus, it looks like a pair of tits coming right at you." Despite all the efforts of the public-relations department, the description had lingered, if for no other reason than it was essentially accurate. Based on the popular Double Drum Stadium in Waco, Texas, the Pomona Bowl consisted of two equal-sized circular areas arranged like a figure eight, surrounded by high, walled-in, blastproof grandstands. In the center of each circular arena was a tall concrete tower, the top of which carried the satellite dishes and microwave transmitters for the television feeds.

At Double Drum, the twin arenas were connected at three separate points. At Pomona, however, this had been reduced to just one, and that was nothing more than a single two-lane drawbridge over a specially constructed moat. The moat could be filled with an inflammable liquid to create a wall of flame when the script demanded special effects.

The Pomona layout was far from being a favorite with duellists. It was cheap and gimmicky, designed primarily to produce good, easy TV pictures and very little else. Larger than the average arena, it operated on just one level and the organization of its games ran close to the limits of AADA rules. It used the huge Skynet TV revenues, its powerful sponsors, and the constant threat of realigning itself with the anything-goes BLUD organization to force the association not to look too closely at possible infringements. Batteries of specialist lawyers were on retainer, constantly looking for fresh loopholes in the AADA regulations.

Many critics complained that Pomona was bringing the sport into disrepute and moving it in the same show-biz direction that had been taken by professional wrestling in the latter half of the twentieth century. Others merely shrugged. It was the way of the future, and what could you do about it?

A similar debate had followed the switch to low-yield ammunition. The critics grumbled that it was yet another move toward the fixing of stadium duelling, but the critics found themselves with little popular support. As every home viewer knew, low-yield ammo made for better spectacle. With low-yield, two opponents could pound away at each other for extended periods of time, where, if they were using full-strength combat charges, it was all too frequently over in a matter of seconds. The critic for *The New York Times* was so enraged by this public betrayal of the purity of the sport that he coined the phrase "moron pressure."

The players' chief complaint was that Pomona lacked any long straight stretches where a driver could work up a decent head of speed. The players found themselves driving in one continuous curve, a source of great visuals, with skidding cars throwing up bow waves of dust, but it put a constant strain on both men and machines.

All this was on Paladin's mind as he picked up speed and drove the Kali out through gate number four and into the fray. The event that he was joining was a "battle royal." Open to all classes of cars and trucks, with a thirty-minute duration expected from each vehicle, it had already been in progress for some time, and a number of wrecks dotted the arena. Gate number four led out into the West Arena, where the major action seemed to be a free-form dogfight between two loosely allied teams of compact cars. Pomona was big on free-form mass events, having discovered through exhaustive market research that the viewers preferred to see large numbers of vehicles going at it hammer and tongs rather than a balanced match between equal individuals. Despite all the magazine articles and pronouncements of TV pundits about the art and finesse of the sport, the figures showed that folks out in TV land were much more turned on by death and mass mayhem than by any of the finer points of vehicle combat.

Paladin looked around carefully as he came through the gate-four tunnel. The chance always existed that some wanna-be hotshot, usually driving a ramcar, would be lurking just inside the gate looking for a quick hit and an easy reputation. The trick was hardly sporting, but sporting wasn't a word that got used too much around Pomona. A few cheap tricks along the way never stopped anyone becoming a star.

As he rolled from the dark of the tunnel into the bright glare of the noonday sun, Paladin gave the Kali a fast burst of power. With its high acceleration, the car could burn its way out of trouble in most life-threatening situations. One of the Omegas that Paladin had earlier seen destroy the Firedrake was coming toward the gate, hugging the wall and looking suspiciously like it might be intending to rush him. From what he'd observed, the Omegas had seemed to be working as a double act, and Paladin quickly looked for the partner, but there seemed to be no sign of him. Maybe the pair had only buddied up to take out the Firedrake. Paladin rapidly armed one of his heavy rockets, but the Omega changed course, swinging off toward the central tower. Either he had recognized the distinctive trim of the Kali and decided that he didn't want to spoil his morning by tangling with Val Paladin, or else the control room had warned him off. Paladin resisted an impulse to let the Omega have it with the rocket anyway, just for being there, and turned the Kali for a first exploratory circle of the West Arena.

As Paladin completed his first quarter of a circuit, the voice of announcer Bo Rheingold boomed over the public-address system. "Well folks, now we ought to be seeing some fireworks. Entering the West Arena from gate number four is Pomona's black knight, Val Paladin, driving the custom built Imperial Kali that has become so familiar to duel fans over the last few months."

At the same time, the voice of Vanna Kreig came over Paladin's helmet phones on the closed channel from the control room. "Control to Paladin, do you copy?"

Paladin grunted into his helmet mike. "I copy."

"Just coast for the moment, okay? I say again, just coast. We want to do your buildup."

"Ten-four on that. Just make sure everyone else knows it."

Even on the closed channel, Kreig sounded pissed off. "Will do. Control out."

Paladin set his match meter to give him regular, two-minute time checks and to beep him after the compulsory thirty minutes was up. Arena combat tended to do strange things to one's sense of time, and under stress, a minute could seem like a lifetime. He didn't want to stay in the arena any longer than he had to. He also turned on the tiny TV in the dash that would bring him the edited satellite feed exactly as it went out to the viewers. If Vanna Kreig really intended to give him a hard time, he might get some warning of what she had planned by the way she set up the shots. Few directors could resist telegraphing their plays by the use of teasers.

Right at that moment, the screen was filled with a high shot of the Kali circling the arena. It made the car look not unlike a cruising shark. Then it cut to a two-shot of Bo Rheingold and his partner Marci Sanger in the commentators' booth. Marci was smiling into the camera. "Yes, Bo, and let's not forget that Val Paladin is sponsored by Himmler Beer. Himmler Old 500, 'the beer that gets you there.' "

The picture on the tiny screen cut to a Himmler Beer commercial. Two scantily clad models, one blond, the other a redhead, each wearing the briefest of leather bikinis, clung to Dan Baron, a top-ranked star at the Omni Coliseum in Atlanta. While cars crashed and burned behind them, Baron popped the top of a can of Old 500 and held it up to the camera.

Paladin looked around, checking on the opposition, but none of the other players seemed to be taking any special interest in him. Nobody was dumb enough to start something during the commercial break and miss out on the glory. The driver of one of the compacts lost control of his car and spun into the outer wall. Now the dogfight was three on two. The commercial ended and the game came back with the two compacts running in front of a coordinated hail of fire from the team of three.

Paladin slowed a little to avoid the chance of stray fire, and was surprised to see an image of the Kali on the screen. Did they have something planned for him already? He scanned the arena for a potential sneak attack but could see nothing. He didn't spot the motorcycle until the very last moment. Some kind of Japanese gasburner, with black and yellow trim and minimal armor, had suddenly come out of nowhere and was running right alongside him, with the rider raising a gloved hand in mock salute and grinning at him through his visor.

Paladin blinked. What the hell was this? It didn't make any sense. A lone motorcycle didn't try to take on a Division 40 car. He snarled into his helmet mike. "What's going on here? Does this biker seriously think he can mess with me?"

The voice of one of the floor controllers came over his headphones. "Don't ask me. According to the stats, those guys are crazy."

"Guys?"

Another bike, with the same black and yellow trim, had appeared on the other side of the Kali. Its driver was also waving at him. Paladin looked from one bike to the other. They were pacing him exactly. "Who are these maniacs?"

Bo Rheingold answered his question for him, running down the background on the pair of bikers for the TV audience. "Although new to Pomona, Joey and Dee Dee, the Krypton Brothers, have been huge hits at both Alladin's Castle and the Arches. And, I'm telling you, folks, with this pair of wackos, you can just throw away the rule book and expect absolutely anything. I mean, just look at them now. Here they are, making their very first appearance at the Pomona Bowl, and what do they do? They only go after the black knight himself!"

Paladin put his foot down, intending to leave the

Krypton Brothers standing in his dust. To his surprise, they also accelerated, staying with him. Those gas-burners had a real turn of speed on them.

Bo Rheingold seemed to find it all highly amusing. "Well, folks, I guess Paladin thought he could power away and give the Krypton Brothers the slip, but that doesn't seem to be the way things work with this pair of cutups."

Paladin was back on the helmet mike, voice terse. "Will you get these clowns off my ass? I really don't need this."

The floor controller's voice took on a snotty edge. "There's nothing I can do about it, Paladin. What the Krypton Brothers do is up to them. That's why this match is called an All-Division Open."

Paladin swung around the arena running close to his top speed for the curve, but the motorcycles remained right there. The Krypton Brothers were starting to get on his nerves. Bo Rheingold's commentary wasn't helping, either.

"So like I said, friends and neighbors, with the Krypton Brothers, you've just got to throw the book away. Maybe they oughta be called the Motorcycle Marx Brothers on account of their monkey business, because you never know what they're going to get up to next. I expect that's exactly what Val Paladin is wondering right now. So far the Krypton Brothers have just been keeping pace with the black knight, but whether they're only doing it to bug him or whether they've got plans for Paladin remains to be seen. Like I said, with the Krypton Brothers, you never can tell. On the surface, it would seem hard to believe that a pair of motorcycles could knock out a heavily armed Division 40 car, but, take it from me, they've done worse than that. I don't know if Paladin is aware of it, but what Joey and Dee Dee don't know about special weapons ain't worth knowing and their tastes run to the strange and the exotic."

Paladin nodded. Thanks for the information, Bo. He spoke into the mike. "I'm giving warning, right now. If I pull ahead of those two jokers, I'm missiling them out. I repeat, out. I will go for the kill. I'm not kidding, I don't need this."

Vanna Kreig's voice was immediately on the link. "I don't want them killed, Paladin. I don't want the Krypton Brothers killed. We spent a lot of money getting them to come here and the company wants to get some use out of them."

Paladin controlled his anger with a lot of difficulty. "So get them off my back."

"The Krypton Brothers are crazy, Paladin. It's not just promo hype. I strongly advised them against this play."

Paladin had a momentary but very satisfying fantasy of crushing Vanna Kreig's head with a hammer. "You advised them? Who's directing this goddamned show?"

"I don't want them killed, Paladin."

"Screw you, Vanna."

He cut the link to the control room and glanced through the Kali's canopy at the two motorcyclists. "Okay, boys, it's just you and me."

He hit the brakes hard and was thrown forward against his web harness. At the same time, he let go with the forward guns. The burst went harmlessly over the heads of the Krypton Brothers, but Paladin wasn't disappointed. He hadn't expected to hit anything. He'd been firing more to make his attitude clear than to actually kill anyone. If they had half a brain between them, the Kryptons would quit bothering him and pick on someone their own size. They might have a rep in Vegas or Deseret but Pomona was his turf, and they could damn well show him some respect or pay the price. Paladin didn't give a damn how much Skynet had paid for the pair of bikers. If they wanted to dog on him, he wouldn't hesitate to have their collective ass.

The Krypton Brothers, however, seemed bent on proving that they had neither brains nor respect. They slowed their bikes and started to turn. Paladin could hardly believe his eyes. They were coming straight back at him. One of them opened up with what looked like a recoilless, and bullets slammed into his armor. The Kali's paint job had lost its cherry. Paladin angrily gunned the Kali forward, at the same time targeting the two bikes on the computer. Just as he had them, though, they both swung away, disengaging and heading off across the arena in opposite directions. Paladin realized that it wouldn't do to underestimate these guys. They had timed the maneuver almost as though they were reading his mind.

Be Rheingold made no sccrct that he thought the whole thing was nothing short of hilarious. "Oh boy, the black knight must be feeling kinda stupid right about now. These Krypton Brothers are just running rings around him. And . . . yes, here they are again!"

And here they were, flanking him again. One on the left and one on the right. What was their next trick? Paladin didn't have to wait long to find out. One of the bikers—Paladin didn't know if it was Joey or Dee Dee, and he didn't particularly care—had something metallic in his hand. It looked like a metal disc of some kind. Instantly, Paladin realized what it was. A limpet mine. The guy was hoping to stick a limpet mine on the side of the Kali. Bo Rheingold had been right; the Krypton Brothers were certainly unorthodox.

The biker was reaching for the Kali, and Paladin swerved toward him, warning him away. Out of the corner of his eye, Paladin saw the other biker moving in. He, too, was holding a limpet mine. Again Paladin hit the power. If he could just get slightly ahead of the bikes, he could hit them with his rear missiles. Once again it didn't work. The brothers still managed to match speed with him.

On the TV audio, Bo Rheingold was becoming excited. "The black knight has himself a bit of a problem here, folks. Paladin's sandwiched between the Krypton Brothers, and while they stay right alongside him, there's no way that Val Paladin can get at them. His guns fire forward and his missiles and his FCD both shoot back, but there ain't nothing on that Kali of his that shoots sideways, and, sooner or later, one of these Krypton boys is going to be able to slap a limpet mine onto his car."

Paladin grunted. "Tell me about it, Bo."

Paladin maintained speed, swerving whenever one of the Kryptons tried to ease in to attach a mine. Each time he swerved though, he eased away slightly from the center of the arena, out toward the wall.

"It seems like Paladin's biding his time folks, waiting for one of the Krypton Brothers to make that fatal slip. Of course, it could be that it'll be Paladin who slips first and ..."

Paladin cut the audio. Bo Rheingold was only making him mad, and that wasn't helping. The brother on the right was coming for him again, leaning out, stretching to plant the limpet. Paladin nudged the Kali slightly to the left at the crucial moment, and the biker missed his shot, almost losing his balance in the process. At the same time, the one on the left made a try. Paladin went hard to the right, hoping to catch the first one before he had fully recovered. He was ready, however, and he swung away as Paladin attempted to sideswipe him.

Paladin sighed. "This could get tired very quickly."

The Kali and the two black and yellow bikes ran

neck and neck for another half circuit, and all the time Paladin kept edging the Kali nearer and nearer to the outer wall. Neither of the Krypton Brothers seemed have noticed what he was doing, so intent were they on matching speed with him and looking for a chance to plant their mines. The outside bike was about three yards out from the wall. Paladin was pushing his speed close to the limit for the continuous curve when he made his move. He gave the Kali the last ounce of power and swung the car suddenly and violently toward the wall. For an instant, the biker thought he had him. He triumphantly raised the limpet mine, ready to slam it down on the Kali's armor. Then he realized that he was about to go into the wall. He desperately struggled to lean his way out of trouble, but it was too late. The only two ways to go were into the wall or into the Kali. The Krypton Brother chose the wall, sliding and trying to step off the bike before he hit.

It was only a glancing blow but enough to send machine and rider somersaulting and bouncing along the ground. The remaining brother tried to tag the Kali on the rebound, but then realized that the car was coming away from the wall too fast and that his brother was down. The biker braked hard, sliding sideways and throwing up gravel. He let it slide out from between his legs and he was off and running back to where his partner had finally come to rest.

Paladin readied a micromissile but held off from firing. A part of him wanted to finish the Krypton Brothers right there and then, but another part couldn't do it. He took the missile off its armed status. "This is just a game, goddamn it. I ain't killing no one for the fun of it."

He turned the Kali and rolled slowly back to where the surviving biker was crouched over his fallen brother. He brought the car to a stop and was about to pop the capsule and ask if the guy was dead or not when the survivor turned and looked at him with an expression that was pure venom. He scrambled to his feet, pulled a pistol from his belt, and pointed it at Paladin and fired. The bullet ricocheted off the armor on the hood. Clearly the surviving brother was a sore loser.

Paladin made a slow circuit of the arena. The bout with the Krypton Brothers had left a sour taste in his mouth, and the crowd seemed to feel the same, because only minimal applause was coming from the stands. He looked around and was surprised to see that he was virtually alone. No other cars were in the West Arena, and the only movements were a tractor hauling away a wreck and the ambulance coming to a halt beside the Krypton Brothers. This situation was far from normal, and Paladin cut the TV back in to see what was happening, but all he got was an Imperial Motors commercial followed by one for Himmler Beer. Finally Bo Rheingold and Marci Sanger were back, grinning smugly against a backdrop of his car in the arena.

"Welcome back to Pomona, folks, where we just saw black knight Val Paladin get the better of two newcomers called the Krypton Brothers."

Marci Sanger smiled into the camera. "And you Krypton Brothers fans will be pleased to hear that Joey Krypton did, in fact, survive that crash into the wall. He's pretty badly beat up, but he is alive."

Bo Rheingold nodded earnestly. "We're all pleased to hear that, Marci." He allowed a slight pause and then got straight back to business. "Okay, folks, and now Val Paladin is still in the arena and it doesn't look as though his troubles are over yet."

Paladin tensed. What was that supposed to mean? He glanced round but could see nothing.

"There was a bit of a confrontation back in the dressing rooms this morning between Paladin and a new driver called Bull Nails."

A brief flashback came on the screen of the scene between Paladin and Nails. Paladin experienced a sinking feeling. This was the setup. The Krypton Brothers had only been for openers. The main event was still to come.

"So get ready, folks, because any minute, we're going to see the outcome of that bit of head butting. They say that talk is cheap, but stay tuned, because when we come back, action is going to speak louder than words."

The feed cut to another commercial break. Paladin brought the Kali to a halt beside the West Arena's central tower. Obviously Bull Nails was going to be coming into the arena at any moment. The question was, through which gate, and what was he going to be driving? After the Krypton Brothers, anything was possible.

The commercials finished, but instead of going back to Bo and Marci, the show returned with a shot that held on the drawbridge connecting the twin arenas. Paladin looked from the screen to the drawbridge itself. At first, nothing was moving there. Then what looked like a heavy truck lumbered into the space, crossing over from the East Arena. It looked big and it looked old. The moment that it came out into the sun, Paladin could see that it was a huge old Crane Wolverine, one of the very first battle trucks, close to seventeen thousand pounds of engine, weapons, and armor. A heavy laser turret sat smug, nasty, and dangerous on the top of the cab, and the skull of a longhorn steer was mounted on the engine grill. This had to be some scripted fix devised by Vanna Kreig to goose up the ratings. How could a punk like Nails get himself this antique monster without help from the company? The question was, how did Paladin figure in the script? Was he the hero or was he the victim?

As soon as the Wolverine cleared the drawbridge, it started to rise, sealing the West Arena. Paladin and Nails were now locked in together, one on one. Just to underline the point, flames roared up from the moat, providing a hellish backdrop for the huge advancing truck.

# CHAPTER TEN

Palm Springs was alive with activity, and all over the outlaw camp, men and machines were on the move, the latter throwing up clouds of dust between the abandoned, sun-bleached buildings. The Horde was gripped by a newborn sense of purpose. They were at long last doing something and going somewhere. A challenge was in front of them, maybe one final chance at old fashioned death or glory, and everyone seemed determined to be ready. A long line of vehicles stretched down Gene Autry Drive, waiting to plug into an outlet at the makeshift charging station that had been rigged by Iggy's original crew when they'd first come into the town. The charging point was powered by the hundreds of twentieth-century windmills on the other side of the San Jacinto Mountains, the still functioning remnant of the old experimental wind-power project from the 1970s. Just forty-eight hours earlier, a line like that would have been a scene of frayed tempers, fistfights, and worse. Now everyone waited patiently for their turn. With a sense of purpose, there also came a degree of discipline.

Iggy, driving his Hades, with Billy Dalton's Security Seven following him, seemed to be everywhere in the camp, stopping at intervals to talk to the men and women preparing themselves for combat. Morale was high and everyone seemed ready to roll and ready to fight. Just one problem came up time after time in these chats with the troops. The supply situation verged on critical. The Horde was out of just about everything.

The outlaws knew that they could go without food for days if need be, but ammunition was a different matter. As one old-timer put it, "We're going to look pretty goddamn foolish if we show up at Pomona and we don't got a damn thing to shoot at them with."

Each time the question was raised, Iggy simply winked, smiled, and tapped the side of his nose with his forefinger. "Don't worry about ammunition. I got something cooking. By tomorrow morning, we'll be looking at a whole different picture."

After he'd used this line four or five times, Dalton felt that he had to call Iggy on these promises. They were halted in front of the ruins of the Dunes Hotel, where the K-90s had made their camp. As Iggy climbed out of the Hades, Dalton jumped down from the Security Seven. "So what's the story, Iggy?"

Iggy looked blankly at Dalton. "Story? What story?"

"You really got something cooking? You can get the stuff we need?"

Iggy grinned. "You worried?"

Dalton nodded. "Yes, I'm worried."

Dalton was starting to notice a change in Iggy. It had begun from that moment when he'd talked the Horde into following him as their undisputed leader. He now moved through the camp with his shields constantly up. He was relentlessly performing, giving a continuous and seamless display of confidence and good humor. It was great for general morale but allowed no individual to get near him. Not even Dalton. This worried Dalton. He had no illusions about Iggy Mengele. He was sneaky and he was crazy, but he'd always taken Billy Dalton into his absolute confidence. Even Iggy had known enough to be straight with the man who watched his back.

Iggy's grin broadened, but he didn't quite look Dalton in the eye. It was as though he were enjoying some deep, private joke. "You worry too much."

Iggy started to turn and walk away, but Dalton stopped him. "Wait up a minute."

Iggy's grin faded. "You got a problem?"

"We gotta talk."

"All I'm doing is talking. You think we could make this later?"

Dalton shook his head. "We gotta talk now. The way things stand, we don't have anything like enough ammo to make a showing at Pomona. We could get ourselves creamed. That's a fact that no amount of bullshit can get past."

Iggy's eyes narrowed. Now he was looking straight at Dalton. "You saying I'm bullshitting?"

"I'm saying that, from where I'm standing, you're going to have to work some kind of swift miracle or this army of ours is going to fall apart before it even gets started."

"Is that what you think?"

"That's what I know. If there ain't food and ammunition arriving in camp by this time tomorrow, your loyal followers are going to have a suitable tree all picked out and be looking for you with a length of rope. A crew like this can change mood real fast. Particularly when they're disappointed."

Iggy's eyes glittered. "And will you be leading the lynch mob, Billy boy?"

"Everyone knows I'm your sidekick. They'll be coming after me, too."

Iggy stared down at the ground, as though thinking. After a long time, he looked back up at Dalton. "You trust me? You trust me, Billy Dalton?"

Dalton wondered what was coming next. "You know I trust you."

"So trust me on this. We'll have everything we need."

Dalton wanted to believe Iggy, but he was having difficulty. "By tomorrow."

Iggy nodded. "By tomorrow."

"But you're not willing to tell me how you're going to do it?"

"You'll find out soon enough." Iggy's expression carried a trace of mockery. "Even you have to allow me a few little secrets."

This was exactly the kind of response that Dalton had been hoping he wouldn't get. As he was wondering what would happen if he pushed Iggy any further, an electronic bleating started to come from Iggy's Hades. Iggy grinned. "Well, how about that. Someone's calling me up."

Dalton was surprised. The tone of the ringing was the kind that came from a cell-system communicator. He hadn't known that Iggy had a line to the outside world. Iggy went back to the Hades, leaned into the car, and picked up the communication handset.

"Yeah."

There was a pause.

"Yeah, this is me."

Another pause, and Dalton shuffled his feet, wishing that he could hear the other end of the conversation but trying not to look like he was listening. Iggy glanced at Dalton and then spoke into the phone. "That was the deal. That was definitely the deal. It's hardly renegotiable this late in the game."

Iggy listened for almost a minute and then violently shook his head. "No. No way. Tonight. It has to be tonight or the deal's off. I said *off*. You hearing me?"

Iggy listened again. His face was grim. "Okay, as long as it's tonight. No foul-ups, right?"

Who the hell could Iggy be talking to outside of Palm Springs? Dalton had a sinking feeling. A lot was going on that neither he nor anyone else in the camp knew about.

Iggy was still talking. "Yeah, okay. It'll be done, just like I said it would."

He was silent for some seconds, and then he nodded with finality. "Good-bye, Vanna, don't let me down. You know what I'm saying?"

Vanna? Who in creation was Vanna? The way that Iggy had said the name made it almost sound like an insult. He turned away from the car, smiling, amused by Dalton's confusion. "I expect you're wondering what that was all about."

Dalton looked at his boss guardedly. "What do you think?"

"I think it's like I told you. You'll find out soon enough. Wait until tonight, Billy. Just wait until tonight."

With that, Iggy turned and strode off toward the K-90s' camp, leaving Dalton to wait for him in the armored truck and nurse his unease and confusion.

## CHAPTER ELEVEN

The truck was nothing less than a goddamned juggernaut. Paladin had seen Wolverines before but never one tricked out like this, and he was amazed that the monster had made it past the AADA judges. From its plasticore tires to the top of its laser turret, it was one vast and virtually impregnable combat machine. With such a weight of armor under the purple and gold western-style paint job, Paladin seriously doubted that he could hurt it with anything but his heavy rockets. On the TV feed, even Bo Rheingold sounded awed.

"Well, friends and neighbors, it isn't often that we see anything like this in the arena here at Pomona, and I'm wondering if it's even strictly legal. I guess it's kind of late to be thinking about that now, though. Bull Nails has brought his rig into the ring and it looks like the door's been closed behind him. I gotta tell you, friends, I really wouldn't want to be Val Paladin right now. When Bull Nails braced Paladin in the dressing rooms this morning we thought we might see a grudge match in the arena today, but none of us suspected that the newcomer was riding a rig quite like this. It kinda looks as though the black knight may just get himself . . ." Rheingold couldn't resist a self-congratulating grin. ". . . nailed."

Paladin snarled. Rheingold was lying through his teeth. Everyone in the control room must have known exactly what kind of vehicle Bull Nails would be driving.

Moving at little more than walking pace, the Wolverine ground its way into the arena. Nails turned it away from where Paladin waited by the central tower and began a slow circle of the ring.

Paladin muttered under his breath. "Pretty confident, boy. Just ambling along, showing off your goodies."

On his helmet speaker, Bo Rheingold's commentary continued. "It seems like Bull Nails doesn't figure there's much the dark knight can do to him. He's coming round the circle now, slow and easy, just like it was a beauty contest. As for Paladin, he really only has just two choices. He can either forfeit the match by leaving the arena right now, and I for one wouldn't blame him if he did exactly that, or he can come out fighting and face this armored beast."

Paladin hated to agree with Rheingold, but in this instance, he was right. He was faced with just two ways to go, either run or fight. If he ran, he'd not only forfeit the match, but it would be the beginning of the end for both his reputation and his career. But if he actually tried to face down Nails in the massive Wolverine, he stood to lose his life.

An electronic beeping filled his helmet. The match timer had gone off. His mandatory half hour in the arena was up and he could leave with no loss of championship points or honor.

Paladin let out a long sigh. "Saved by the bell."

He was about to open the link to the control room and inform Vanna Kreig that he was checking out when the reality of his situation dawned on him. "The hell I've been saved by the bell!"

He hadn't been saved by any damn thing. Vanna Kreig had probably timed this out to the second. The bitch had him locked tight in a trick bag. Sure he was entitled to leave the arena, but no one would see it that way. If he retreated in the face of Bull Nails, he'd never lose the chicken tag. No matter how much he insisted that he was within his rights, the story would be all over how Val Paladin had turned coward, how, when the big one had come at him, he had run away.

"Okay, Nails. You asked for it. You may be big, but you're probably pig stupid as well."

Paladin angrily gunned the Kali forward, flashily spinning the car round so it was running head on, straight at Nails' juggernaut. The Kali shuddered as he thumbed a burst from the twin ATGs. The mixture of HESH, AP, and tracer burst over the front of the Wolverine and the longhorn skull blew into tiny fragments. Paladin tempted fate by glancing briefly down at the tiny TV monitor, and was gratified to see that the explosion of Nails' mascot had been recorded in loving close-up. It was only symbolism, but in a life-and-death situation, even symbolism could provide a crucial edge.

The Wolverine powered forward as though it had been stung, and as it came through the smoke, Paladin saw what he had feared. The damage, even from his antitank guns, was minimal. He was using low-load stadium ammunition, designed for visual effect rather than destructive force, and this rig had a hell of a weight of armor to chew through before he could hope to disable it. A light flashed from the laser turret, sweeping across the arena straight at the Kali. Paladin swung the car into a skidding turn and then gunned it away, around the central tower and out of the field of fire. His only chance was to keep jumping in at an angle, hitting the Wolverine hard, and then getting the hell out before Nails could respond. It was a gadfly play and he only hoped that he had enough ammunition to go the distance.

Nails put the hammer down but he didn't try to come after Paladin. In terms of speed, the Kali had the big rig shut down from the get-go. Turning the duel into a race would be pointless. Instead, Nails started charging round the center of the track. After the first half circle, a sudden burst of flame exploded from the back of the Wolverine. Paladin didn't dare hope. Could he really have made a lucky hit with his first burst? Then Paladin saw that it wasn't luck but a rear-directed oil jet. Nails was laying fire, seemingly at random. While Paladin watched, the tractor dropped a second flaming slick. Nails' move was a smart one. The rack on an FOJ held either ten, twenty, or twenty-five loads, and even with ten, Nails could create obstacles all over the arena that would hamper Paladin's hit-and-run tactics.

Either knowingly or not, Nails was giving himself an added advantage. Paladin's heavy rockets were low-throw heat seekers, and the multiple fires were more than enough to confuse the hell out of them. Nails was proving to be far from pig stupid. He seemed to know entirely too much about the weapons that Paladin was toting. He could only assume the Vanna Kreig had marked Bull Nails' card for him in advance.

The Wolverine was now zigzagging, laying fire in an irregular pattern, and Paladin decided it was time to put a stop to this game. Swerving wildly to avoid the areas of fire, Paladin floored the Kali and quickly closed with the tractor. The laser turret was coming around to the rear firing position. Paladin's vision was suddenly obscured by black smoke as Nails tried to turn the oil jet on him. Paladin slackened speed and dropped back. He armed his first rocket and tried for a snap shot, but the rocket started going wild even before it hit the Wolverine's trail of flame. It missed the cab of the truck by scant inches and shot on to explode against the wall. That was another reason that increasing numbers of stadium promoters insisted that players use only low-throw and low-yield ammunition. It helped preserve both the spectators and the real estate.

The laser made a fast rear sweep and touched the Kali. The car's smooth forward motion hardly rippled or rocked as the beam carved a slice on the empty half of the Kali's lucite double-cockpit bubble. If Paladin had been packing a gunner or passenger, they would now be headless. The interior of the car was filled with the stench of burned plastic, and Paladin had to raise his visor to wipe his stinging eyes. "This ain't right, goddamn it!"

A low-yield laser shouldn't be able to do that much damage. Even at full power, it shouldn't cut that deep. "The son of a bitch has got himself a boosted weapon."

Convinced that the fix was in, he stamped down on the juice and surged past the juggernaut. The laser turret wasn't fast enough to pan with him, and once again he could power his way out of immediate harm.

Paladin had entered what he called the detachment, a place in his mind beyond fear, where everything was managable and reactions flowed smooth as silk. It was a place he could only get to in the heat of combat, a place of total focus where everything was excluded except for the moment-to-moment process of battle. He couldn't even hear the roaring of the crowd or Bo Rheingold becoming hysterical on the TV feed.

The Kali was pushed to the left as a burst of machine-gun fire smashed into its right rear armor, and

Paladin all but felt the bullets before they hit. Steering the car away from a burning oil slick, he instantly triggered a pair of rear-mounted micromissiles. One missed but the other flared, blinding white, high up on the top of Wolverine's cab, close to the laser turret. Even in his detachment, Paladin dared to hope. Without knowing it, he was talking quietly to himself.

"Oh yeah, burn good, baby! This might just be the chance I need."

With white phosphorus searing his roof armor, it was possible that Bull Nails might have become a little distracted. Paladin heel-and-toed the Kali into a full 180° turn and let go with a second heavy rocket, straight at the oncoming truck.

"Yeah, go!"

Right up to the last minute, it looked as though the rocket was going to go straight into the Wolverine, but then, ghosted out by the nearest patch of burning oil, it swerved off course and exploded in midair. The explosion was enough to rock the Kali on its springs, and it must have done a lot more than just distract Bull Nails. He appeared to spin the wheel without thinking, as Paladin followed up with a burst of HESH. The cluster of shaped shells burst just above the truck's right front wheel. The Wolverine seemed to stagger forward, all but nosing into the ground as the tire burst.

"Okay, sucker, how you like them eggs over easy?"

Nails wasn't through, however. The laser beam whipped across the Kali, burning into its armor. Again Paladin used his acceleration to get away. The laser really was doing too much damage.

It must have touched something vital, because a cluster of warning lights on the damage-control panel flicked into life, blinking ominously. The drive systems on both rear wheels seemed to be rapidly overheating.

Paladin glanced back. Although it was bouncing on one front rim, and half the cab was smoldering, the Wolverine kept on coming. Worse than that, thick black smoke was pouring from the underside of the Kali.

Paladin knew that he was in trouble. The FCD was on the underside of the Kali, and if the flame loads blew, there wouldn't be enough of him left to bury. The car's voice warning cut in, a calm female voice, totally at odds with the dire situation. "The vehicle is on fire. The FCD is disabled and the magazine will eject in ten seconds. Repeating—The vehicle is on . . ."

Paladin's left hand shot out and hit the override. The voice died. He knew he was taking an insane risk, but it might be the only way to stop Nails. The car was now a short-fused bomb, and he'd cut off all automated help. One false move, and he'd be charbroiled. He quickly glanced back to see if the Wolverine was still behind him. It was right on his tail, bearing down on him across the burning ground. Paladin took a fast breath and placed his hand on the manual magazine ejector. "Hold it, boy. Can't give the sucker time to swerve."

The Wolverine was right on his ass.

"Okay!"

He jerked the toggle. The magazine was gone, and the Wolverine rolled right over it. A series of loud bangs came from somewhere in the rear of the Kali, and the power died. Looking like it was riding on a wave of fire, as the flame loads cooked off right under it, the juggernaut bore down on Paladin. The Kali's mill refused to turn over. Paladin knew that bailout time had come. The world went slow motion. It seemed to take forever to fumble himself free of his safety harness and open the bubble top. All the time, the giant tractor was sliding straight into him. And then the top popped. Paladin grabbed his shotgun from beside the seat and jumped for his life. The last thing he saw before he hit the ground and rolled was Bull Nails, right above him, diving from the cab of the Wolverine with his leather coat burning.

The Kali folded in half as the Wolverine hit it, and the sound of tortured metal was like the foundries of hell. Paladin covered his head and curled his body into a fetal ball as explosion followed explosion. The Wolverine's momentum carried the whole mess almost to the wall before it came to a stop with a blast that sent debris high into the air and sections of the crowd fleeing for cover.

Paladin wasn't sure how long he lay on the ground. His head was spinning, he was having trouble focusing his eyes, and his arms and legs seemed unwilling to respond. His ears were filled with the inferno roar of the Kali and the Wolverine in their death embrace. Bo Rheingold was somewhere at the end of a long tunnel, shouting over the PA.

"What a firefight! What a spectacle! What a firefight!"

About twenty yards away, a smoke-blackened figure was struggling to get to its feet and, at the same time, clawing for a gauss gun on his hip. Then people were all round the two of them, men running with cameras on their shoulders, firemen in flame suits, and paramedics in green jumpsuits. Bull Nails was being restrained and emergency vehicles were screaming from every gate. Hands were helping Paladin to his feet, leading him to an EMS cruiser. It looked as though he and Bull Nails weren't going to be allowed to slug it out to the end, man to man. Both would live to fight another day.

As Nails was led away to a different ambulance, he turned and yelled at Paladin. "You wait, Paladin! I'll get you yet!"

Paladin's mouth curved into a perfect sneer as a camera homed in to capture his reaction. "You think Skynet'll buy you a new toy truck after what you did to the last one?"

He could imagine Vanna Kreig hastily squelching that last bit of audio.

# CHAPTER TWELVE

"Remember, the airships are on our side! Don't fire at them. Don't fire at anything in the sky! Don't fire at the airships! The airships are on our side! Don't fire at the airships!"

All over the ghost city, bull horns and speakers barked out the same order over and over again.

"Don't fire at the airships! Don't fire at the airships!"

It was night in Palm Springs, but no one was sleeping and no one was getting drunk. All eyes strained, looking for shapes in the sky. Iggy and Billy Dalton were once again on the roof of the Ritz Carlton, staring along with the rest into the night sky to the west where the glow of Los Angeles was reflected by the clouds.

Iggy kept glancing at Dalton, repeating the same question every couple of minutes. "You see anything yet?"

Each time, Dalton shook his head. "Not yet."

Iggy was more nervous than Dalton had ever seen him. His whole body crackled with tension, like a penned-up wildcat, and when he wasn't pacing, he couldn't stop himself from rocking backward and forward on his heels. Nerves fluttered and twitched down the left side of his face as he talked to himself. "They're coming. They'll be here soon. They gotta be coming." As they waited, Billy Dalton grew increasingly uneasy. Could it be that Iggy Mengele was actually losing his mind?

Iggy had given the word just before sunset. Supplies were on their way. Three big cargo blimps would be coming in after dark, loaded down with everything the outlaws needed. Surprisingly, few in the camp questioned how Iggy managed this miracle. Iggy was the leader now and all they needed was his assurance that it was going to happen. The Horde seemed willing to blindly follow anyone who offered them the hope of a future. Of those few who did wonder about the source of these mysterious supplies, most preferred not to question Iggy. As the sun went down and the stars appeared, the strain on Iggy was starting to show, and they knew that Iggy Mengele under strain was best left alone.

"You see anything yet?"

Dalton had forgotten how many times he'd shaken his head that night. "Not a damned thing."

"Keep looking."

Billy Dalton had been wondering if this almost magical ability of Iggy's to summon food and ammunition from out of the sky had some connection to the period when Iggy had gone missing. Iggy had never talked about that time to Dalton, or to anyone else as far as he knew. As with most things, no one had ever summoned the courage to quiz Iggy directly about it. The fact remained, though, that Iggy had been gone for over a year and rumor had been rife all along the border country that Iggy was dead. A guy by the name of Ed Brand had even been going round claiming that he'd shot him, a highly dangerous boast if there was no truth to it. Nothing would piss Iggy off more than to have some character going around claiming to have killed him. But Iggy never showed up to put the record straight, and his running partners, the original Horde and the remnants of the Losers, held a wake for their lost leader and then went on with business as usual.

And then suddenly, out of the blue, he had returned. He'd simply walked into the camp one night, with no comment, certainly no explanation, wearing the same slightly insane grin. Within a matter of days, he'd been the boss again.

The way Dalton figured it, Iggy must have formed some weird alliance during the time he'd vanished. How else could he line up enough outside help to suddenly bring in supplies by airship? And then there'd been that afternoon's unexpected call from someone on the outside. Dalton looked at Iggy. He was pacing again. Dalton burned to confront him and demand to know what was going on. Dalton knew, however, that in his present mood, Iggy would be more inclined to whip out a pistol and shoot him dead rather than come up with any answers.

"You see anything?"

"No . . ." Dalton hesitated. "Wait a minute."

Iggy was instantly beside him. "What?"

"Over there."

"Where?"

"There. Between the two mountains . . . I don't know, maybe it's just a cloud formation. Would these blimps be coming in without lights?"

Iggy nodded. "Quite likely. I doubt they want to advertise what they're doing."

Dalton looked sharply at Iggy. "What the hell does that mean?"

"Confused, Billy boy?"

"I'd just like to know what we're getting ourselves into."

Iggy grinned unpleasantly. "I imagine you would."

Dalton tried hard to keep his own temper in check. "So, are you gonna tell me?"

Iggy's grin widened and, at the same time, became nastier. "All in good time, Billy. All in good time."

"Jesus, Iggy, you're pushing me."

"All in good time." Iggy's attention was back on the night sky. "I think I see them."

Dalton also peered. Three shapes were definitely drifting toward the city. Others must have thought that they saw something too, because beams of light stabbed into the air, spotlights searching the sky. The shapes came nearer and it was clear that they were far too symmetrical to be clouds, and also, in confirmation, the rhythmic slap of engines was becoming audible.

Iggy was elated. "It is them! They're coming!"

A couple of spotlights hit one of the airships, and its bulbous, triangular shape was plain to see. More spotlights came to bear, lighting up all three ships. A trio of heavy lifters, probably C-995s, fat helium-filled deltoids with a crew capsule, twin container pods, and six rotary engines with long paddle propellers slung beneath them. Like most of the big cargo blimps that since the gas crisis had all but replaced truck and rail transport, the C-995 had a shaped gasbag that added aerodynamic lift to that of the helium.

The speakers were blaring again. "Do not fire on the airships! Do not fire on the airships."

Iggy grabbed Dalton by the arm. "Come on, we gotta go."

"Go where?"

Iggy grinned like a wolf. "The airport."

Dalton shook his head. "What are you talking about?"

Iggy pointed into the dark emptiness of the long abandoned Palm Springs Municipal Airport and, as he did, the single surviving runway blazed into life.

Dalton's jaw dropped in amazement. "What the hell . . . ?"

It was a night for party tricks and Iggy obviously relished the role of conjuror.

"A little routine I cooked up with Tod Slaughter earlier. Gotta give those guys a landing marker."

Dalton could see that the airfield's original landing lights were supplemented by the headlights of a parade-ground lineup of cars, trucks, and bikes.

Dalton couldn't believe what he was seeing and hearing. "Tod Slaughter knew all about this?"

"I explained a few things to him this afternoon."

Iggy was anxious to go, but Dalton dug his heels in. "Explained what to him?"

"How I was going to get these guys to fly in here with a load of supplies."

"And how did you do that? I'd be real interested to hear."

Iggy, who was already heading for the stairs that led down from the roof, turned and faced Dalton. "It was easy. I sold the TV rights to this little war that we're about to start."

With that, Iggy Mengele was hurrying down the stairs. Billy Dalton raced after him, yelling into the stairwell. "What the hell are you talking about?"

Iggy's voice floated up above the sound of his boots crashing down step after step. "I did a deal."

Dalton plunged down the stairs after him. "Who with?"

"Skynet."

"The satellite network?"

"The very same."

"You're putting me on."

"I swear."

"What kind of a deal?"

"They keep us supplied and we give the greatest live-action show of all time."

"What live-action show?"

"The Last Hurrah of the Outlaw Warriors."

"You're insane."

Iggy's laugh sounded deranged as it echoed up the stairwell. "Yeah? So?"

By this time they were down to ground level. Iggy headed straight for the vehicle park without stopping for anything. Dalton remained close behind. As they approached the parked cars and trucks, Iggy turned and gestured to him.

"We'll take your truck."

Dalton shrugged and climbed into the driver's seat of the Security Seven. Iggy swung himself up into the gun turret. As Dalton started the motor, he glanced up at him. "You want to run all this by me again? You're saying that Skynet, the satellite TV network, is supplying us with everything we need... so we can go and attack their own autoduel arena at Pomona?"

Iggy nodded. "You're a real bright boy, Billy. You got it in one."

"And how did Tod Slaughter take this piece of news?"

Iggy grabbed for a handhold as Dalton jammed the truck into drive and lurched forward. "He had a bit of trouble with it at first. He ain't as smart as you are, Billy, I had to lay it out for him a couple of times before he got it. He came round to my way of thinking in the end, though."

The truck hit forty as Dalton gunned it down the hotel driveway. Through the windshield, he could see that the three cargo blimps were right over the town, lit from below by dozens of spotlights, looking like three fat UFOs.

"How come you didn't lay it all out for me?"

Iggy smirked. "You jealous or something?"

"Starting to feel kinda left out of things. Like you don't trust me no more."

"Sure, I trust you. That's why I thought it was okay to keep you in the dark until everything panned out. I mean, you're my loyal henchman, ain't you?"

"And what about that rousing goddamned speech this morning about how selling out to TV was like having your balls cut off?"

"A leader has to do a lot of things to keep up morale."

"This is some weird twisted logic."

Iggy cackled as Dalton swung the truck onto Date Palm Drive and pushed it up to seventy. "So what else is new?"

Dalton gripped the wheel very tightly. He was having trouble dealing with these revelations. "The men are liable to hang us all if they find out what you've been up to."

"Then they better not find out."

"Are we really going through with this?"

"Through with what?"

"This attack on Pomona."

Iggy had the turret flap open and was gazing up at the three airships. "Sure we're going through with it. There may be a few changes in the script, though."

"Like what?"

"Like I suspect the idea is that we're all supposed to get ourselves killed. I was thinking more of winning."

The truck passed the old Palm Springs Drive-In on

the corner of Date Palm Drive and Ramon Road. An ancient flickering print of Elvis Presley in *Girls, Girls, Girls,* more scratches than picture, was playing, but it was being totally ignored. Most of the outlaw audience had climbed up on the screen or the projection booth to get a better view of the airships. Dalton glanced back at Iggy. "Is there any more stuff you've been keeping me in the dark about?"

Iggy shrugged. "Plenty, but there isn't the time to go into it right now."

Dalton swung the Security Seven left onto Ramon. The airport was coming up on the right. A crowd had already gathered outside the south vehicle entrance and was being kept there by a squad of armed K-90s. Dalton hit the horn as he came up to the gate and the onlookers scattered. A K-90 toting an old-fashioned M-60 signaled for the truck to stop, but Iggy stuck his head out of the turret and they were immediately waved through.

The first C-995 was drifting majestically down to the overgrown main runway. When the big blimps were in the air, it was impossible to really gauge just how huge they were. Close to the ground, their two hundred feet of wingspan and massive inflated bulk dwarfed the line of cars and trucks that were supplying the makeshift lights. Vast as it was, however, the first C-995 settled with the delicacy of a feather. With its engine pods angled up and throttled back, the lead blimp gently descended until the skids on the bottom of the cargo pods kissed the ground.

Directly the skids touched, and the gang of outlaws who had been recruited as ground crew and cargo handlers dashed forward. They cast long crisscross shadows as they moved in front of the massed headlights, ducking through the sandstorm whipped up by the prop wash from the blimp's engines. As the ground crew moved to their places, though, the ball turret on the underside of the C-995 crew capsule swiveled to cover them with its snub-nosed twin cannons. Obviously the crew of the blimp was taking no chances on this unique and unorthodox mission. When the handlers went straight to work, however, the gun turret returned to its rest position. Apparently the crew was satisfied that no double cross was going to be pulled on them.

For men who were totally untrained, the hastily assembled ground crew uncoupled the massive steelweb H-tags that attached the two cargo containers to the blimp in double-quick time and dragged the containers to one side to make room for the next airship. The second blimp was already coming down as Dalton steered the Security Seven into the blaze of light around the landing area. He brought it to a halt where Tod Slaughter was supervising the operation.

Iggy immediately swung down from the turret. "How's it going?"

Slaughter nodded. "It's going good, real smooth."

Iggy grinned. "Okay."

"The K-90s don't screw around."

"I'm beginning to realize that."

It was Slaughter's turn to grin. "You'd better believe it."

The ground handlers were throwing aside the wide steel-mesh strips and signaling to the blimp's crew that they were free to take it up. As the second blimp started to lift, the team all moved to one end of the first container pod and strained to push it along on its skids, out of the immediate landing area.

Slaughter glanced at Iggy. "What do you want us to do once we get the last blimp unloaded?"

Iggy looked up at the rapidly lifting airship. "I guess you could start breaking down the cargo pods. You better put a serious guard all round them, though. Pick men you can absolutely trust. I wouldn't put it past some of these crews to take it into their heads to hijack the whole consignment. It might also be an idea to organize an issue of booze to the whole camp."

Tod Slaughter's face registered surprise. "Booze? What booze?"

The familiar wolf grin spread across Iggy's face. "There's fifty cases of bourbon in one of those containers. A dozen bottles to the case. I figure some of that firewater might be good for morale."

Tod Slaughter frowned doubtfully. "Is that such a good idea? Most likely everyone in the camp will get as drunk as a skunk."

Iggy nodded. "That's the idea. I want every last one of them to be feeling no pain when we move out tomorrow."

Slaughter's eyebrows shot up. "Tomorrow? We're moving out tomorrow?"

Iggy spread his hands and his grin turned into a look of guileless innocence. "We've got to go with the element of surprise, and there's no way you can keep a secret very long in an outfit like this. Why? You got a problem with that?"

Slaughter shook his head. "No, I guess not. One time's as good as another. What about ammunition? You want us to start issuing that as well?"

Iggy shook his head. "No, we'll hand out the ammunition right before we move. If we give it out now, these lunatics will spend the night either killing each other or shooting into the air trying to hit the moon."

# CHAPTER THIRTEEN

Val Paladin had made up his mind. He was going down to the Leper Colony to get roaring drunk in full view of everyone. At first he had been inclined to stay in his quarters, nursing his contempt for commercial autoduelling, the Skynet Corporation, and the whole idiot business. Then something inside him had revolted. Damn them all. Why in hell should he keep his feelings to himself? The day had started out nasty and then turned nastier by the hour. By the time that the floodlights had come on and the games had gone into their nighttime mode, he was actually relieved that he'd been called into the ring early to face the Krypton Brothers and Bull Nails. Those two contests had only been preliminary bouts in a day that had broken all records for lethally bloody unpleasantness. By the close of play, the death toll stood at nineteen, and even the crowd in the stands had become subdued in the face of such unprecedented slaughter.

The final game had been an insane free-for-all that finished up looking like the aftermath of a nuclear attack, with vehicles left to burn in the arena. Drivers had died without medical attention because the paramedics wouldn't risk going into the inferno of tracer and oily smoke. The moat blazed, lasers flashed from the twin towers, and the cameras went for tight close-ups of the dead and dying that were repeated over and over in rolling computer montages on the big screens. Vanna Kreig seemed to believe that nothing was too brutal or disgusting that it couldn't be beamed out to the viewing audience in the name of entertainment. She didn't even hesitate when a gunner, bailing from a cripped Polaris that was about to be turned into scrap by a rammer, had his head splattered by a biker who came up behind him wielding nothing more sophisticated than a 36-inch prybar. She not only went for the tight hi-def close-up but then ran two slo-mo, stop-action replays.

As Paladin stood in the pits, watching the mounting insanity, he knew that autoduel, as it was played at Pomona and relayed to the world by Skynet, had crossed the line. Once it had been a sport, no matter how dangerous. Now it was nothing but a blood spectacle, laid on for the sick amusement of the burgerheads of America. In the real world, the dumb bastards were probably too terrified to even leave their apartments after dark. Paladin was sickened by the whole idea and he didn't give a damn who knew it.

He voiced his disgust as he and Mac Connolly passed a pint of J.T.S. Brown back and forth. They were staring glumly at what was left of the Kali. "I ought to take my fucking shotgun and grease that bitch Vanna Kreig. And her whole gang of suits."

"So why don't you?"

Paladin took a hit on the bottle and sighed. "I gotta tell you, Mac, I think I seen enough killing for one day."

The Irishman shot him a sidelong glance. "There's always tomorrow."

"You got a point there."

"You're not the only one that's thinking like that."

Paladin looked at him. "You?"

"I'd like to see them suffer first. The old-time IRA used to have a trick they used on informers. They blow off the victims' kneecaps. Apparently it hurt worse than you could imagine."

When Paladin got back to his quarters, his first impulse was to rip off the fancy combat suit and hurl it as far away as possible. He wanted to climb into the shower and let the water, as hot as he could stand it, course all over his body for at least a half hour. As he tugged at the velex fastening, though, his attitude abruptly changed. To try to shower away the day was pointless. The poison wasn't on his skin or his costume; it had penetrated all the way into his soul, and no amount of water could get rid of it. He'd not only go and get as drunk as a skunk, but he'd do it in the full Val Paladin regalia, sweaty and with the flash burns still blackening his armor.

The Pomona Bowl was silent as Paladin left his quarters and walked across the darkened enclosure, but he could feel the atmosphere. A cloud seemed to hang over the place, a cloud of anger and frustration, waiting for the dawn to see what the next day might bring. Somewhere a man and woman were yelling at each other, probably out on the campsite where over half the audience went to spend the night in their cars and RVs.

A movement overhead caught his eye. Three dark shapes were drifting across the sky from east to west. Paladin halted and stared upward, craning to make out exactly what the things were. The shapes looked like deltoid cargo blimps, and Paladin wondered how come they were flying high without lights in the dark of night. He could only assume that they were up to no good, maybe running contraband of some kind, either in or out of the Free Oil States. He watched them until they vanished behind the arena wall, shrugged, and walked on. The blimps, if that indeed was what they were, had nothing to do with him. So what if they were doing something clandestine and illegal? At least they were headed for somewhere other than Pomona.

The sullen, brooding atmosphere was at its worst inside the Leper Colony. Normally, after a day's play, even a day that had racked up a heavyweight body count, the players' bar was a scene of loud and uncontrolled rowdyism. Men and women, who'd been given no guarantee that they'd even live to see the sun go down, celebrated their survival and tried to lose themselves for a while in drunken oblivion. Tonight, however, the players and mechanics sat hunched over the tables, staring morosely into their drinks while the sound system played maudlin country music.

A number of drivers appeared to have had the same thought as Paladin. They'd come to the bar straight from the ring in their stained armor and dirty leathers, to put a final alcoholic termination to a day that, as far as they were concerned, would live in infamy. At regular intervals, one of them would sit up, shake his head, and recount some incident from this seemingly unbelievable afternoon.

"I mean, sweet Jesus, did you see that Jackhammer burn? I was right up close to it. The poor bastard driving didn't have a chance. I saw him through the canopy just before the unit blew. He couldn't get the goddamned thing open and he was screaming. I could see him, but I couldn't hear anything. His mouth was open and every vein in his face and neck was standing out like a rope."

Around this point the story would run out of steam as

the numb disbelief took over again. "I'm telling you. This shit is getting unreal. You know what I'm saying?"

Heads all over the room would nod in agreement. "Unreal."

The same heads turned as Paladin walked into the place. Vito Kurtz, one of the top ram drivers on the circuit, was standing near the door, and he scowled at Paladin. "You were lucky, man. You went in early, before the fun'n'games got totally out of hand. Do you have any idea what that bitch was doing?"

Vito was red in the face and his skin was covered with an oily sheen of whiskey sweat. He'd plainly been taking his drinking very seriously. Somewhere along the line, he'd stripped off the top half of his trademark scarlet armor and was naked to the waist. Paladin shrugged and walked past him, heading for the bar. "By 'that bitch' I take it you mean Ms. Vanna Kreig? Our beloved director for the day?"

Kurtz followed Paladin to the bar. "That's exactly who I mean. What the hell was she trying to prove?"

Paladin glanced back at Kurtz. "What do you think she was doing? She was making the ratings. That's what it's all about in the noble sport of autoduel, isn't it? TV ratings points?"

Kurtz growled. "I think we just got into the human-sacrifice business."

Paladin scowled. "If fucking Kreig has her way, that's gonna be the way of the future."

He gestured to Gasoline the bartender to pour him a shot of the usual and to give Kurtz the same again. Kurtz looked Paladin up and down. "I don't know about you, but I ain't too keen on being a damned sacrifice. I mean, I don't mind taking chances, but if she ain't stopped, she's going to turn this ring into a slaughter house."

A majority of the people in the Leper Colony were now looking at Paladin and Kurtz. As a star-rated player, they wanted to hear what Paladin had to say about the situation. Paladin nodded. "Mac Connolly wants to shoot off her kneecaps, IRA style."

Kurtz barked out a harsh laugh. "I always did like that Irish mick."

Paladin downed his shot in two gulps and looked to Gasoline for a refill. "I guess we could all up and quit. If she ain't got the players, she can't pull no more shit."

Petaluma Annie, a large biker in a suit composed entirely of leather straps, shouted from where she sat at one of the tables in the back. "Is that the best you can come up with, Paladin? If we don't like it, we should quit?"

Paladin raised his glass and smiled amiably at her. "How you doing, Annie?"

Petaluma Annie glared at him. "I'm doing lousy, Paladin. I almost got myself killed in that last free-for-all. That bitch in the control room wants us all turned into roadkill."

Paladin glanced at Gasoline. "You better send Annie a drink over too."

Petaluma Annie hauled herself to her feet. "I don't want a fornicating drink, Val Paladin. I want to know what we're going to do about that bitch Vanna Kreig."

Every eye in the room was now on Paladin, who looked straight back at them. "I didn't call no union meeting."

Vito Kurtz indicated that Gasoline should leave the bottle for him and Paladin to help themselves. "This ain't no union meeting. If the fun'n'games keep going the same way as they did today, we're all going to wind up dead."

Vicky Bligh, the woman sitting with Annie, puffed

on her cheroot. "This shit could catch on. We all know that. It's just the kind of bullshit the numb fucking meatheads could go for. It ain't real to them."

Petaluma Annie was nodding. "It's real to us."

Kurtz poured both himself and Paladin a shot apiece. "We can't sit still for no more of this shit."

Paladin downed the shot in one and suddenly grinned. "Maybe we oughta go and brace Kreig about what's happening. Let her know how we feel about her bullshit."

Petaluma Annie growled. "I'll show her how I feel about it."

Slick Bowdry, a minor leaguer who had been drinking since well before noon, got unsteadily to his feet. "My twelve-gauge Mossberg could show her how I feel."

The crowd muttered comments of "Right on" and "Kill the bitch." Paladin grinned and picked up the bottle. "So do it. You don't need me to tell you it's okay."

The booze was starting to kick in. Paladin suddenly found the idea of an angry and drunken mob of drivers and gunners marching across to the admin building to confront Vanna Kreig very appealing. Vito was looking at Paladin through narrowed and bleary eyes. "So are you with us?"

Paladin laughed. "Sure I'm with you. I don't want to wind up dead."

Slick Bowdry looked round at the inmates of the Leper Colony as though it had all been his idea. "So what are we waiting for?"

After a moment's hesitation, Petaluma Annie nodded. "Yeah, right. What are we waiting for?"

The cry was taken up. "What are we waiting for?" Suddenly everyone in the Leper Colony was on his or her feet. A mass surge toward the door started. Paladin continued to smile. "Fastest lynch mob I ever did see."

He glanced at Gasoline. "Hold the fort here. I imagine we'll all be back sooner or later."

As the players elbowed their way out of the bar, Paladin scanned the faces. When he'd first walked into the Leper Colony, he'd expected to see Bambi Starr there, possibly even waiting for him to show. He hadn't seen her all afternoon, but from the way that she'd talked to him that morning, he'd read her as at least marginally interested in getting to know him better. As he followed the crowd out into the enclosure, carrying the bottle with him, he dismissed the thought from his mind. Maybe he'd read her wrong.

The Pomona admin building and the Leper Colony were some seventy yards from each other along the perimeter wall. Along the way, the crowd grew in size and became considerably noisier. Loud voices were shouting out the news that they were on their way to confront Kreig about the day's carnage. Drivers streamed from their quarters. Crews dropped their tools and left the pits en masse. By the time the front ranks of the crowd reached the main entrance to the admin section, Pomona security had also been alerted, and five blue-uniformed Action Corps security men, in flak jackets and riot helmets with protective visors locked down, stood blocking the doorway with machine pistols and autoload shotguns at the ready.

The mob halted a few yards back from the door. Vito Kurtz, taking role of leader and spokesperson for the players, made a drunkenly placating gesture to the arena security. "Why don't you just step aside boys? Whatever happens, we're going to get Vanna Kreig, and, if you back off now, nobody else will get hurt. You know what I'm saying?"

A security officer with sergeant's stripes took a step forward. "We can't do that. We got our orders." He raised his voice so all of the mob could hear it. "You all best either go back to your quarters or go back to the cantina before this gets out of hand!"

A rumble ran through the crowd. Kurtz took a step toward the sergeant. "I'm warning you. We're going in there to get that bitch Kreig, either round you or through you."

At the back of the crowd, Paladin took a long pull on the bottle and then started to ease his way through to the front. He got there just as the security men moved back and closed ranks. Their weapons were pointed directly at the chests of the crowd. Paladin moved up beside Kurtz and faced the sergeant.

"You're really making a big mistake."

It was hard to see the sergeant's face through the locked-down visor, but the man showed no sign of wavering. "I don't think so."

"You know what's going to happen, don't you?"

The sergeant said nothing. Paladin shook his head sadly. "At least let some of us through so we can see Kreig."

"It wouldn't matter if I did. She's not even here. She took a chopper back to L.A. There's only the night tech crew left in here."

Kurtz's jaw jutted beligerently. "She ain't here?"

The sergeant nodded. "That's what I'm telling you."

Paladin glanced at Kurtz. The rammer was very drunk and liable to do any damn fool thing. Paladin was a little drunk himself, but he had yet to reach the self-destructive phase. "You better let a few of us in so they can make sure she's not there."

"I can't do that."

Paladin was starting to lose patience. "Get real, will you, man. If you don't make some sort of compromise, this bunch is going to go and get their weapons and then all hell is going to break loose."

A slurred voice came from behind. "Some of us got our weapons already." Paladin didn't look round, but he suspected it was Slick Bowdry. He continued to face the security sergeant. "You see what I mean?"

The sergeant held his ground. "If this bunch doesn't disperse, I'm going to have to give the order to open fire."

## CHAPTER FOURTEEN

By a quarter to three in the morning, a good third of Palm Springs was on fire. Cars and motorcycles roared up and down the main streets, and the air was filled with nonstop shouting, screaming and howling. The Horde was breaking camp in the most literal sense. They had supplies, they had ammunition, and they had the will to fight. They were on their way to Pomona and beyond. Most of them also had a skinful of whiskey and could hardly remember their own names. After the K-90s had issued the whiskey, the Horde's farewell to its temporary home grew to truly epic proportions.

Gangs of men and women, both in vehicles and on foot, roamed through the ruins, drunk out of their minds, randomly destroying any structure that took their fancy. Arson became the night's sport of choice, along with the usual sex, mindless violence, and probably a good deal of score settling. The outlaw philosophy dictated that if you had a beef with a guy and a battle was coming up, it was best to get in early and kill him yourself before some total stranger did it for you.

The Jetboys had played a particularly prominent part

in the general pyromania, bringing to it a supercharged boyish enthusiasm, a couple of backpack flamethrowers, and a supply of homemade incendiary devices, the main ingredients of which were household granulated sugar and a common herbicide. They also packed a healthy explosive force, and just three of them were more than enough to totally eliminate the bronze statue of Sonny Bono at the corner of San Rafael and Indian. The Jetboys hadn't merely contented themselves with destroying statues, however. As they became drunker, their ambitions grew more elaborate. Around midnight, they had set fire to the Palm Springs Convention Center, reducing it to a blackened ruin in a little over an hour, and by 3 AM, they were working on razing the Dunes Hotel.

Within minutes of the whiskey being passed out, Iggy knew that he had made exactly the right decision when he had told Slaughter to hold the ammunition until the morning. The Horde would indeed have spent the night shooting at the moon, if not at each other.

Through the hours of darkness, Iggy moved through the city, presiding over the festivities. Standing in the back of a commandeered open car, he knew he was the total warlord. He laughed as each new building went up in flames, waving and cheering as he encouraged his drunken followers to greater and greater excess. He had a lot to be pleased about. The ambition that had dogged him for all of his life was being fulfilled. Whatever the outcome of the attack on Pomona, he had already made his mark. He had raised one of the biggest outlaw armies that the Southland had ever seen, and that alone was enough to guarantee his place in renegade history. He was also burning his first city.

As he roamed the city, he felt a sense of elation that he had never experienced before. Was this the way the old-time despots had felt when they burned a town?

Was this how Attila had felt, or Alaric, Tamerlane, or Genghis Khan, Quantrill as he burned Lawrence, Kansas, even Napoleon as he watched Moscow go up in flames? Had Sherman felt this elation as Atlanta burned or the SS generals as they put Warsaw to the torch? Tonight it was Palm Springs burning; in the coming days, he would take Pomona. After that, who knew? Maybe Los Angeles itself? Conquests were only as small as the imagination of the conqueror.

He felt like raising his head and howling at the stars. It was a pinnacle in his life. He would always be remembered as the man who had set fire to Palm Springs and no one could take that away from him.

A crowd had gathered to watch the Jetboys trying to destroy the Dunes. Charlie Fats was driving the car for Iggy, and as they approached, Iggy indicated that they should stop for a while. The crowd had been partying for so long that it was no longer in a condition to be impressed that their leader had come among them. Iggy was largely ignored as most of those gathered went on with their drinking and concentrated on the show. Then a figure detached itself from the crowd and started walking toward him.

Iggy's hand dropped to his gun. Ever since the airships had brought in the supplies, an undercurrent of suspicion had been noticeable among the more thoughtful outlaws. Questions were starting to be asked about how exactly Iggy had managed to pull it off. Who was his mysterious contact on the outside? Maybe the approaching figure was someone who wanted to press the point. It seemed to be a good-looking woman in tight leathers, but that in no way excluded the possibility that she could be looking for trouble. He eased the gun out of its holster, thumbed off the safety, and held it down by his side, out of sight. When the woman spoke, it came as something of a surprise.

"Iggy? Iggy Mengele? Is that you?"

Iggy was stunned. It was the voice of Ilsa McCoy, but Ilsa McCoy as Iggy had never seen her before. The shapeless coveralls had gone. She walked toward the Hades swaying her hips in a skintight leather bodysuit and long high-heeled boots. The zip that ran up the front of the suit was unfastened all the way to her navel. Her hair, which had always previously been tied up in a dirty, functional bun, swung, bushed out and free, well past her shoulders.

"Ilsa McCoy?"

McCoy halted. Smiling and with one hip sexily tilted, she looked up at Iggy. "You gotta feel real good tonight."

Iggy noticed that she was wearing purple lip gloss.

"You're looking kind of different."

Ilsa half turned, posing, pin-up style, hand on hip. "You like it?"

"I didn't know you could look that way."

"Sometimes I make the effort. When the motivation's strong enough."

"And what was the motivation tonight?"

McCoy indicated the burning city.

"Seemed like a special occasion. One way or another, things are going to be different after tonight."

Iggy grinned. "Yeah, they are."

Ilsa pointed to the sidearm that Iggy was still holding down by his side. "If you're so pleased to see me, how come that gun isn't your pocket?"

Iggy looked down at the gun in his hand. He had completely forgotten about it. He slipped it quickly into its holster. "Can't be too careful."

McCoy was holding a bottle. She offered it to Iggy. "You want a drink?"

Iggy nodded. "Sure."

He took the bottle. McCoy leaned against the side of the car. "You gotta be pretty pleased with yourself."

Iggy actually looked smug. "I guess I've come a long way for a poor boy."

"You're a real warlord now. Just like in the stories of the old times."

Iggy nodded. "Yeah, I guess I am."

Up on the seventh floor of the Dunes, an explosion ripped out a section of wall. McCoy turned and looked up. "Shouldn't they be saving their energy for Pomona?"

Iggy shrugged. "I ain't about to tell the Jetboys what to do. If they want to party, let 'em. Besides, I like to see a city burn."

"We ain't gonna run into any surprises when we hit Pomona, are we?"

Iggy's face darkened. "What's that supposed to mean?"

"There's a few people wondering where the blimps might have come from."

"Are you one of them?"

McCoy shook her head. "I'm wondering, but I ain't asking. I figure you'll tell everyone in your own good time."

"I like that attitude."

"I kinda hoped you would."

"For better or for worse?"

McCoy treated Iggy to a long, sultry look. The firelight was reflected in her eyes. "I'd prefer if it was for better."

"You seem pretty determined."

McCoy leaned closer to Iggy. "I can be, when I want something."

Iggy could smell that she'd put on perfume. He wondered where she'd found it. Maybe it came with the leather suit and the lip gloss. He hadn't smelled perfume in a very long time. "You want to get in the car? Maybe go for a last ride around town?"

McCoy nodded. "I'd like that."

Charlie Fats glanced back and grinned at Iggy. Iggy opened the rear door of the car and Ilsa McCoy got in.

"Where to, boss?"

Iggy laughed. "Somewhere dark and quiet."

Fats started the car. "You got it."

McCoy sat very close to Iggy. "I never got close to a warlord before."

"You are now."

"I could maybe get to like the sensation."

"Depends what you want."

She ran a hand under his poncho. "Maybe I want to feel what's in his soul."

Iggy's face twisted into the wolf grin. "Who says I got a soul?"

## CHAPTER FIFTEEN

The blinding white light of a sungun blazed down from the top of the perimeter wall, taking the drunken mob from the Leper Colony by surprise. A bullhorn crackled through the night. "Everyone move back! Move back right now! Move back or we fire."

Paladin recognized the voice straight away. It was Howard Shemp, the head of security at Pomona. Paladin had butted heads with Shemp more than once since he'd been at the stadium. He was a nasty piece of work, a balding onetime merc who took a control freak's pleasure in applied violence. Paladin knew that he wouldn't hesitate to open fire on the crowd given the slightest excuse.

The sudden blaze of light confused the hell out of the mob, totally distracting them from the confrontation in front of the administration building. By far the majority reacted by peering up, straight into the beams, looking for its source, and temporarily blinding themselves in the process. Paladin managed to keep a minimum of smarts about him and shaded his eyes against the glare, looking instead to either side of the light. He was quickly able to make out a number of dark figures ranged along the guard catwalk that topped the wall. He could count a dozen or more black shapes, doubtless Shemp's Action Corps security goons, standing, waiting for the order to fire, with automatic weapons already trained on the mob. The whole scene was taking on an unfortunate resemblance to some old-time prison-break movie.

The bullhorn barked again, confirming all of Paladin's suspicions. "This is Shemp, head of security, and I'm ordering you all to disperse immediately. I have fifteen armed officers up here with me and I'm giving you sixty seconds before I order them to open fire."

Paladin knew, if the situation wasn't instantly defused, the result could be a massacre. He yelled up into the light. "Hey, Shemp, you can't be shooting us. How they going to put on a show tomorrow, if you kill us all?"

Shemp's tone altered slightly. "Is that you, Val Paladin?"

"Sure is, Shemp."

"Then get this drunken rabble back where they belong, Paladin, or you're going to be responsible for a whole lot of them getting greased."

Paladin fought the booze running around in his head and tried to keep his patience. "Don't piss me off, Shemp. All we want to do is talk to Vanna Kreig. We got some problems down here, Shemp."

"Just get this scum back in the Leper Colony where they belong."

Enough was enough. "You wouldn't be talking to us like that if you didn't have a bunch of guns backing you."

Even distorted by the bullhorn, it was possible to hear the gloat in Howard's voice. "Yeah, well I do, boy, and that's all the argument I need."

The mob from the Leper Colony was now looking to Paladin for some kind of direction. Even drunk as they were, most grasped the reality that Shemp and his men had the drop on them.

Vito Kurtz was among the minority who continued to mutter and fume. Like a lot of ram drivers, he had a strong stubborn streak, and he glowered at Paladin. "Are we going to take this garbage?"

Paladin looked up at the figures on the wall and then at Kurtz. "You got a better idea?"

The original group of Action Corp men, who had first stopped the mob from entering the administration building, still stood in the doorway, nervously watching for a sign as to which way the deal might go down. If Shemp ordered the men on the wall to fire, the door guards knew that they were dead.

Paladin saw, to his relief, that Kurtz was at least taking the time to think blearily through his position. If the ram driver gave up and went back to the bar, the rest of the crowd would follow. Shemp, however, was putting on the pressure.

"You got thirty seconds left!"

Paladin yelled up at the wall, playing for time. "Some of these boys have been drinking, Shemp. They don't think so fast when they're like that."

"That's not my problem."

Paladin glanced urgently at Kurtz, and Kurtz shrugged. "I guess they got the drop on us."

Paladin was just breathing a sigh of relief when Slick Bowdry decided to get in his nine-cents' worth. "This is garbage. That son of a bitch can't tell us what to do."

He emphasized the statement by brandishing the cut-down shotgun that he carried on a strap over his right shoulder, and Paladin's flesh crawled. It was all too easy to imagine bullets smashing into his body. No one could reason with a booze-stupid drunk like Bowdry.

Paladin hauled off and swung. The punch wasn't scientific, but science didn't play much of a part when it came to punching out drunks. The blow landed on the left side of Bowdry's jaw, and he went down without a sound. Before anyone else could react, Paladin faced the crowd, gesturing to where Bowdry lay crumpled on the ground.

"Get him up on his feet, and let's get the hell out of here."

As the mob of players and their mechanics started sullenly back to the Leper Colony, Paladin looked up at the security chief on the wall. "You won this one, Shemp, but don't think this is the end of it."

Grumbles of agreement came from the crowd. To people who made their living autoduelling for TV, even the most minimal saving of face was important.

Two hours later, back inside the smoky gloom of the Leper Colony, the booze flowed and old-time militant rock and roll played on the sound system, and the stories became taller and more grandiose. A new arrival wouldn't have known that the abortive march on the admin building was the drunken, ill-considered, ineffectual incident that it was. Players were up on their hind legs and haphazardly yelling at each other.

"Strike! That's what we want! All-out strike! We all walk. No more fucking fun'n'games until we get some ground rules."

"Come on. All they'll do is bring in a bunch of amateurs who don't know any better."

"We ain't letting no scabs in here!"

"We know how to handle scabs!"

A big gunner, with a bottle clutched in his beefy fist, climbed up on the bar. "This ain't a strike, goddamn it! This is a fucking mutiny! If we stick together, we could take over this place! We got the numbers! We got the weapons!"

While all this was going on, Paladin was wondering how much of this after-the-fact belligerence would survive the morning's hangover. Kurtz, on the other hand, seemed to want to go all the way with it. "This ain't even a mutiny. If we wanted, this could be a uprising! A full-scale revolution. A revolt of the gladiators!"

Petaluma Annie was one of the few voices of reason. "Vito thinks he's a goddamned Spartacus."

Kurtz rounded on her angrily. "What's so wrong with that?"

"You know what happened to Spartacus. He finished up nailed to a tree."

"All I know is that I'm mad as hell and I ain't going to take it."

A lot of voices took up the old cry. "We're mad as hell and we ain't gonna to take it! We're mad as hell and we ain't gonna take it!"

Paladin didn't take part in the yelling and bluster. It wasn't his style and he couldn't see much point in it. Something had to be done about Vanna Kreig, no doubt about that. In the morning, though, the picture could be very different. He wasn't about to get himself in an uproar before he saw that picture. His first rule of life was *Take it as it comes*. The players had made their protest and blown off some steam. Nobody had been killed, and it was time to move on to other business.

Right at that moment, the business that Val Paladin most wanted to move on to was Bambi Starr. Screw tomorrow. Tonight was far from over. The idea of Bambi Starr seemed real appealing. Images of her long legs and tight little ass under the denim cutoffs floated across his inner vision, but where the hell was she? All evening, he'd been expecting her to show, but still there was no sign of her. He would have thought that, if nothing else, she would have appeared during the commotion around the admin building.

He hung around drinking for another hour, while the others players waxed louder and more flamboyant about what they were going to do to Kreig and the rest of the Skynet suits. Still Bambi Starr failed to come walking into the Leper Colony. By the end of the hour, Paladin was swaying on his feet and trying to find enough brains to accept the inevitable. The woman wasn't coming, and it was looking more and more likely that he'd misread the signals. She hadn't been coming on to him at all, just playing it up for the camera. It was a hard thing to admit with a skinful of booze, but just before the room swum out of focus, Paladin set the bottle down on the bar and nodded to Gasoline, "I guess I'm going to call it a night."

Gasoline nodded back. "Then I guess I'll see you tomorrow."

Paladin sighed. "I guess you will."

The chill of the night air hit him hard at first, making his head swim. He stood swaying, taking deep breaths, well aware that he was going to feel unusually bad in the morning. Paladin was in no way prepared for the voice that came out of the darkness.

"Val Paladin."

Paladin groaned to himself and slowly turned. Now what? "That's my name, don't wear it out."

He had to make an effort to not see double as he peered onto darkness. Two figures were standing in the shadows between the Leper Colony and the spare-parts store next door. One was tall and broad shouldered, the other short and skinny.

The voice spoke again. "You don't look quite so big now." The taller of the two figures stepped into the light. "I gotta tell you, Paladin, you really don't look so big now."

Paladin recognized the figure as Bull Nails, and groaned again. "What the hell do you want?"

Nails sauntered toward Paladin, with his thumbs tucked in his belt. "In fact, you don't look like anything more than a pathetic, over-the-hill drunk right at this moment."

Paladin noticed that the man was wearing a new set of coveralls. Presumably his old clothes had burned up at the end of their earlier fun'n'games. "Listen, asshole, it's late. You want to cut the crap and get to the point?"

Bull Nails halted. "I think we got a score to settle."

The second figure stepped into the light. It turned out to be one of the Krypton Brothers. Up close, the man was short, with sallow, unhealthy skin and the not-quite-focused eyes of a psycho. "I think we both got scores to settle."

Paladin took a step back and slowly shook his head. "I really don't need this right now."

"We don't give a damn what you need."

Dee Dee Krypton stepped up beside Nails. "They say my brother Joey may not walk again."

"Didn't anyone ever teach you that what goes down in the arena stays in the arena?"

Apparently no one had ever taught Bull Nails any such thing. His eyes glinted dangerously. "You cost me a truck and a shot at the bigtime this afternoon."

Krypton nodded. "And you cost me my brother."

Paladin looked covertly round for something that he might use to his advantage. Nothing presented itself. "You're making a big mistake here, boys. This ain't no blood feud, this is show business."

Nails was shaking his head. "This is no mistake."

Krypton had a gun in his hand. "It's the payoff for you, Paladin."

The night became very quiet and suddenly Paladin wasn't drunk at all. Nails and Krypton had to be completely out of their minds. It wasn't uncommon for a bad loser to try and pick a fight with the winner of a bout. Paladin had assumed that the two might be looking to rough him up a bit. The gun changed the whole picture. These two psychos were looking to chill him out of pure psychotic meanness.

Very deliberately, Krypton raised the pistol until it was pointing straight at Paladin's head. "Get down on your knees, you son of a bitch."

Bull Nails was grinning, clearly enjoying the whole thing. Paladin ignored Nails and looked Krypton in the eye. "Forget it."

Now Bull Nails also had a gun in his hand. "He told you to get down on your knees."

"And I said forget it. If you want to shoot me, you can do it while I'm standing up."

To Paladin's dismay, this didn't seem to bother Krypton. He actually saw the muscles in the man's hands start to tighten. He couldn't quite believe that, within the space of a second or less, a bullet was going to cause his head to splatter like an overripe melon. After all he'd been through in his life, it was absurd that it should have to end like this.

And then a loud bang split the air, and it was Krypton's head splattered and not his. Chunks of brain tissue splashed the front of his combat suit. Bull Nails seemed to be as surprised as Paladin. His jaw dropped, and spinning around he saw Bambi Starr standing by the corner of the parts store, holding a deadly little automatic that still had smoke curling up from the barrel. She looked coldly at Nails. "I'd drop the piece unless you want to end up like your buddy."

Nails didn't need to be told twice. The gun fell from his hand and thudded to the ground. Paladin quickly kicked it out of reach. Bambi all but spat at Nails. "Now get the fuck out of here and don't be messing with any of my friends again."

Nails glowered but didn't say anything as he slunk

away. When he was gone, Paladin turned and faced Bambi Starr, doing his best to put a casual, devil-may-care face on the shock that was still making his heart pound and his stomach churn.

"What took you so long? I've been expecting to see you all evening."

Bambi Starr moistened her lips. Killing seemed to do something for her. "I was hoping that you might come looking for me, but I got tired of waiting."

## CHAPTER SIXTEEN

The Horde was on the move, strung out for almost a mile along the highway and throwing up a cloud of dust that hung in the sky like a threatening storm. With outriders on the flanks and scouts up ahead, they were clear of the smoke-blackened ruins of Palm Springs, and the leaders were onto what was left of Interstate 10, rolling past the abandoned shell of the old Wheel Inn. Back in the twentieth century, the Wheel Inn had been the biggest truck stop in Southern California. Famous for the life-sized concrete dinosaur statues that had been constructed on the parking lot back in the 1960s, it had remained a landmark and a tourist attraction for almost a century and had been featured in a half-dozen Hollywood movies and countless TV shows. When the Wheel Inn had been destroyed by road gangs back in the '20s, the dinosaur statues had miraculously survived. According to legend, the gang leaders had issued strict orders to their men that the dinosaurs should on no account be damaged.

Before the Horde had rolled, Iggy had given the self-same orders. In front of the entire assembled army, he had made it clear that he'd personally shoot anyone who attempted to trash them. He had as good as made it a point of honor. Anything as absurd as a collection of giant concrete dinosaurs had a right to be preserved.

The Horde wasn't moving quite as fast as Iggy wanted. He had always fantasized about an army screaming down on a target like a mechanized wolf pack, hammers down, pedals to the metal, throttles wide open, pennants flapping from their whip antennae and grinding metal music pumping from speakers. His years along the border had taught him that, until the final assault, this Errol Flynn stuff was nothing more than fantasy. Even under the most favorable conditions, an army in transit could only move at the speed of its slowest vehicle. The bigger the army, the more things there were to go wrong.

Although some repairs had been made to the highway system around Los Angeles in the last four or five years, the 10 was still a poor-ass, ruined excuse for a highway, little more than eight lanes of fissures, craters, and collapsed overpass bridges. Before the column would reach Pomona, it would have to deal with stretches where earthquakes had broken up the road surface and flash floods had washed out the foundations, reducing the interstate to an expanse of boulders, rubble, and rusting steel that could have doubled for the surface of the moon.

The column frequently slowed to a crawl to thread its way around obstacles, negotiate bottlenecks, or even detour out into rough desert and then run parallel to the highway until the surface was once again usable. Breakdowns were frequent and engines overheated after covering miles at a stop-go snail's pace in the heat of the sun. In the first ten miles alone, no less than seven vehicles had to be abandoned by the side of the road. Their crews climbed onto someone else's rig, riding the top or clinging to a turret, resigned to the fact that they had been relegated to the role of infantry in the coming fight. The half-dozen tow trucks that belonged to the Horde were working overtime, hauling working vehicles out of trouble and dragging the ones with cracked axles, stripped gears, and blown-up mills to their last resting place at the side of the road.

Iggy was everywhere as the column inchwormed its way forward. He had given Charlie Fats charge of the Hades until they got to Pomona and borrowed a spare dirt bike from the Jetboys so he could go as fast as possible along stretches of highway that would be impassable to a four wheeler. All through the rising temperatures of the morning, he'd roar up on his bike, a hunched figure coming out of the swirling dust with a bandana over his mouth, hair streaming behind him, and eyes hidden behind tinted goggles, ready to untangle a traffic snarl, take a report from a scout, or redirect the column out into open country when the highway was impassable. As he yelled, cajoled, encouraged, and threatened, his energy and optimism appeared limitless. It seemed as though, if needed, he'd carry the whole army to Pomona on his back.

Roaring up and down the column, fast and on his own, Iggy wasn't in any one place long enough for anyone to notice how he was constantly scanning the sky up ahead. His big fear, which he was at pains to conceal in his ceaseless attention to detail, was that Vanna Kreig would pull a double cross and the military in L.A. would launch some kind of air strike against the outlaw column. If that happened, they wouldn't stand a chance. They were strung out and slow moving, ultimately vulnerable on the ruined highway, and it wouldn't take more than a handful of helicopter gunships to make mincemeat of the Horde. They would only need to make a few passes, dropping napalm and HE, and Iggy

Mengele's dreams of glory would go up in a flash of flame and a column of dirty, oily smoke.

Each time bikers returned from scouting ahead, Iggy urgently quizzed them as to what was happening along the road closer to L.A. Every time he got the same answer.

"There's nothing up there, Iggy, I swear to God. The only thing I saw in eight miles was a bunch of homesteaders in a pickup truck."

Iggy still wasn't satisfied. He turned away from the biker, a low-echelon Jetboy, shading his eyes and staring down the road running away to the west. "So what were these homesteaders doing?"

The Jetboy pushed back his goggles. "Looked to me like they were running for their lives. They had all their stuff piled on the back of the truck."

"So I guess they knew we were coming."

The Jetboy grinned at the line of combat vehicles making their way along the highway. "I figure we're kinda hard to miss."

Noon came and went and the scouts continued to bring back favorable reports. Their forward sweeps were now taking them almost within sight of the Pomona Bowl, and there was still no threat of any kind. One after another, they told identical stories. Nothing up ahead that could stop them.

Even though the physical haul to Pomona was proving hard and taking its toll of the vehicles, morale was high with so much good news coming in. Drivers and gunners yelled to each other as they sweated along the freeway.

"Yo, you all ready to get some killing done?"

"Ready and willing."

"Suckers at Pomona won't know what hit them!"

"Fucking-a right. We ain't no TV show. We be a goddamned nightmare."

Iggy did nothing to discourage this kind of talk. The Horde would find out soon enough that Pomona wouldn't be any pushover.

True to form, the Jetboys, who made up the majority of the forward scouts, were so emboldened by the seemingly empty road up ahead that they started talking about taking the fight to Pomona right away. On a break, during which both Iggy and Zap Celine, the new leader of the Jetboys, happened to be drinking beer and taking a breather at the same time, the biker came up with a proposition.

"Hey, Iggy, why don't a bunch of us head up there on our scooters and give them a taste of what's going to come?"

Iggy shook his head. "Forget it. I don't want any of you getting whacked before the shit starts happening for real. You're a bunch of damned freaks but I need your numbers."

Straightaway, Celine came up with another scheme. "Suppose a bunch of us went up there pretending to be spectators, or a crew of ronin bike tramps trying to sign on as amateur cannon fodder. That way, when you launched the main attack, you'd have a crew on the inside that you could do one hell of a lot of damage. Like the Trojan Horse, you know what I'm saying?"

Iggy nodded slowly. It wasn't such a bad idea. His eyes narrowed and he looked sideways at the Jetboy's leader. "You think you could pull off a stunt like that?"

Celine grinned. "Piece of cake."

Iggy wasn't so sure. "Yeah?"

"What could go wrong?"

"You could get all drunk and shoot your mouths off, and, when the rest of us show up, your heads are up there on poles decorating the main gate."

Celine looked offended. "We can hold up our end."

Iggy was silent. Could he really trust the unpredictable bike gang not to screw up? Maybe if he sent a few of the K-90s in with them ...

Heads turned and Iggy's train of thought was abruptly derailed as the slap of helicopter blades came out of the west. Iggy was on his feet in an instant, yelling to the men around him. "Aircraft! Take cover! Incoming aircraft."

A terrible sinking feeling gripped his stomach, telling him that his worst fear was coming true.

"Aircraft! Everyone get down."

All around him men were galvanized into action. Some dived for cover, while others ran for their vehicles. Weapons were cranking up to maximum elevation. The helicopter noise was louder now and men were pointing skyward. Iggy pulled off his goggles and squinted down the road. Further ahead in the column, men were shouting.

"There it is!"

"Looks like there's just one of them."

Iggy could see the helicopter. As far as he could tell, it was on its own. It also wasn't behaving like any attack ship that he had ever seen. It came straight down the middle of the highway, flying low and presenting a perfect target for fire from the ground. Celine was standing beside Iggy, also watching the approaching chopper. "What the hell is wrong with that crazy bastard? He's just begging to be brought down."

Iggy snarled from between clenched teeth. "And he's going to get what he's begging for."

He turned and gestured to the gunner sitting in the turret of a nearby half-track, behind a pair of matched, heavy-calibre Vulcans. "Bring that thing down! Right now!"

The gunner hauled back on the machine guns, swinging them round as the long chopper zipped overhead. Close up, it was easy to see its red and white paint job and the Skynet insignia on the side. Iggy ground his teeth. Vanna Kreig had gone back on her word. She'd promised that no cameras would be in the air until the Horde reached Pomona. The gunner frowned at Iggy, obviously confused. Like the rest of the rank and file, he knew nothing about Iggy's wheeling and dealing with Vanna Kreig and Skynet. "It's just an eye-in-the-sky, camera chopper! You still want me to shoot?"

Iggy's temper went critical, wiping out his previously apparent good humor. "I don't give a damn what it is! Blind it! Bring it down! Kill the damned thing."

The gunner fired a burst but missed. More guns, farther back down the column, opened up, and the chopper instantly took evasive action, swinging up and out, away from the highway. Iggy was beside himself with fury. "Get that thing! Kill it!"

For a moment it looked as though the Skynet chopper was going to get away, and then someone loosed off a heat-seeking missile. The white contrail went straight for the chopper, a white line across the sky, and the two connected in a suddenly expanding ball of smoke and flame. The chopper hit the desert at the same time as the sound of the explosion reached the men and women on the ground.

Iggy slowly turned and faced Zap Celine. "I guess that screws your Trojan Horse plan. We're probably on live TV in instant replay right now."

# CHAPTER SEVENTEEN

As Paladin had expected, the day started with most of the players sharing the same murderous hangover. What he hadn't expected was that the entire day would deteriorate at truly mind-wrenching speed from his opening his eyes in Bambi Starr's trailer, wishing he had died in his sleep.

When Paladin woke and groaned, Bambi was already up, sitting in front of a mirror that took up almost one whole wall of the trailer's bedroom, wearing nothing but a pair of the briefest lace panties and brushing out her blond curls. After about a minute, she noticed he was moving and turned and smiled a knowing, heavy-lidded smile that seemed to indicate her memories of the previous night were a good deal clearer than his.

"How are you feeling?"

Paladin looked around the bedroom and noticed that Bambi had decorated most of the wall space that wasn't mirror with pictures of herself. A lot of them showed her in ultra-provocative poses. Right at the moment, the come-on images didn't do anything for him. "I feel terrible."

Bambi put down the hairbrush and started to work on her lips, applying a scarlet gloss with a brush. "You want some coffee?"

Paladin propped himself up on one elbow. "How come you're so perky this morning?"

"I didn't drink as much as you did."

"Were you serious about the coffee?"

"Sure. I made it a while ago but it's still hot. I'll get it as soon as I've finished this paint job." She made the finishing touches to her lips and put down the brush. "How do you like your coffee?"

"Black, please."

Bambi grinned. "You feel that bad?"

Without looking, Paladin knew that his face was a pale shade of green. "Worse."

"So how do you figure you're going to drive today?"

"I'm not going to drive today. Not if I can help it."

Bambi frowned. "How do you expect to get out of it?"

"Simple. I don't have a car. Remember, I totaled the Kali yesterday."

"Big star like you doesn't have a replacement?"

Paladin nodded. "Yeah, there's a backup, but I'm hoping it won't be ready to roll today."

Bambi looked surprised. "You don't want to drive today?"

Paladin laughed. "Honey, when you've been doing it as long as I have, you don't want to drive any day. Besides, I've got a bad feeling about today. I think Kreig is planning something truly nasty."

Bambi stood up. "I'll get you that coffee. Maybe it'll take the edge off these paranoid feelings."

Paladin lay and watched her as she walked, all but naked, to the trailer's tiny kitchenette, wishing he could remember more about their long encounter in the darkness before he finally passed out. From the look of her, the way that she moved without her clothes, and the hot fragments that he could still pull up from his aching brain, it should have been memorable. His most vivid memory was of the two of them being in the shower together, bodies pressed together under the deluge of hot water. That had only been the start of things.

Moments later, Bambi was back with a steaming mug in her hand. "Here, drink this."

As she handed him the coffee, she leaned close and kissed him on the cheek. Her voice was hot and breathy in his ear. "You were pretty good for a guy who'd put away two bottles of bourbon."

She kissed him again and this time the kiss lingered. Something inside of Paladin forced its way up through the hangover fog. More memories were coming back and, even in the morning, Bambi Starr looked exceptional. He put down the mug on the bedside table and smiled. The smile hurt but he didn't care. All he could think about was the full, defiant curve of her lower lip and the way that her perfume mingled with her real, fresh-from-bed, woman smell. Very gently, he pulled her down on top of him.

Thirty-five minutes later, the coffee was standing cold and untouched, and Bambi Starr slid slowly out of bed, with her hair freshly messed up, her fresh lipstick smeared, and a smug smile on her face. Paladin held out a hand. "Come on back here."

Bambi grinned and shook her head. She took a pair of leather jeans from the wall closet and started pulling them on. "I can't. You've already made me late for the show."

"Screw the show."

"That's easy to say. You've made a name for yourself. I'm still fighting to get to the front of the pack."

Paladin suddenly became serious. "Listen, be really

careful out there today, okay? I think Kreig is about to go crazy."

Bambi was pulling a tank top over her head. She stopped and gave him a look that was both searching and amused. "Are you actually saying that you care, Val Paladin?"

Paladin slowly smiled. "I'd hate to see anything happen to you so soon after we got acquainted."

Bambi's eyes flashed. "Acquainted? Is that what you call it?"

Paladin's smile slowly spread. "What do you want to call it?"

Bambi shook her head and picked up her leather bike jacket. "This is real romantic, Paladin, but I have to go. Will you lock the trailer when you leave?"

"Take care, okay?"

Bambi paused in the doorway. "I won't get into anything I can't handle. I promise."

The decline and fall of the day started in earnest as soon as he left Bambi's trailer. He was dressed in the clothes he had worn all through the previous day's action and the night's drinking. Back in his wild days, he had smelled bad most of the time and it hadn't bothered him in the slightest. He sighed. Goddamned civilization was making him soft.

As he walked across the players' enclosure, Paladin saw security everywhere. Shemp had uniformed Action Corps men, complete with riot helmets and flak jackets, positioned all along the wall, and the administration block was completely cordoned off. Nobody went through the door without intense scrutiny by an Action Corps team complete with X-ray units and mass and metal detectors. Obviously Shemp was taking no chances after the previous night's confrontation, but this beefed-up enforcement, on top of everything that had gone before, was doing nothing to improve the dispositions of the players and mechanics. Their tight, angry faces and attitudes gave fair warning they were reaching the end of their tolerance.

Paladin's first stop was at the pits to make sure that the reserve car wasn't ready to be rolled out. Mac Connolly looked at him with the contempt that the chief mechanic reserved for total idiots. "What do think? That I didn't have anything better to do with my time than go without sleep for a second night running? You think all I want to do is to ready up another unit so you can go out and wreck it? And even if I'd felt so inclined, it would have been hard to get any work done with you ignorant players trying to start a drunken riot. We haven't even cleaned the Cosmoline off the guns."

Paladin laughed. "I didn't want to drive today anyway."

Connolly's grin was wicked. "Then I guess you're a happy man."

"Unless the suits try to find me another car."

Connolly shook his head. "They won't find a car that you can drive." He linked his fingers in a gesture of unshakable solidarity. "Us crew chiefs have our own code. Our drivers don't go out in any car that we haven't worked on personally. That's the rule, whatever the suits might think. If anyone wants to put you in another car, you just send them to talk to me."

With matters in the pits squared away, Paladin started out for the Leper Colony to check on the mood of the other drivers. Although he didn't anticipate any of the previous night's drunk talk to have survived the harsh morning, he wondered how they might be reacting to another day of fun'n'games under Vanna Kreig's direction. Along the way, he stopped at the bank of TV monitors to see what was going on in the arena. What he saw was pretty much what he had expected. No one was trying too hard. The drivers seemed to be playing a noncontact form of ring-around-the-rosie in which they simply circled the arena, firing off their guns or even the odd rocket now and again, but making every effort to avoid any serious engagement. It was hardly a strike or a riot, but at least his colleagues were doing something to demonstrate how they felt about the situation. It was early in the day, however, barely noon, and a lot could still happen. Pomona had plenty of would-be stars like Bambi. Sooner or later, someone would try to heat up the action. When that happened, he knew that Kreig wouldn't be slow to exploit it.

Paladin turned from the screens and immediately noticed a pair of security men, in their dark blue military-style uniforms and with guns at their hips, walking determinedly toward him. He quickened his pace. What the hell did they want anyway? Was he going to be arrested?

The goons caught up with him just as he was about to go inside the Leper Colony. He was pushing open the bat-wing doors when one of the pair called out to him.

"Hey, Val Paladin, we want to talk to you."

Paladin stopped and turned. "Can't this wait? I need a drink."

The Action man who'd called out to him looked him up and down sourly. "From what we heard, you had quite enough to drink last night."

Paladin's face hardened. "I didn't know my drinking was anything for security to be concerned about."

"Maybe it is when it leads to a near riot."

Paladin sighed. "If you know so much, you'll be aware that I didn't start that thing. In fact, go check with Shemp. He'll tell you that it was me that talked the boys out of a riot."

The second goon decided to get in a couple of licks. "That's Commander Shemp to you, Paladin."

"The hell it is."

"You've got a bad attitude, Paladin."

"That's Mr. Paladin to you."

The goons ignored the crack and moved in closer to him. "So you're saying you didn't start that thing last night?"

Paladin was getting tired of this. Customers in the Leper Colony were standing up to get a better look at the confrontation outside the door. "You want to tell me what this nonsense is all about?"

"Maybe you're also saying you didn't kill Dee Dee Krypton?"

"I didn't."

"But maybe you know who did?"

Paladin shook his head. "I don't have a clue. Maybe you ought to talk to Bull Nails. I heard him and Krypton were hanging together last night."

The goons looked a little uncomfortable. "Nails is gone."

Paladin half smiled. "Gone?"

"He seems to have left Pomona."

Now Paladin was grinning all the way. "No kidding? Isn't one of the first principles of police work to suspect the guy who's taken it on the lam?"

The first goon's lip curled. "You think you're pretty smart, don't you, Paladin?"

"Smart enough that I ain't no flunky rent-a-cop."

The second goon tried to muscle him. "You want to watch your mouth."

Paladin refused to be muscled. "Yeah, well, this is all really amusing but, like I said, I need a drink so, if you boys will excuse me."

The first goon shook his head. "Not so fast, buddy, you're coming with us. Vanna Kreig wants to see you."

This caught Paladin off balance. It was the last thing that he had expected. "Kreig wants to see me?"

"Seems like you don't know everything."

Paladin was thoughtful. "I guess I don't."

The Action men took Paladin through the cordon without any of the searches or inspections that seemed to be the order of the day for everyone else going into the administration building. When he was brought into the dimly lit control room, with its glowing screens and pinpoint lights on the electronics, Kreig was standing behind the big control board looking at the main bank of monitor screens over the shoulders of the technicians and assistant directors doing the actual hands-on work. In black slacks and a practical white shirt, she was perfectly costumed for the gig, leaving no doubt that she was ultimately the one in control. Kreig was feeling the strain, though, and she smoked continuously, chain lighting each new cigarette off the butt of the last.

Kreig totally ignored Paladin for the first five minutes that he was in the room, too absorbed in the monitor screens and her headset to notice a mere player. When she finally found the time, she regarded him with the weariness of a superior forced to deal with an irritating underling. "I hear you were causing trouble last night." She stepped closer to him. "God, you smell bad. Have you been living in those leathers?"

"I was too busy causing trouble to change."

"So what was that all about last night?"

"A few of us wanted to talk to you."

"I wasn't here. I'd flown back to L.A. on business."

"So we were told."

Vanna Kreig raised a supercilious eyebrow. "And what did you all want to talk to me about?"

"Some of the players didn't like the way you were directing the show yesterday."

Vanna Kreig's face darkened. "Oh no?"

"No."

Her lips became a thin tight line. "When I want the opinion of players, I'll ask for it." She pronounced the word "players" with noticeable contempt.

Paladin just shrugged. "Some of them were getting a little worried that they might not live through this current slayfest to even have an opinion."

"If they don't like it, they can always quit."

"Quit? With the contract you guys hand out, it's kinda hard to just quit. A lot of crap about being in breach and never working in autoduel again."

Kreig made a dismissive gesture. "They should have thought of that before they signed."

Paladin nodded toward the monitors. In the arena, cars were still circulating in a passive, lackluster fashion. "I think those guys out there are trying to let you know how they feel. They're thinking it's been getting a bit beyond a sport lately. As one of the boys put it, we seem to be getting into the human-sacrifice business."

Vanna Kreig took yet another thin silver-tipped cigarette from an engraved case and lit it with a matching lighter. "Is that what they're saying? It doesn't matter. Any player is replaceable. We build them and then we blow them up. That's what the show's all about. If the turnover seems to get a bit hectic, too bad. The audience gets jaded, Paladin. All the time, we have to give them more to keep them watching. If we didn't, someone else would. TV violence follows all the patterns of classic addiction."

"And you're the one peddling the dope?"

"I just deal in numbers. They can always turn the thing off."

"Anything for the ratings?"

Kreig inhaled and then blew a lungful of smoke

straight at Paladin. "You better believe it, boy. Nobody is exempt."

She signaled to one of her assistants, who spoke softly into his headset, too quietly for Paladin to hear what he was saying. Vanna Kreig stubbed out her cigarette, half-smoked. "Watch the monitors, Paladin."

Paladin looked at the ranks of control-room monitors. Bambi Starr, sexy in black leather, riding her trike out into the arena, suddenly flashed up on a dozen of them. She entered fast and started a rapid show circuit, waving a clenched-fist salute to the cameras.

"It's your new little girlfriend, Paladin."

"You know a lot."

"I know she shot Dee Dee Krypton, and that you were a witness."

Paladin was silent. Vanna Kreig laughed. "You're surprised?"

Paladin looked at her with cautiously narrowed eyes. Something was going on here, but Vanna Kreig was, once again, taking her time to let him know that. "Yeah, I'm surprised."

"We've even got the incident on tape."

Vanna Kreig nodded to the AD who seemed to be cuing tape for her. A picture from a surveillance camera came up on two screens. It showed Paladin facing Krypton and Bull Nails. It was shot from a high angle and, as far as Paladin could tell, by a remote camera mounted either on the roof of the Leper Colony or the building next to it. Paladin looked questioningly at Kreig. "How did you get this?"

Vanna Kreig grinned smugly. "It's not a widely advertised fact, but most everything that happens in this facility is recorded on tape. We have one of the most extensive big-brother systems in the southwest."

"Has Shemp seen this?"

"No."

On the screens, Krypton slowly raised his gun and Paladin saw his own face looking at death. "It ain't too flattering."

Krypton's head silently blew apart and his body instantly dropped to the ground like a puppet with its strings cut. It lay in the dirt, continuing to twitch like a freshly slaughtered hen, as Bambi stepped into the frame. The tape ran out and the two monitors cut back to Bambi in the present, now running her second lap of the West Arena, playing to the cameras for all she was worth.

Paladin stared at Vanna Kreig. "So what are you going to do about her?"

"Why should I do anything about her?"

"She killed Krypton."

Vanna Kreig shrugged. "So? He was no loss without his brother. She, on the other hand, is full of energy and very ambitious." She looked sideways at Paladin. "Unless I decide to chill her in this bout, just to see your reaction. Have some rammer just take her out. Quick and painless? I can do it."

Paladin's face was like stone. On the TV, Bambi had started in pursuit of a second, male biker. "Anything that happens to her today is going to happen to you. You don't have the power to stop me getting you if I wanted to."

Vanna Kreig looked at him disbelievingly. "You care that much?"

"Maybe I just don't like to see anyone playing God. Particularly someone who never put their own ass on the line."

"You're getting depressingly sanctimonious."

"Perhaps it's a sign of the times."

Vanna Kreig smiled. "You want to see another sign of the times, Paladin? I've got another piece of tape I want you to watch."

"What's that?"

On the monitors, Bambi had just squeezed off a burst at the biker in front of her. Then the image changed. Instead of Bambi, Paladin found himself looking at multiples of a highway. It seemed to be taken from an aircraft, probably a helicopter, running low and fast, right down the center of the road. The highway was busted, pockmarked, and long neglected, and it looked like some stretch of the I-10, somewhere further east.

Paladin frowned. "Is this supposed to mean something?"

Vanna Kreig was a sadistic tease. "Just wait."

Something was up ahead. It looked like a bunch of vehicles, coming down the road, throwing up a cloud of dust. Paladin was about to ask "So what?" but the question froze in his throat.

"Jesus Christ."

The helicopter was over what he had taken for just a few vehicles. In fact, there were a hundred, maybe more. It was hard to tell. A battered column was strung out along the highway to well beyond the range of the helicopter's camera. The cars and trucks were ragtag and dirty but quite ready for combat. It was years since Paladin had seen a force like this, all together in one place and all headed in the same direction. Brown, sweat-streaked faces looked up at the chopper as it skimmed overhead.

Paladin was stone faced. "That's a lot of vehicles."

Bursts of flack blossomed beside the helicopter, and the camera tilted violently as the ship took evasive action. The next moment, the screen went dead and all that remained was a snowstorm of empty static. Paladin had a dozen questions. The first one was "Where did you get that?"

Kreig was supercool. "It was shot just over an hour ago."

"Where?"

"That bunch, at the speed they're traveling, is about half a day from here."

"Does the military know about this?"

"They don't feel it's their concern."

Paladin felt the need to sit down. "What happened to the chopper?"

"Unfortunately we had to write it off."

"And where the hell did they all come from?"

From her triumphant smile, it was clear that this was the question Vanna Kreig had been waiting for. "That's Iggy Mengele's army, Paladin. Remember I told you about it? You thought that I was being handed a load of bull."

Paladin silently nodded and Kreig's smile widened. "So how do you feel about it now, Val Paladin?"

Paladin slowly shook his head, and Kreig laughed. "What's the matter, Paladin? At a loss for words?"

# CHAPTER **EIGHTEEN**

A half-dozen Jetboys roared up the highway, whooping and hollering. Iggy sat astride his bike and watched them coming. As the afternoon wore on, the bikers were becoming an increasing problem. Being so much faster and more maneuverable on the damaged highway than the rest of the column, particularly the heavy armor, they were hard to hold in check, and Iggy couldn't afford to have them jumping the gun on him. In this motorized combat, the bikers were his light cavalry, and he couldn't have them charging in without any heavyweight support. Napoleon had fallen into that trap at Waterloo, and Iggy was well aware how Waterloo had ended for Napoleon.

The last rider in the bunch seemed to be dragging something behind his bike on a length of rope. It looked like a body. Now what were they up to? Iggy gunned the bike and accelerated to meet them. As they came level, he swung around so he was running beside the last biker, the one towing the thing at the end of the rope. "What you got there, kid?"

"A deserter."

"A what?"

"A deserter."

Iggy didn't like this. "We got people deserting?"

The Jetboy shook his head. "No, he ain't one of ours. This one deserted from Pomona."

Iggy hit his brakes and the Jetboy did the same. Iggy dropped the bike and ran back to where the body lay in the dust. On close examination, the deserter was a bundle of bloody rags. Iggy turned to the Jetboy. "So what's the story?"

The Jetboy pulled off his helmet and wiped the sweat from his face. "We were making a run up by Pomona and, on the way back, we found this guy camped in the desert beside his bike. He looked like he'd been drinking and passed out."

"So you woke him up?"

The Jetboy grinned nastily. "Yeah, we woke him up. At first he didn't want to talk to us, but, after we worked on him some, he got a bit more outgoing."

Iggy walked around the body. It showed no signs of life. "Outgoing?"

"It's amazing what a generator and a couple of jumper cables can do for a guy's willingness to talk."

Iggy liked the Jetboy's style, even though he'd probably forgotten more about torture than the kid would ever know. "So what did he have to say for himself?"

"He said he'd been a driver at the Pomona Bowl, but there'd been a murder last night and he'd had to lam out of there."

"He did the murder?"

The Jetboy shook his head. "He passed out before we got to the details. We figured we'd bring him back to the column and let you decide what to do with him."

Iggy nodded. "Yeah, you did the right thing."

The Jetboy beamed, and Iggy was touched by the way, for all their wild violence, these Jetboys were so damned anxious to please, even though he'd killed Johnny Zone and Masthead. The biker tugged tentatively at the rope that was tied around the body. "So what do we do with him?"

The other Jetboys had turned and driven back to where Iggy was standing. They gathered around, gunning their engines, excited as kids who'd scored some rare trophy. Iggy rubbed his chin. "I take it he's dead."

The original Jetboy who'd done the dragging shrugged. "He was still breathing when we tied him to the back of the bike."

Another Jetboy climbed off his machine. "One way to make sure." He put the bike on its stand and walked quickly to the body. Without hesitation, he swung his steel-shod boot hard into the deserter's ribs. The body grunted and curled itself into a fetal position.

"Seems like he's still alive."

The second Jetboy looked at Iggy. "You want I should kick him again, just to make sure?"

Iggy stood over the body, looking at it. The guy was so torn up that he was scarcely recognizable as a man. Iggy could see that, after Pomona fell, the Jetboys might well get radically creative with the survivors. "You find out if this thing's got a name?"

"Said his name was Bull Nails. Said he was some big-ass stadium driver until the company gave him the shaft. Went on about some bitch in a suit called Vanna Kreig. Seemed to think she was the cause of all his troubles. Around then, though, we figure Nibbo must have given him a few too many volts, because, after that, he got kinda incoherent."

The Jetboy called Nibbo, a pale, weasel-faced individual with black spike hair and dead, hooded eyes, looked unhappy. "It's hard to judge when they start yelling. You know what I'm saying? Besides, it's the amps that really hurt them, not the volts."

Iggy was thoughtful. "He say anything about us? I mean, do they know about us at Pomona?"

Nibbo shook his head. "No. He seemed kinda surprised to see us."

The first Jetboy was more cautious. "He claimed he left Pomona around dawn. We were only just getting on the road at dawn. They might have heard about us since. Quite a few of them homesteaders and desert rats running in front of us. And then there was the camera chopper."

Iggy pondered on this and then peered around at the Jetboys. "Any of you boys got some of that moonshine you make?"

The Jetboy in the purple and black armor reached into one of his saddlebags and hauled out a mason jar. "We having a party?"

Iggy's face folded into the wolf grin. "Me and Mr. Bull Nails here are going to have ourselves a little drink and get acquainted."

He took the mason jar and unscrewed the top. He gestured to Nibbo. "Get his head up."

Nibbo crouched down and lifted Nails' head until his chin was resting on his chest. Iggy squatted on the other side of Nails, holding the mason jar. He took a quick hit of moonshine for himself and then nodded to Nibbo. "Okay, open his mouth."

Nibbo used his thumbs to pry Nails' jaw open, and Nails let out a weak moan. Iggy poured a generous double measure of the raw spirit into Nails' mouth. Nails spluttered and coughed and turned blue under the caked dirt and blood. When he found his voice, he started in pleading.

"Oh God. Don't hurt me no more. Please ... no more. I can't ... take no more."

Nails' voice came out muffled through a cut and bruised mouth and broken teeth. The Jetboy in black and purple watched with an expression of contempt. "He don't look so bodacious now."

Iggy took the mason jar away from Nails' mouth and glanced at Nibbo. "Get him up a bit higher, okay? I want him to see what's going on."

Iggy and Nibbo lifted Nails so he was half sitting, and he screamed all through the process. When he was up, Iggy pointed to where, back down the road, the column was coming around a curve. "You see that, boy?"

Nails coughed blood. "It looks like ..."

Iggy's laugh was harsh. "It looks like an army, boy. That's what it looks like."

Nails seemed to be fading fast. He sagged against Nibbo and Iggy. "... an army?"

"You hear about my army?"

Nails coughed again. It sounded as though his ribs were all busted up. "No ... I didn't hear nothing."

"Anyone at Pomona talking about my army?"

"I ... never heard anyone say anything."

"And who's running things at Pomona?"

Nails groaned. "You mean ... the ... company."

Iggy impatiently shook his head. "No, I know all about the company. Who are the top players?"

"Son of a bitch by the name of ... Val Paladin thinks he's ... the number-one hot dog." He sighed. "Son ... of a bitch."

Iggy's eyes glittered dangerous. "Val Paladin?"

Nails didn't answer and his eyes slowly closed.

Nibbo looked at Iggy. "You want to give him another shot of booze?"

Iggy shook his head. "No, we ain't going to get anything useful out of him." He let Bull Nails drop with casual finality. "Hang him."

Nibbo, apparently the one most versed in torture and execution, looked sadly at Iggy. "We could have a problem with that."

Iggy looked surprised. "We could?"

Nibbo gestured around to the empty desert. "There ain't a good tree in three miles of here. Not in any direction, not a hanging tree. Unless you were thinking about stringing him up from a yucca or one of them big cacti."

Iggy was as disappointed as the kid. He stood up and looked around. It was true what Nibbo said. He couldn't see a single tree anywhere that would hold the weight of a man. He spat on the ground. "Goddamn it to hell." Without further ado, he pulled out his pistol and shot Nails in the head. The Jetboys turned without a word and walked back to their bikes. Iggy quickly called after them. "Hey, where do you guys think you're going? I got a job for you."

The Jetboys looked at him expectantly. Iggy pointed to Nails' body. "I want you to take him back to Pomona."

Nibbo frowned. "Back to Pomona?"

"That's what I said."

"Ain't that going to tip them off about us coming?"

Iggy had become even more wolfish. "I figure they got to know about us by now. Like you said, between the homesteaders and the helicopter, they got to have heard we're on our way. I think it's time we sent them a message."

Nibbo was grinning. "The stiff's gonna be a message."

Iggy nodded. "You got it. I want you to take this lump of meat back to Pomona. Leave it right in front of the main entrance to the stadium and then hightail it out of there without getting yourselves killed. I want those showboats at Pomona to know what's in their future."

# CHAPTER NINETEEN

"You're planning to show this?"

"It's ready to go out on the feed right now. As a program interrupt."

"And you're also going to show it on the screens in the arena?"

"The satellite feed always comes up on the screens in the arena. The crowd doesn't believe it's real unless they see it on a TV screen."

Paladin looked at Kreig as though she was crazy. "There are nearly four thousand spectators out there."

Vanna Kreig glanced down at a computer display. "Three thousand, seven hundred and eighty-two paying customers."

Paladin's face was grim. "They'll panic."

"So what would you have me do? Leave them in blissful ignorance until this outlaw army is actually beating on the gates of the arena?"

The technicians in the control room had stopped work to watch the confrontation.

Paladin shook his head. "No, but ..."

"So we run the tape without further delay."

"Just like that, no softening up? No breaking it to them gently?"

Kreig's expression was icy. "What do you want from me, Paladin? How exactly do you break the news gently to a crowd of four thousand that an army of motorized barbarians is rushing down on them and will be here before the end of the day? Maybe you'd like to go on camera and tell them that there's no cause for alarm?"

Paladin was having trouble keeping his anger in check. "You've known about this for a while, so how come you didn't do something up front?"

"Like what?"

"Like canceling this three-day ratings extravaganza."

Vanna Kreig regarded Paladin as though he was insane. "I'm in the autoduel industry, Paladin. We produce the shows that keep the masses quiet. I can't concern myself with a mere four thousand of them. In an emergency like this, they are to be looked on as expendable. They knew they were taking a risk when they came out here. Leaving the city is still a dangerous business. You could say that they were part of the show now."

"You still have a responsibility to them. You took their money and . . ."

Vanna Kreig's cool slipped a little. "Responsibility? I have just two responsibilities and one is to Skynet and the other's to the TV audience, fifty million of them. In both cases, I have to keep putting out a show no matter what the circumstances. Do you know what would have happened if I'd tried to cancel this three-day event? They'd have canned my ass inside of an hour, and installed someone else to put the whole thing back on line."

"So you're telling me it was more than your job was worth?"

Vanna Kreig's eyes had become dangerous slits. "I'm not telling you that at all. I didn't even consider canceling the show and I don't give a damn what happens to that crowd of morons in the stands. They're more than happy to see you drivers injured or killed. so why the hell should you worry now that the boot may be on the other foot? Iggy Mengele is going to bring me the biggest live-action TV spectacle of the century, and nothing is going to stop me putting that out on the air. You hear me, Paladin? Nothing is going to stop me."

After this outburst of megalomania, she quickly redirected her attention to the crew in the control room, seemingly embarrassed that she had given away so much of herself. "And what are you all looking at? You don't have jobs to do? Cue that tape and be ready to send direct to feed. Have Bo Rheingold on standby for voice-over. Get to it."

One of the ADs raised a nervous hand. "You want that routed to the arena?"

Her voice was acid. "Of course, I want it routed to the arena. I've heard Mr. Paladin's objections and I've decided to ignore them. In fact, have a full spread of cameras on the crowd for reaction shots."

She looked back at Paladin to see how he was taking this, only to find that he was already walking to the door, too angry to speak.

"Where do you think you're going?"

Paladin halted in the doorway. "You don't need me here. I'm going out to see what happens when you run that tape."

"I want you back here in an hour, you understand?"

Paladin's expression was bleak. "For what?"

"To decide what we're going to do about Iggy

Mengele. I want you here, along with some of the other top players, Shemp, and my tech people."

Paladin looked even bleaker. "That should be interesting. I've never been in a war that started with a script conference."

With this parting shot, he walked out of the door. Vanna Kreig shrieked angrily after him. "Listen, Paladin, I'm warning you ..."

But Paladin was gone. One of the ADs glanced up at Vanna Kreig. "You think he'll be back?"

Vanna Kreig nodded confidently. "Oh yes, he'll be back. He wants Iggy Mengele as badly as I do."

The admin block had an elevator that ran all the way up to the top of the perimeter wall, and Paladin went straight to it. It was the fastest way to a vantage point from where he could watch the crowd when they learned that Iggy Mengele and his wolf pack were coming.

Paladin put on his sunglasses as he stepped out into the glare of the afternoon. He was at one of the highest points on the high outer wall. It gave him an uninterrupted view of not only both arenas but also the surrounding country for a couple of miles in any direction. Below him, cars and bikes circled in the arena and the crowds packed the stands. It could have been a normal day at Pomona, except that an unusually large number of armed Action men patroled the catwalks that ran along the tops of the walls. Paladin wasn't sure if this was an early response to the threat from Iggy Mengele, or if Shemp was still worried about some sort of industrial action by the players.

Paladin turned his attention to the country outside the wall. To the south, he could just make out the broken ribbon of Interstate 10 running to L.A. in one direction and to Phoenix and beyond in the other. So far, he could see no sign of Iggy and his motorized Huns except that a sinister dust cloud was hanging over the highway at a point beyond the horizon. Paladin slowly scratched his chin. If that was the dust of Iggy's horde, the outlaws were close. They could well be in Pomona before sunset.

Much of the land around the Bowl was flat, featureless desert. The area had once been part of the outer suburbs of Los Angeles, but then the water had stopped coming. Like all the other suburbs, the town of Pomona had dried out, withered, and become part of the huge ghost city that surrounded L.A. When Skynet had built the Bowl, much of the immediate area had been bulldozed flat, first for the campground and the airship terminus, and then, farther out, in preparation for future development. The long-range plan, as it had been sold to the investors, was to make the Pomona Bowl the centerpiece of a whole vast amusement complex with autoduelling as its theme. Paladin suspected that Iggy Mengele was about to put a crimp in this extravagant scheme.

Paladin realized that he was looking over the surrounding area as a potential battleground. Old instincts really did die hard. This one from his days out in the wild seemed very much alive and functioning. If he remembered rightly, it was the Duke of Wellington, when talking about Waterloo, who had said that the winner in most battles is the general who decides where it will be fought. He couldn't pass up another chance at Iggy Mengele. With people like Vanna Kreig and Howard Shemp around, though, organizing the defense of Pomona could quickly turn into a custom-built nightmare.

A change in the tone of Bo Rheingold's commentary distracted Paladin from the surrounding terrain. "Hold on there a moment, folks, some kind of news flash is coming in. Just bear with us here a moment."

Rheingold sounded flustered. Apparently nobody had bothered to warn him about Iggy and his outlaw army. A hush fell over the crowd as though they sensed that this was something important and not just some new, tricky lead-in to a beer commercial. In the arena, a few of the cars came to a halt, and the satellite feed went momentarily to dead air while Bo Rheingold held a muttered conversation with someone off camera. When he turned back to the audience, the commentator looked frightened and it was obvious that he was reading from a cue card.

"Friends, even as we speak, reports are coming into the control room here at Pomona that a very large column of outlaw vehicles is right now moving east on the I-10 in the direction of Los Angeles. We are getting reports of some two to three hundred vehicles on the road, all traveling together, and, if these reports are accurate, this would be the largest concentration of armed outlaws that has assembled in a decade."

The helicopter clip came up on the screen. It might as well have been a huge flashing sign that said PANIC in big red letters. By the end of the clip when the helicopter blew up, large sections of the crowd were on their feet, looking at each other with confused consternation. What exactly did this all mean?

A picture of Iggy came up, standing on a hill, silhouetted against a blood-red sunset, poncho flapping in the wind. He slowly turned and wolf grinned into the camera. Paladin was stunned. Where the hell did they get that piece of tape, unless there was actual collusion between Skynet and Iggy? And what were they trying to do? Turn the son of a bitch into a movie star? If this was the case, the whole Skynet setup was even more fucked up and degenerate than he had ever imagined.

The image of Iggy cut to Lars Martinez, the Skynews anchor, safe and comfortable behind his desk in New York. "The leader of this dangerously large band of outlaws is reputed to be a character called Iggy Mengele. Mengele, a one-time border raider, is known to be a ruthless killer, and law-enforcement sources in Los Angeles, El Paso, and Phoenix describe him as a 'homicidal psychotic' and 'some kind of barbarian throwback.' The situation is further complicated by the fact that this army of outlaws appears to be headed straight for the Pomona Bowl where a large crowd is, right at this moment, watching some of the top stars of autoduel engage in mortal combat. Of course, here at Skynews, we are in a unique position to . . ."

The crowd didn't wait to hear any more. They were moving for the exits like ants when the anthill is stomped on. It was at the exits that the first trouble started. The access tunnels that led out of the stands had never been designed to deal with the entire crowd at once. What started out as a bottleneck quickly turned into a pushing, shoving crush of people. The helicopter tape was showing a second time and a lot of the crowd was acting as though the images weren't just on the screen but right there behind them. Even as high as he was, Paladin could see that the jostling and pushing around the exits was becoming more serious. Violent ripples and eddies in the crowd seemed to indicate that fists were already flying.

The Action men on the catwalks were listening to their radios. Then they began moving quickly, down into the stadium. Apparently Shemp had pulled them in for emergency crowd control. A new image had come up on the arena screens. A smart cameraman had made it to the parking lot and was feeding back pictures as the crowd came boiling out of the access tunnels and onto the parking lot and campsite, racing for their cars, vans, and campers. Within a minute, the first vehicles were on the move, instantly creating their own version of the snarls in the stands. Paladin glanced behind him to the airship docking facility. A good two-thirds of the crowd had come to Pomona by commercial airship out of L.A., and that was also their only way out. Right at that moment, there wasn't a single airship at any of the three mooring masts. Another one wouldn't be coming in until just before sunset, unless someone had taken the trouble to bring out extra dirigibles. The airship terminal would be the next scene of chaos as panicking fans fought for the first places on line.

Paladin decided it was time to move and hurried back to the elevator. He wanted to get down on the ground and see for himself what was going on, and how Shemp and his Action men were handling the situation, before he went to any meeting with Vanna Kreig. He discovered the Action men weren't handling anything. Shemp's crowd control had been a matter of too little, too late, and the fleeing spectators were rapidly turning into a fear-driven mob. Paladin used a private drivers' exit that the public hadn't yet managed to penetrate and got to a point near the main entrance. The condition of the people staggering from the tunnel told what was going on back in the stadium. Men and women were cut, bruised, and bleeding. Some were being helped along, supported by friends or relatives. A man carried a little boy of maybe eight or nine in his arms, unconscious or worse.

Gunfire sounded from the other side of the parking lot where the traffic was channeled into the approach roads. Paladin spun round, hand going to his pistol. Were the outlaws here already? Paladin relaxed a little, realizing that it was only hysterical spectators resorting to their own firepower in the bumper-to-bumper traffic that jammed the exit roads. That was a Californian tradition as old as the freeways themselves.

Paladin walked a short distance out onto the parking lot. Under normal circumstances, he wouldn't have been able to do that without being mobbed by fans wanting autographs and the kind of weird contact that so many of them seemed to crave from celebrities. In their panic, though, they no longer gave a damn about famous names. Fueled up by two days of death and destruction in the arena, they had completely abandoned themselves to atavistic self-preservation.

Paladin halted as more gunshots rang out across the lot. This time the shooting was more frenzied and prolonged, as though someone was really laying down a field of fire. People were screaming and starting to run in the opposite direction, back toward the stadium, as though trying to get away from something behind them. Then Paladin heard the gunning of motorcycles.

When the six bikers appeared, like a focal point of horror in all of the dust and confusion, Paladin knew straightaway that they weren't any part of the fleeing audience. He had only run across the Jetboys on a couple of occasions, but once you saw a Jetboy, you never forgot. They roared through the crowd with no regard for their own safety or anyone else's, wild and threatening, in their bright multicolored armor and with their weird dyed and braided hair streaming behind them. If one of the crowd got in their way, that was just too bad, and if anyone tried to stop them, they simply opened up with their machine guns.

The leading rider had a dark bundle draped across his gas tank that looked uncommonly like a body. Paladin drew his pistol and held his ground as the crowd on the parking lot milled around him. He could only assume that this was some kind of precursor to the coming of Iggy Mengele.

The Jetboys swept past him some twenty yards away to the right. Too many spectators were in the way for Paladin to get a clear shot at any of the riders. He hurried after them, pistol still in hand, going against the tide of humanity who wanted to put as much distance as they could between the Jetboys and themselves. The Jetboys seemed to be headed for the main entrance to the arena.

An Action Corps armored personnel carrier was making its way through the crowd. Paladin waved to the driver, indicating that he wanted to ride along. Paladin didn't know if it was the pistol in his hand or his general air of authority, but the carrier slowed almost to a stop beside him, and Paladin was able to grab a handhold and haul himself up onto the vehicle's running board. With Paladin clinging to the outside of the carrier, it bumped off in pursuit of the Jetboys.

They arrived at the main gate just in time to see the apparent leader of the dirty half dozen dump the body. It flopped in front of a group of Action men who had been trying to impose some minimal order on the chaos surging out of the arena. Paladin dropped from the carrier, seeing no need to make himself more of a target than need be.

A standoff seemed to have been reached between the Action men at the gate and the Jetboys. The two groups had weapons pointed at each other, but neither seemed to want to start the firefight. The arrival of the armored carrier drastically upset that balance, though. As the body from the motorcycle hit the ground, the leading Jetboy, a strange, weasel-faced figure with spiked-out black hair, screamed out to anyone who might be listening.

"We brought Bull Nails back to you! Take a look at him! Take a look at what we done to him, because we're going to do the same to all of you when Iggy gets here! And he's going to be getting here real soon!"

With that, he gunned his bike and wheeled away. The personnel carrier opened up with its front-mounted machine guns as the rest of the Jetboys took off in his wake. One of the bikers went down immediately, but not before he'd flipped a grenade back into the group of Action men in front of the entrance. Paladin ducked away from the blast as the grenade went off, instantly killing three of the security guards and hideously maiming two more. The gunner in the personnel carrier got another Jetboy before one of the bikers dropped a proximity mine that stopped the carrier in its tracks. A moment later, the four remaining bikers were safely into the cover provided by the frightened crowd, charging back the way they'd come. Paladin noticed a cameraman getting up from a crouch with a broad grin on his face, clearly delighted that he had just got himself a major scoop. Pictures of the whole sorry incident were almost certainly on their way out to the world.

Paladin hurried to the bodies by the gates. A brief glance told him that there was nothing he could do to help the security men who had been cut down by the grenade, and he turned his attention to the other figure on the ground. The corpse had been so viciously abused and mutilated that Paladin would have been hard-pressed to recognize Bull Nails. Then he noticed the steer's head tattoo on the corpse's right shoulder where the blood-caked shirt had been ripped away. It was Nails. The man had been an asshole, but nobody deserved to die like that.

An Action man from the carrier hurried up. "What the hell was that all about?"

Paladin gestured to Nails. "Iggy Mengele just left us a calling card."

The Action man whistled in amazement. "This guy Mengele is really serious."

Paladin nodded. "Don't doubt that, pal. Don't ever doubt that."

# CHAPTER TWENTY

It was the angriest sunset yet. The sky went through a series of colors, bright crimson to livid purple. The lead vehicles of the Horde swung off the highway, crested a low ridge, and there it was in front of them. The Pomona Bowl. For Iggy, it was the crowning moment of his life. He's given the motorcycle back to the Jetboys and was riding the top of Ilsa McCoy's armored scout car, the first four-wheeler in the column, posing like Rommel at the peak of his glory. His goggles were pulled down, and his headset hooked him into a radio net connecting all the leaders of the individual crews.

The first sight of Pomona rendered Iggy momentarily speechless, but as soon as he got his voice back he barked into his headset. "Okay, everyone hold it. Everyone halt. We're there. We've made it."

Iggy could hear cheering behind him as the column ground to a halt. Ilsa looked up at him from inside the scout car. "So how does it feel?"

Iggy's eyes gleamed. "I gotta tell you, baby. I feel

like one of those old-time conquerors back in the Middle Ages. That's the fucking fortress, and it's gonna fell to my legions."

With its high white walls and tall TV masts silhouetted against the dying day, the Pomona Bowl was, in every respect, the modern equivalent of a medieval citadel.

"It ain't gonna to take no months of siege, though. No battering rams and siege towers in his assault. Oh no. No waiting around for them to starve or get the plague. We're gonna to blast our way in there inside of a day."

Ilsa looked at him curiously. "You sure of that?"

Iggy nodded. His grin bordered on crazy. "Instant gratification, baby. Even in warfare."

Iggy had already decided, after a roadside meeting with Tod Slaughter, Zap Celine, and some of the other leaders, that they wouldn't attempt the main assault until the following day. "Let our people rest up. The suckers inside the walls won't be going nowhere. They can sweat through a sleepless night and we'll come at them out of the dawn."

Zap Celine hadn't particularly liked the idea of waiting until dawn. As usual, the Jetboys were hot to trot and wanted to take the fight directly to Pomona. Iggy had managed to cool them out by promising that they could run off some of their pumped-up energy by harrying and killing anyone who was dumb enough to be outside the walls during the hours of darkness. As well as stopping the Jetboys from going ballistic before the rest of the Horde was ready, it also provided Iggy with a watchdog service that would give him early warning of any sneak attack from inside the stadium. He'd used the wolf grin on Celine. "Okay, so that's the deal. You and your boys own everything outside the walls through the hours of darkness. You can do whatever you like with whoever you find."

Only minutes after they arrived at Pomona, Iggy realized that maybe he'd spoken too soon. A lot of people were still milling around outside the walls. More important, two large, cigar-shaped commercial airships floated in the air on the far side of the stadium building. One was tethered to a mooring mast and the other was just nosing its way up to dock at a second one. Iggy was amazed. They hadn't evacuated the spectators yet. Whoever was in charge inside the Bowl had been given plenty of warning of the Horde's coming, but they still hadn't managed to get all of the crowd out of harm's way. Iggy was more than a little disappointed. He didn't give a damn if a bunch of civilians had to die before he could take the stadium. What bothered him was that it showed a massive incompetence on the part of the defenders. If they couldn't organize something comparatively simple like getting the bystanders out of the way, what kind of actual defense were they going to put up? He had wanted his first major conquest to be achieved against a worthy opponent, but it looked like he was dealing with a bunch of dummies. He hardly wanted that going down when history was written.

Iggy spoke quickly into his headset. "Slaughter, Celine, Dalton, Charlie Fats, all of you, get up here fast."

When the crew leaders were assembled, Iggy came straight to the point. "There are two things that need to be done right now. Those people running around in front of the walls have to be removed and I want those airships taken out."

Iggy noticed how Charlie Fats' eyes gleamed at

the mention of taking out the airships, and he grinned. "You want that one, Charlie? You want the airships?"

Charlie Fats nodded like an eager kid. "Sure do, boss. Never had me an airship."

"They ain't filled with hydrogen. They ain't going to burn like the *Hindenburg* in the old newsreels."

Charlie Fats shrugged. "Yeah, well, you can't have everything."

Celine was more interested in the people. "What about them? Who greases the crowd?"

Iggy let the leader of the Jetboys have his head. "Take your bunch and some of the other bikers. But don't do it on your own, hear? Take some light four-wheelers as backup."

A task force was quickly organized. Charlie Fats and a crew rolled out in a trio of Barcelonas, heavy tractors with triple rocket platforms, borrowed from the K-90s and Ilsa McCoy's crew. A bunch of gunners carrying various shoulder-mounted missiles clung to the back and sides of the big trucks, looking to go along for the ride. It seemed that more of the Horde than just Charlie Fats had a desire to bring down an airship.

The tractors carrying the rockets were quickly followed by the Jetboys, augmented by most of the nomad bikers in the Horde and a dozen or so compacts plus a couple of flatbeds loaded down by men and women armed with shotguns and machine pistols. It was plain that, after the journey from Palm Springs, just about everyone was ready to get in on the action. Even those who weren't going to participate had left their vehicles and moved up to the front of the column for a better view.

The bikers and the compacts drove directly toward

the stadium, while the three-rocket trucks took a more circuitous route, keeping out of range of any possible fire from the walls as they closed on the airships. As a result, the Jetboys were the first to make contact. Sounds of screams and gunfire drifted back to the column as they roared into what was left of the spectators from Pomona. Iggy stood on top of the scout car watching through a pair of powerful field glasses. Even with binoculars, though, it was hard to make out any real details through the cloud of dust that was being thrown up by the attack. Now and again Iggy would see a flurry of muzzle flashes or a car or bike emerge from the general confusion, but for the most part, the attack was little more than dark figures moving inside a maelstrom of flying sand.

Heads turned as the first rocket blasted into the sky, and a loud cheer went up from the outlaws as it exploded amidships of the nearest dirigible. A second and third rocket followed, both hitting the same target. With one airship taking all of the punishment, the pilot of the other one made a desperate move. He ran his engines full astern, pulling away from the mast, presumably hoping that he could snap the mooring cables with this surge of power. One cable gave way as planned, curling away into empty air. The other, however, held firm, causing the airship to suddenly swing to one side. Its tail section tangled with the damaged and burning midsection of the blimp that had taken the rockets, and for over a minute, the two huge craft hung locked in unholy embrace. Another rocket hit and a fuel tank on one of the airships exploded. Fire slowly ran along the outer skins of both ships, and almost as one, they started to disintegrate. The cheering from the outlaws grew louder, and Iggy, peering through his field glasses, thought that he could just make out tiny figures falling from the airships along with the debris.

Ilsa looked up at Iggy from inside the scout car. "Some spectacle, huh?"

Iggy laughed. "And whoever's left in there has got no way out except past us."

# CHAPTER **TWENTY-ONE**

Shemp looked round excitedly at Vanna Kreig. "There aren't that many of them. There's a lot less than we expected."

Paladin glanced at the burning wreckage of the two airships before he spoke. He couldn't take many more of the security chief's idiot assumptions. "That bunch down there is most likely only the tip of the iceberg. Unless we send out some reliable scouts, we can't assume anything, except that we don't have a clue how many of them may really be out there."

Shemp ignored him. "I'm going to order out my men."

Paladin shook his head. "You're crazy. Most of the spectators are dead now anyway. What's the point?"

Shemp swung round and glared at Paladin. "Oh yeah? And what would you do?"

"I'd hold my fire and wait for the main assault. That's just a skirmishing party. That's just the Jetboys showing off, plus a few other bikers and a handful of compacts. Even from that one bit of tape, we know there are a whole lot more of them than that. This bunch is just Iggy flexing his muscles."

Shemp started to puff up inside his uniform. "You sound like you're scared of this Iggy Mengele."

Paladin did his best to keep his temper in check. "I'm not so dumb that I'd underestimate him."

"And I'm not so cowardly that I'm going to skulk behind the walls of this place and do nothing."

Paladin glared at Shemp. "I think I'd rather be a coward than a damned fool who goes rushing out without a clue."

Shemp appealed to Vanna Kreig. "Even if there are more of them out of sight, I could run off this bunch before any more of them get mobilized."

The meeting was taking place on the same high point of the wall where, earlier, Paladin had stood and watched the crowd in the stands start to panic. Now a lot of that crowd were dead, either burned in the wreckage of the airships or gunned down by Iggy Mengele's advance party. The outlaw bikers were riding up and down in full view, right in front of the walls, flaunting their victory, finishing off the stragglers and turning the Pomona parking lot into a killing field. Paladin could understand that Shemp wanted to do something, but he knew instinctively that it wasn't the time.

The emergency meeting had been hastily called after the Jetboys had dumped Bull Nails' body on Pomona's doorstep. It had continued for some time, rapidly getting nowhere. Then the Jetboys had returned in force and waded into the crowd, and the two airships had been destroyed. With sudden and bloody mass murder going on right in front of them, the meeting had taken on a new tone of urgency. In addition to Paladin, Shemp, and Vanna Kreig, those present included Vito Kurtz, Petaluma Annie, Rhino Joe, and a half-dozen other drivers; Mac Connolly and four other chief mechanics; and a handful of the senior Skynet technicians. Vanna Kreig seemed to have abruptly become a democrat in the face of the outlaw threat, or at least she was going through the motions.

Unaccustomed to playing politics, Paladin found that his strongest support was coming from the other players led by Petaluma Annie. Formidable and muscular in her scanty leather costume, she was more than ready to confront Shemp or Kreig. "Maybe we'd better move some of the spare heavy weaponry up onto the walls."

At this, Shemp bristled. "I already thought of that."

Vito Kurtz grunted. "That's a miracle."

Again Shemp turned to Kreig as the ultimate authority. "Do I have to listen to this? As far as I'm concerned, this business with Iggy Mengele is strictly a security matter. I don't even see why performers have to be involved at all."

Hackles rose all round at the tone Shemp used when he said the word "performers." Paladin voiced it for all of them. "We're going to need every gun we've got, and maybe a few guns that we don't got, before this thing's over, so don't be telling us that it's 'strictly a security matter.'"

Shemp was going red in the face. "How do I know I can even trust these goddamned players? Half of them are little better than outlaws themselves."

Rhino Joe and Petaluma Annie advanced threateningly on Shemp, and Paladin and Kurtz had to step into the way to stop a fistfight breaking out right there and then. Vanna Kreig angrily raised her arms. "Will you all stop this, goddamn it! Stop this right now!"

The meeting calmed down a little, although Shemp and the drivers continued to glare at each other, while Vanna Kreig took the unprecedented role of mediator. "I agree with Paladin. We're going to need every gun we've got. But I also think that the security forces should be given a chance to clear the area outside the walls."

Petaluma Annie wasn't going for this. "Are you sure that you just don't want to get some quick action tape to put out on the air?"

Vanna Kreig treated the big woman to an icy look. "I'm not even going to dignify that with an answer." She turned to Shemp. "Order your armored units out into the field, and let's see what happens."

Paladin shook his head. "We're going to lose some armored units, that's what's going to happen."

Vanna Kreig was at the limits of her patience. "Shall we just see what happens?"

Shemp spoke into a hand communicator, and just a few moments later the main gates of the stadium rolled open. A number of the closest bikers spun their machines round, thinking that there might have been some kind of foul-up and that they were going to have a chance to rush inside the Bowl. Instead of a lucky chance, however, the bikers found themselves facing a column of ten white-painted armored personnel carriers with the Action Corps logo on the side. They were already rolling fast, and with tracer and laser beams flashing from the turrets.

On top of the wall, Petaluma Annie spat into space. "Well, damn me, don't they look pretty? Ain't they the cutest little white tanks you ever did see?"

For the first few minutes, the cute little white tanks had it all their own way, sweeping across the space in front of the Bowl, inflicting casualties and driving the outlaw bikers and compacts in front of them. It didn't last, though. Bit by bit, the outlaws recovered from their surprise and started to take the fight back to the Action Corps men. It was immediately obvious to Paladin that the outlaws were much better at it than Shemp's boys. He winced as a lone Jetboy rode up alongside one of the security carriers and, in a solo replay of what the Krypton Brothers had tried to do to him in the arena, slapped a limpet mine on its side and peeled away, ducking low as the mine exploded, gutting the security vehicle.

Two of the big Barcelonas that had taken out the airships were now altering course. They had been heading back toward where the main body of the outlaw force presumably waited, but now they seemed to have decided to join the fray. They came at the Action Corps vehicles, lights blazing in the gathering twilight, Paladin saw a flash of fire on the leading Barcelona's rocket platform. Instantly a vapor trail flashed upward and quickly arced down again. Another of the personnel carriers exploded.

Paladin glanced at Shemp. "Your boys don't seem to be doing too well out there. Maybe you ought to call them in before they get themselves creamed."

The security chief neither looked round nor answered him. He seemed to be transfixed, staring aghast at the battle raging below them. Petaluma Annie sniffed loudly. "You're looking a little pale, Shemp."

Shemp was at a loss for words. He turned, stricken, to Vanna Kreig. "I . . ."

Kreig, however, was also watching the scene below, where a half-dozen bikers were dogging one of the carriers, which, try as it might, seemed unable to shake them off. An outlaw clinging to the sissy bar of a big trike swung a line, lariat style, and managed to get a grappling hook on the security vehicle. The trike made a close pass and the outlaw jumped, swinging like a monkey, up the side of the moving carrier. He crawled along the top of the swaying machine, dragged open the top hatch cover, dropped a grenade inside, and jumped clear. The carrier came to an abrupt stop and smoke billowed from every open port as the grenade went off.

Kurtz whistled under his breath. "Damn, but these guys are good."

Petaluma Annie nodded. "We used to be like that, but, while these boys have been out on the border keeping themselves hard and mean, we've been getting soft playing charades in this circus."

Vanna Kreig rounded on Shemp. "The players are right, Shemp. This is pathetic. Do like Paladin says and call your men back."

As she spoke, another carrier was caught by a flamethrower mounted on one of the outlaw compacts. Liquid fire ran down its sides as the crew bailed out only to find themselves cut down by machine-gun bullets. Shemp hadn't moved and Kreig barked at him in disgust. "Do it now, Shemp. While you've still got some men left to call back."

Shemp's shoulders sagged and he spoke quickly into his hand communicator. From the desperate haste with which the surviving carriers turned tail and ran for the main gate, the order couldn't have come too soon for them. The outlaws didn't try to follow. They let the retreating carriers go, gathering instead in front of the walls of Pomona in a gesture of arrogant defiance. They gunned their engines and, led by the Jetboys, set up a weird, savage howling that echoed through the gathering dusk. They'd be back, and the next time, no one would escape.

Vanna Kreig faced the others who'd been watching from the wall. "So what does all this teach us?"

Vito Kurtz pointed to where the outlaws were whooping back to their own lines. "Those guys are the best I've seen in a very long time."

"I think you already said that."

"It don't make it any less true."

Paladin stared hard at Shemp. "Your boys just don't cut it."

Shemp scowled. "You players could do better?"

Petaluma Annie answered before Paladin had a chance. "Sure as hell couldn't do much worse."

Vanna Kreig faced Paladin. "So what would you do?"

Shemp started to protest, but Kreig silenced him with a look. Paladin thought for a moment. "Seems to me, from what I know of Iggy Mengele, the outlaws will attack at dawn. Which means we've got maybe eight hours, ten hours tops, to get our shit together."

The other players were nodding. Paladin continued. "The first thing I'd do is what Annie said, haul all the heavy ordnance we can find up onto the tops of the walls and mount it so we've got a good, all-round field of fire. That way, at least we'll own the area immediately around the stadium."

Petaluma Annie looked sharply at him. "You saying we should hole up in here and let them come to us? Make this into a siege?"

Paladin shook his head. "No, I think that's the last thing we should do. But we've got these walls and we might as well use them."

Rhino Joe didn't look exactly happy about this. "So what about us? What are us drivers supposed to be doing? I don't see myself manning the barricades."

Paladin smiled grimly. "We take the fight out to the enemy. By all accounts, the outlaws have us outnumbered, and we have an awful lot of half-load stadium ammunition, while we can assume that Iggy's boys will be firing the real deal. . . . Hey!"

He stopped in midsentence. One of the Skynet ADs had taken out a pocket-sized camcorder. Paladin pointed angrily at the man and faced Vanna Kreig. "What the hell is that supposed to be? Making a little tape of this strategy meeting so you can run it on the air and let everyone with a TV set, including Iggy Mengele, know what we're planning?"

Kreig gestured to the AD to put the camcorder away. Kurtz was looking belligerent. "Yeah, what about this? Are you still going to be rolling tape when the outlaws attack?"

She looked at Kurtz in amazement. "Of course I'll be taping. You think I'd miss out on one of the greatest battles of all time?"

"But you won't be taping any of the planning or the setup of the defenses?"

"Of course not."

The light of low cunning dawned in Kurtz's eyes. "And we'll be getting paid for whatever goes down?"

Kreig couldn't believe what she was hearing. "I suppose so. I hadn't really thought about it."

"Maybe you should. I figure we ought to be getting some kind of bonus for all this."

This was too much for even Petaluma Annie. "You think we could leave the union meeting until later to try and figure out what we do about Iggy Mengele? I mean, if goddamned Iggy gets in here, whether we get paid or not is going to be pretty academic." She looked to Paladin. "So what's the plan, big boy?"

Shemp appealed to Kreig. "You can't just let them take over...."

Vanna Kreig coldly cut him off. "I already have."

"What qualifies a committee of stadium players to organize the defense of this place?"

Paladin looked hard at Shemp. "At least we know how to fight."

"This couldn't have anything to do with the fact that there's old bad blood between Paladin and Mengele?"

Paladin took a deep breath, only controlling himself with great difficulty. "You're asking that, with an outlaw army beating on the gate?"

Petaluma Annie glanced at Paladin. "So what did go down between you and Iggy Mengele?"

Paladin shook his head. "There isn't time to go into that now."

Kreig sighed. "When you and your people have a defense plan together, come and tell me about it. I have some problems of my own to deal with right now."

Shemp looked outraged. "What about me?"

Kreig looked at him with withering contempt. "You come with me. I've got plenty for you to do."

With Shemp trotting behind her like a whipped dog and her technicians and ADs bringing up the rear, Vanna Kreig walked quickly back to the elevator. As the elevator doors closed behind her, the players breathed a collective sigh of relief. Annie got quickly to the point. "Okay, so what do we do?"

Paladin looked round at the others. "I figure the only things we have going for us are speed, weight, and organization. The big problem for the nomad outlaw is always range and fuel, and I'm guessing that by far the majority of the people with Iggy will be driving cars that are on average considerably lighter than ours. So when we hit them . . ."

Rhino Joe interrupted him. "We are going to hit them?"

Paladin nodded. "Oh yeah, we're going to hit them all right. When they come screaming at us out of the dawn, we're going to be outside the walls waiting for them, with the heaviest rammers leading the charge." He glanced at Kurtz. "I'm going to need you to organize that. The ramcars are crucial to this. I want every one of them charged up and ready to go by 4 A.M., okay?"

Kurtz grinned. "You got it." The rammer seemed much happier now he had something to do.

Annie was frowning. "What makes you so sure that they're going to come at dawn?"

Paladin trusted his gut feeling. "I know Iggy. Nothing would make him pass up the drama. He thinks he's some kind of reincarnated Attila the Hun. He'll come at dawn."

"We'll look pretty stupid if he doesn't."

"He will, trust me." Paladin looked out to where Iggy's army waited. It was now completely dark. "Listen, we gotta get moving. Let's go down and start things happening. We can talk on the way."

For the next four hours, Paladin constantly moved through the stadium, overseeing the increasingly frenetic preparations. Since there was no chance of bringing the second Kali on line, he'd put Mac Connolly in charge of the wall fortifications. Every surplus rocket, spare cannon, and heavy machine gun was hauled up onto the walls and installed in its own sandbagged emplacement. Connolly was such a painstaking perfectionist that Paladin knew that there would be no problems with these defenses. When he went up there just before midnight to see how things were progressing, the crew chief looked up from attaching the fuel hoses to a bank of down-pointing flameguns and grinned at him.

"I'm telling you, Paladin, even if you showboats on the ground screw up and let Mengele through to the walls, we'll teach him a lesson he won't forget."

Unable to raise any cooperation from Shemp, Paladin had instructed Kurtz to take a squad of drivers and gunners and break into the Action Corps armory. The orders had been simple. "Get in there any way you can and bring out all of the full-load ammunition. We'll use their stuff first and fall back on the Mickey Mouse stadium charges if we're pushed to it."

By one in the morning, the defense of Pomona had taken on a life of its own. Paladin decided that he could take a little time off without everything collapsing, and, not having spoken to her since the morning, he made his way to Bambi Starr's trailer. He found Bambi sitting cross-legged on the floor beside the big bed, dressed in a decidedly nonsexy coverall, meticulously cleaning and oiling a small collection of shotguns, pistols, and automatic weapons. He blinked at the number of guns.

"You planning on packing all of those?"

Bambi looked up with hair hanging in her face and a smudge of oil on her cheek. "A girl can never have enough hardware."

Paladin sat down on the bed. "You want to take a break for a few minutes?"

Bambi finished reassembling the AR25, put it to one side, and stood up. "So what did you have in mind?"

Paladin shrugged. "Hell, I don't know, maybe a drink? Maybe hang out for a half hour or so."

Bambi moved to the kitchenette and took a bottle of scotch and a pair of glasses from one of the wall cupboards. "So what is this, Paladin? The old 'let's get it on because tomorrow we might be dead' routine?"

Paladin leered. "I can't think of a better excuse, can you?"

Bambi Starr leered right back and poured a liberal dose of scotch into Paladin's glass. "You think you gotta use an excuse on me?"

Paladin took a drink. "I figured it was better than just coming over here assuming."

Bambi Starr sipped her own drink. "Honey, you can assume all you want with me."

Her hand went to the zipper that ran all the way down the front of her coverall. With a languid, seductive smile, she slowly teased it down. "How long can you stay?"

Before Paladin could answer, someone started

hammering on the door of the trailer. "Paladin? Are you in there?"

Bambi Starr's seductive smile faded and the zipper came to a stop just above her navel. "What the hell . . ."

The voice belonged to Rhino Joe. "Paladin, we gotta talk to you."

"Can't it wait?"

The voice of Petaluma Annie joined that of Rhino Joe. "Get your pants on, boy, and get out here. We got a problem."

Bambi Starr pouted. "He hasn't even got his pants off yet."

"This is serious. Kreig is leaving the stadium. The bitch says she's going to the outlaw camp to talk to Iggy."

Paladin was on his feet. "You gotta be kidding. Has she gone insane or what?"

Bambi Starr was pulling up her zipper. "We ought to shoot that bitch right now. She's more trouble than she's worth." She picked up the AR25 and jammed a clip into it as though she intended to shoot Kreig personally. "Shall we go?"

Paladin looked surprised. "Who said you were coming?"

Bambi didn't seem in the mood to accept any kind of argument. "After this little disappointment, I'm not letting you out of my sight for the rest of the night."

Vanna Kreig was being detained just inside the main gate by a squad of armed players. The gate was barred and reinforced with steel beams, and no one seemed willing to open it. Kreig sat in the command seat of one of the surviving Action Corps personnel carriers, while a dozen or more players with shotguns and assault weapons surrounded the vehicle. The carrier was bathed in the white light of four sunguns blazing down from the wall above, lending the whole scene a bizarre air of stark unreality, as though it was taking place on a movie set. To complicate matters, the situation was yet another standoff. Kreig had her own armed muscle behind her in the form of Shemp and ten of his Action men. The gunner, who sat behind the carrier's twin, turret-mounted Vulcans, seemed quite ready to use them. Paladin walked angrily into the pool of brightness as though he was immune to all the firepower. He had no time for any more internal nonsense. The whole focus had to be on fighting Iggy or they were dead.

"What the hell is this all about?"

It was almost as though Kreig was unable to grasp what was going on. "I was leaving the stadium until these cutthroats of yours decided to stop me."

Paladin took a deep breath, wishing that he'd thought to bring the bottle of scotch from Bambi's trailer. "And where did you think you were going?"

"That's my business."

"I heard you were going to the other camp. To see Iggy Mengele?"

"And what if I was?"

Paladin couldn't believe that he was hearing this. "What if you were? In that case, I'd say you were insane."

Bambi Starr elbowed her way to the front of the group of players. "Why not shoot her right now? She's gotta be planning to sell us out."

Paladin looked up at Vanna Kreig. "You really believe that you can talk to Iggy Mengele?"

Vanna Kreig slowly nodded. "I think he'll listen to me."

Rhino Joe's lip curled. "Listen to you? He'll have your head on the end of a pole before you can even open your mouth."

"I've been instructed to offer him a deal."

"What kind of deal?"

"A Skynet deal. A contract."

It was Petaluma Annie's turn to voice her contempt. "Iggy Mengele isn't going to go for some contract. All Iggy cares about is the chance for looting and burning."

Vanna Kreig looked hard at Annie. "You took a contract, didn't you?"

Annie clearly didn't like the way the argument was going. "Yeah, but I ain't Iggy."

"You were the same as him once."

Even though none of the players said anything, they all knew that Kreig had scored. She looked directly at Paladin. "Are you going to make this rabble let me go?"

Paladin was at a loss. "There's more to this than you're telling."

Vanna Kreig repeated herself. "Are you going to let me go?"

Bambi Starr emphatically shook her head. "She's gotta be selling us out."

Paladin raised a hand. "Let her go. Open the gates."

The players turned to him, shocked and angry. "You're crazy."

Paladin shook his head. "Let her go. With her gone, we can fight this thing on our own terms. I'll feel a whole lot cleaner if she's out of here."

"She knows all about the defenses. She can tell him everything."

"If Iggy hasn't figured out what we've done so far, he's an idiot, and whatever he might be, Iggy Mengele is no idiot. Let her go. I mean, what do we have to lose?"

Reluctantly, the gates were opened. The carrier rumbled forward, through the exit tunnel and out into the darkness. Paladin followed the carrier and watched as it drove away toward the flickering fires of the outlaw camp. Bambi Starr came up behind him. "Why the hell did you let her go?"

"I feel safer with her out of here."

"I think you've made a big mistake. She's going to screw us."

Paladin suddenly felt very tired. "She doesn't know everything I've got up my sleeve."

The sound of distant drumming came from the outlaw camp, with a lone trumpet playing an eerie Mexican refrain. Bambi moved closer to Paladin. "You know what tune that is?"

"The trumpet?"

"Right."

Paladin shook his head. "I don't have a clue."

"I don't know the name of it but it's the song that Santa Anna's men played to the defenders at the Alamo."

"It is?"

"It was supposed to send them a message."

"A message?"

"No quarter."

# CHAPTER **TWENTY-TWO**

One of the pickets was shouting back to the camp. "There's something coming!"

Iggy was on his feet. "What is it?"

"Looks like one of them Action Corps ice-cream trucks."

"Just one?"

"Only one that I can see. And you know what else?"

"What?"

"It's got a white flag hanging from its turret."

Iggy couldn't believe what he was hearing. "You're putting me on."

"I swear. They're waving a white flag. You figure they want to surrender?"

Iggy laughed. "There's only one way to find out. Let them come ahead."

The armored personnel carrier moved slowly forward, approaching the perimeter of the camp. Every pair of eyes watched it with suspicion and every gun was trained on it, although Iggy spoke quietly to his men, warning them not to open fire unless they wanted their health to take a turn for the worse. The drumming stopped and the whiskey bottles were set aside. The men crouched around the fires got slowly to their feet, and Julio the trumpeter lowered his instrument. Everyone watched and waited to see what this enemy vehicle with its white flag might do.

It would have been hard to imagine more of a contrast than the one between the Action Corp unit and the vehicles of the outlaws. The carrier's pristine, straight-from-the-factory paintwork gleamed in the light of the campfires, while the Horde's cars and trucks stood silent, ramshackle, and dust covered, decorated with everything from ancient battle flags and psychedelic designs to hides and human skulls.

For Vanna Kreig, peering through the narrow view slit in front of the carrier's command seat, entering the outlaw camp was like going to another planet. Up to that point, her dealings with Iggy Mengele had been strictly at arm's length and her role had been played out exclusively in the antiseptic, air-conditioned world of phones, faxes, and satellite communications, corporate boardrooms and corporate finance. A network of agents and field operatives had done the dirty work. She had seen videotapes of him and even brainreads and a DNA scan, but she had never met him in person. Another consideration was that, if the scheme blew up, she wanted to make sure that it wasn't her face it blew up in. Deniability was a major factor in all corporate intrigue. You also tried to never call anything by its real name. The death and destruction that was the stock-in-trade of Skynet's autoduel operation had always been expressed in terms of replacement figures and insurance claims, audience ratings and the relative value of one piece of tape over another. They were abstractions that wore safe, acceptable faces.

Here among the outlaws, death was raw and naked.

In the camp of the Horde, death was immediate, primitive, and tangible, with a form and an overpowering smell. It lurked in the haunted, hollow eyes of the men and women that watched her arrival, it permeated their dirty, sweat-stained clothing and danced in the flames of the campfires. Most important of all, it could be instantly conjured, in all its bloody reality, by the weapons that were, at the moment, trained on her.

As the carrier came to a stop, she glanced at Shemp. Her security chief was as white as a ghost. Putting on a braver face than she felt, she glanced at him and smiled sardonically. "Worried?"

"I hope you know what you're doing."

"Just trust me."

Shemp slowly shook his head. "That's why I'm worried."

Vanna Kreig shrugged. "Think of it this way, Shemp. If you'd stayed back at the stadium, the players probably would have killed you before the night was out. This is our best bet for coming through the situation alive, believe me."

A group of outlaws were walking toward the halted carrier. Vanna Kreig recognized Iggy Mengele from pictures and tape footage. The images she had seen, however, had never indicated quite how small he was. He seemed almost dwarfed by the hulking oddities who surrounded him like a personal guard.

The gang around Iggy Mengele were exceptional in their scarred and brutal ugliness. None of them were the kind that you would want to meet on a dark night. Although, as Vanna Kreig reflected as she prepared to step out of the carrier, meeting them on a dark night was exactly what she found herself doing. What did surprise her was the presence of a tall, good-looking woman in the group around Iggy. She was dressed in black leather and walking right beside him. Vanna Kreig wondered if this was the would-be conqueror's mistress.

As one of the Action men levered back the bolts on the carrier's forward hatch, Vanna Kreig turned back to Shemp. "If anything goes wrong, if anything happens to me, blast your way the hell out of here as fast as you can."

Shemp looked bitter. "I thought nothing was going to go wrong."

"It isn't. I'm just trying to be your concerned superior."

"It's a little late for that, isn't it?"

Vanna Kreig snarled. "Screw you, Shemp."

With that, she slipped down through the hatch.

Iggy and Vanna Kreig found themselves face to face. For the first moment both seemed at a loss for words. It probably didn't help that Kreig was the taller of the two. It was Iggy's turf, though, and he was the first to recover. He resorted to the familiar wolf grin. "So, what is this? You've come here to surrender the fort?"

The men around Iggy were also grinning. Even the woman in leather had a half smile on her face. Vanna Kreig took a deep breath and then wished she hadn't. The outlaws had only been camped for one night and already the whole area smelled of sweat and beer and excrement, and something strange and unique that could have been some old evil from the desert. The stench was something else that Vanna Kreig had failed to take into account.

"I've come to talk to you."

Iggy continued to grin. "Talk to me? This isn't unconditional surrender?"

"I need to talk to you before this goes any farther."

"And who might you be?"

Vanna Kreig wondered if Iggy was always like this or if he was putting on the demented grin for her benefit. "Please don't play cute. You know who I am. We've talked on enough video links."

"Video links can be deceiving."

She sighed wearily. "I'm Vanna Kreig, and I don't have time to play games with you. Can we please go somewhere where we can talk in private?"

"You can say anything you need to say in front of my men."

Right at that moment, a pale weasel-faced kid in a filthy leather and Kevlar battle suit leaned forward and inspected her closely. The kid's hair was greased into spikes that stuck straight up from the top of his head, and his breath stank of something so disgusting that Vanna Kreig didn't care to imagine what it might be.

Iggy seemed to be amused by her reaction. "Nibbo likes you."

Vanna Kreig looked round at the other men with Iggy. Every one of them seemed to have some kind of disfiguring combat scar. The face of one man was almost entirely burned away, little more than pink scar tissue with eyes and a mouth. With all of them, the eyes were the most troubling. The glint of craziness even lurked in those of the woman in leather. How the hell had she come to fall in with this bunch? She was actually wearing makeup. The woman's face hardened as their eyes met. Ilsa McCoy seemed to know what Vanna Kreig was thinking. "Just so there's no misunderstanding, girlie. I'm one of them."

At that moment, Vanna Kreig realized that she had made one small but very crucial mistake. She had been assuming that they were more or less rational. It was rapidly becoming clear to her that this was not the case. The whole camp reeked of insanity, and her only chance was to get Iggy away from his entourage and talk to him one on one.

"Some of the things we need to discuss would be better talked about in private."

"I have no secrets from my men."

"So you said, but . . ."

Nibbo was going on with his inspection. He sniffed Vanna Kreig's neck and glanced at Iggy. "This one smells like a plotter, boss. A born conspirator."

Ilsa McCoy was shaking her head, "Don't trust her, Iggy. She's poison. I've met her kind before."

Vanna Kreig's frustration was threatening to overwhelm her. "This is ridiculous. I can't talk to you about the TV coverage of your invasion with half your camp standing around."

Iggy was thinking. "She may have a point there." He took Vanna Kreig by the arm. "Come to my tent. We'll talk there."

Ilsa McCoy obviously didn't like this. "You want me to come with you?"

Iggy shook his head. "I don't think we'll be discussing anything you need worry about."

McCoy stiffened angrily. "With a full-scale battle coming up, I can find plenty to worry about. Particularly when one of the enemy shows up and wants to talk to you in private."

Iggy glared at her. "You saying that you don't trust me to take care of her?"

McCoy reddened. "No, but . . ."

Iggy didn't let her finish. "Then it's okay?"

Ilsa McCoy didn't say anything but she was clearly more than a little angry. Some of Iggy's male henchmen also didn't seem to be taking kindly to the idea of their leader having a confidential talk with this strange woman from the outside world, and Vanna Kreig drew some dark looks as she and Iggy walked away together.

Iggy's tent proved to be surprisingly spartan. Vanna Kreig had expected something fit for a barbarian warlord, complete with animal skins and chests of loot. Instead, she found that the only furniture consisted of a narrow cot, a small table, and a couple of folding chairs. A hand-drawn but extremely accurate map of the Pomona Bowl was pinned to a board that rested on an easel. The place was dimly lit by a single propane lamp.

"The simple life?"

Iggy shrugged. "There's plenty of time for luxury." A bottle of tequila was on the table. "Drink?"

Vanna Kreig shook her head. "No, thank you."

Iggy poured himself a shot. "You should have a drink. It might help you come to the point. It must be real important to bring you out here in the middle of the night. I mean, aren't you scared of us wild men?"

Vanna Kreig took out a cigarette case, extracted one, and lit it. "Yes, I'm scared. But I thought it was worth the risk."

"So?"

Kreig blew smoke into the air between them. "So, up to this point, I've been secretly financing your little expedition."

Iggy nodded. "That's true."

"And I arranged with the army to drive large numbers of outlaws from borders up in this direction so they'd join up with your troops."

Iggy's expression wasn't giving anything away. "You did that?"

"I've also kept the military and the L.A. militia from becoming involved in any of this. Both here and while you were in Palm Springs."

"I should be grateful?"

"I've come for the payoff."

Iggy's eyes flashed suspiciously. "Payoff?"

Vanna Kreig caught the flash. It encouraged her that the idea of payoff could worry this madman. At least something worried him. She leaned forward. "You think it was all charity? Tomorrow's battle is going to give me the biggest TV spectacle of the decade. You must know that."

"So make your film. I ain't stopping you."

"I just want to make sure of that."

Iggy pushed his hair out of his face. "Why should I want to do that?"

"There are people around who'll pull a double cross just for its own sake."

"And you think I might be one of those?"

Vanna Kreig didn't want to go down this road. She quickly changed the subject. "Val Paladin has taken over the defense of Pomona."

Iggy said nothing. Vanna Kreig raised an eyebrow. "You know Val Paladin?"

Iggy nodded. His eyes were hooded. "Of course I know Paladin. You know I do. You've been over my history."

"You have his people outnumbered by more than two to one."

"So I've got nothing to worry about? Is that what you came into the lions' den to tell me? Or are you worried that it'll all be over too soon and you won't have enough material to justify the money you've spent?"

"That is one consideration."

"So I'll see that my boys take it slow. That's no problem. Most are them are homicidal sadists anyway. Taking their time is a treat for them. You got anything else on your mind?"

Vanna Kreig nodded. "Paladin has heavily fortified the walls. He's got a lot of weaponry mounted up there."

Iggy didn't look too concerned. "I figured someone would pull something like that."

"And it doesn't bother you?"

"Why should it? All we gotta do is stand well back and rocket the hell out of them. Shouldn't take more than a half a day before they give up."

"That could cause a lot of damage to the facility."

Iggy laughed. "Is that what's bothering you, Ms. Vanna Kreig? That I might damage your goddamned stadium? What the hell did you expect?"

"It's not the stadium that bothers me. All my production facilities are there. If you blow up the stadium, I'm screwed."

Again Iggy didn't see it as much of a problem. "So bring out more gear from L.A."

"That would take time."

Iggy slowly nodded. "Ah . . . I think I'm starting to get it. You came here to make sure I'd follow the script. Am I right? First you want the boys to take it slow when we're whipping their mobile force on the ground, and now you want us to hold off on trashing the Bowl until you've got another production facility on line."

"That's one way of looking at it."

Iggy's face went blank and his eyes hooded again. It gave him the expression of a reptile. "That's the way I am looking at it."

Kreig lit another cigarette. "I did make all this possible."

"You provided the money and supplies."

Vanna Kreig's face twitched. "Maybe you should give me that drink."

Iggy poured her a shot of tequila. His face was still unreadable. "You got a lot of balls to come out here like this."

"I'm playing for big stakes."

"Is there anything else that you want?"

Kreig took a sip of her drink. "I need your guarantee of protection for the duration of the conflict."

Iggy poured himself a second shot. It was almost a moment of intimacy. "You're asking me for my protection? Why didn't you come to me before?"

"Previously I hadn't expected that Pomona was going to fall to you. Now you're obviously going to win, I have to have you on my side. I can't get any guarantees from Paladin if he's dead."

"The payback on the investment?"

"The final part of the transaction."

Iggy's face lit up with childlike delight. "You really do have it figured out, don't you?"

"I'm doing my best."

"There's one thing that you left out."

Vanna Kreig's face twitched again. "What's that?"

Iggy glanced in the direction of the tent flap and raised his voice. "Nibbo! Ilsa! Get in here."

The tent flap was pushed back and Nibbo and Ilsa McCoy came in. "What up, Iggy?"

Iggy pointed to Vanna Kreig. His voice was calm and measured. "I want you to take Ms. Vanna Kreig here outside and hang her."

Vanna Kreig's face was a picture of total disbelief. "What did you say?"

Iggy smiled. "I told these two to take you out and hang you."

"You're joking, right?"

Ilsa McCoy drew a pistol and pointed it at Vanna Kreig's head. "Iggy doesn't joke."

Iggy was now grinning broadly. "You see, that's what you forgot. We're just degenerate savages who have no concept of even the most minimal code of behavior."

Vanna Kreig had turned white, and panic was edging into her voice. "I don't believe this. Tell me this is some kind of joke."

Iggy ignored her. "You can't do business with people

like us and expect a payoff. We don't respect deals. In fact, we take an unholy delight in reneging on them. That's why they call us renegades."

"You're reneging on our deal? Everything?"

"I'm going to take Pomona tomorrow and I don't give a damn if anyone films it or not."

"But why kill me?"

Iggy answered the question as Nibbo pulled out a short length of cord. "The reason I'm having you hung is that I don't like the way you come into my camp with your white flag and your shooting script and your bullshit and think that you can just take over. I don't need that, Ms. Vanna Kreig. If I let you live, you'd make my life just too damned complicated. There'd be no end to your demands."

Vanna Kreig was shaking her head. "You can't do this, Iggy. I made you. I created you. You can't kill me."

Ilsa McCoy looked at Iggy. "What's she talking about?"

Kreig glared up at McCoy. "I created him. I saw that his severed head went to a private freezer clinic after he was killed by Ed Brand. I arranged the cloning and, while his personality was reconnecting, I ordered a little tailoring to juice up all the hate and compulsion to destroy in him. I built me the greatest of the outlaws. The perfect villain for live-action TV. After that it was easy to let him loose and have him gather an army. I made sure that he always had weapons and that he always had money and his fueled-up ambition did the rest."

"All that for a fucking TV show?" A tremor in Iggy's voice indicated that this ultimate truth was causing him more grief than he cared to admit. "All that for a fucking TV show."

Vanna Kreig smiled bitterly. "Creating you was no trouble. I enjoyed it. This show was going to be my masterwork. I guess you could call it the ultimate media manipulation."

Iggy was white. "I ain't no fucking TV show!"

"You're what I made you."

"I got nearly two hundred guns out there that prove what I am."

"And I gave them to you."

Iggy grasp on sanity was gone. "You're going to suffer. I'm going to think up ways to make you suffer. You're gonna scream, you bitch! You're gonna scream for hours! You're gonna beg for death!"

"How do you think your followers are going to react when they find out you're nothing but a clone?"

Nibbo shrugged, suddenly changing the whole picture. "It don't bother this follower none."

Iggy looked hard at Ilsa McCoy. "How about you?"

Ilsa was a little slower in answering. "It bothers me, but it doesn't change anything."

Iggy stood up and spread his hands. "Seems to me that the real reason you came out here is that you just couldn't resist seeing your creation in the flesh. You had to look at the monster, and now, like Frankenstein, you got to pay for the privilege."

He gestured to Nibbo, and Vanna Kreig screamed as her arms were pulled behind her and the cord was looped around her wrists. More men were in the tent and hands were dragging her out into the darkness. Amid all of the confusion, she heard Iggy's voice asking a question. "There is a place where we can hang her, isn't there?"

Nibbo answered. "Sure, we built a gallows to hang those homesteaders and the other prisoners."

"Don't hang her yet though."

Nibbo laughed. "You want the boys to have her?"

"As many times as they want. And tell them to be creative. Make sure the real perverts get a piece of her."

"You got it, boss."

"And make sure there's a tape of it. Tape every goddamned moment. Every twitch and every whimper." He smiled horribly at Vanna Kreig. "After we take Pomona, maybe we'll put it out on satellite. Should get some rating, huh?"

Vanna Kreig began yelling at the top of her lungs. "Don't listen to him! He's a clone!"

Iggy's voice was curt. "Gag her!"

Some foul-smelling rag was being forced into her mouth. She fought against it, but there were too many of them. They lifted her off her feet, and, kicking and struggling, she was carried out into the night and the outlaw camp.

# CHAPTER TWENTY-THREE

Paladin stood beside the lead truck, Vito Kurtz's customized, Division 60 Sabre Omega, with its RV body and massive ramplates. He looked slowly round at his preparations. Even leaving as little to chance as possible, the tactics that he'd set out were still one hell of a gamble. He'd brought out every serviceable vehicle in the Bowl and still he only had a total of seventy-three units under his command, as opposed to Iggy who, as far as anyone could tell, could muster just shy of two hundred. It was like going into a chess game with half your pieces already taken, although the battle in front of the walls of Pomona wasn't going to be fought like any chess game. Chess was a contest of time and dignity, thought and finesse, and there'd be precious little of any of those when the two sides started rolling. The Battle of Pomona would be short, ugly, and brutal, and Paladin's only hope, being hopelessly outgunned, was that he could outsmart Iggy Mengele. He knew the keys to winning by smarts against a much stronger force were preparation and planning. But now the plans were laid, the preparations were made, the vehicles were in place and ready. Nothing remained for him to do, and still he worried. He glanced for the hundredth time at the eastern horizon. Were his eyes playing tricks on him? Was the sky actually lightening?

Kurtz leaned out from the cab of the Omega 60. "You want to take it a little easy, boy, or you are going to burst something."

"There're a lot of people counting on me."

Kurtz got down from the ramtruck and lit a cigar. "There are a lot of people counting on each other. If this plan of yours don't do it, there ain't going to be anyone blaming you."

Paladin smiled. "That's the only consolation in all this. If the plan doesn't do it for us, I almost certainly won't be around for anyone to blame."

The core of Paladin's play was the assumption that Iggy's forces would come in howling and undisciplined, spreading their attack across a wide front, hoping to sweep everything in front of them in the first charge. Paladin was well aware that the weakness of this headlong rush was that the lighter, faster vehicles invariably raced well ahead of the rest of the pack, softening the impact, getting in the way of the heavier machines, and screwing up their fields of fire.

Taking this into account, Paladin had divided his forces into two narrow columns that would hit the outlaw onslaught at two specific points on the line. With his ramtrucks taking the lead, these two concentrated assaults might be able to smash their way clear through Iggy's line, then turn and come at the outlaws from behind, driving them straight into the fire from Mac Connolly and his gunners up on the walls. The plan was a long shot, but it was the only shot they had.

"I just hope that I haven't overlooked anything obvious."

Kurtz bit off the chewed end of the cigar and spat it into the dust. "If you have, it's too late now."

Now both men stared to the east. Faint streaks of gray really were visible over the mountains. Kurtz unzipped his pants and started to relieve himself right behind the vehicle. "I guess it's getting close to show time."

When the light came, it came quickly. The streaks broadened to a wide band of gray and the darkness rapidly faded. Paladin glanced at Kurtz as a lone motorcycle engine started up back down the column and then began coming up the line toward them. "What's this? Someone chickening out already?"

Kurtz grinned. "I don't think it's that."

A moment later, Paladin discovered why Kurtz was grinning. Bambi Starr was speeding along beside the column on her flamboyant trike, just as though it was a normal day and she was just putting on a show in the arena. Her only concession to the fact that they were all about to engage in genuine combat was that she had dressed in cut-off desert fatigues. The other drivers laughed and applauded as she passed, and Bambi acknowledged them as though they were all her loyal fans and not men who were about to go into battle.

She brought the trike to a stop beside Kurtz and Paladin and grinned at the two men as though it was all the start of a fabulous adventure. "So how you holding up, Paladin?"

Kurtz laughed. "He's just discovered that he's a worrier."

Bambi's grin broadened. "What are you worried about, baby? We're going to win, ain't we?"

Before Paladin could reply, Bambi stood up on the trike's footrests, struck a cheerleading pose, and shouted back down the line. "We're going to win, ain't we?"

Paladin moved toward her warningly. "Keep the noise down."

Bambi gestured to the bright sky in the east. "What's the point? They can see us now, can't they?"

Paladin had moved his forces into place, under cover of darkness, silently and with the minimum of lights. Bambi was right though; now the sun was coming up, secrecy was no longer possible. Paladin was still having trouble, however, dealing with this sudden outbreak of frivolity. "I'm not sure we need a pep rally."

Bambi's smile dropped. "Maybe that's exactly what we do need. This isn't the last day at the Alamo yet. Besides, today is going to make me famous." She bawled back down the line again. "We're gonna win, ain't we?"

The first response was thin and ragged and Bambi tried again. "We're gonna win, ain't we?"

The second response gathered strength as the drivers and gunners seemed to decide that they might as well go out with a shout as a whimper. "Yeah! We're gonna win!"

"We're gonna win, ain't we?"

"Yeah! We're gonna win!"

"We're gonna *win*, ain't we?"

"Yeah, we're gonna win!"

Paladin shook his head, although he couldn't help smiling, "So now we got a cheerleader. I should have ordered pom-poms."

Kurtz ground out his cigar with his boot. "You were wondering if you forgot something."

Bambi went at it with renewed vigor. *"We're gonna win, ain't we?"*

"Yeah, we're gonna *win*!"

Sound travels a long way in the desert. Two miles off, in the outlaw camp, the noise from the other side set things in motion. Iggy crawled from the sleeping bag that he had been sharing with Ilsa McCoy and began struggling into his clothes. "Come on, baby, let's get moving. I got a stadium to burn."

As Iggy swaggered through the camp making for the Hades, a crowd quickly gathered behind him. A lot of his people had been awake and drinking all night and now were in exactly the right mood to go out and commit indiscriminate murder. With that the priority of the day, it was only fitting that his walk to the Hades took him past the gallows where the naked and hideously mutilated body of Vanna Kreig swung in the morning breeze. Buzzards don't fly by night, but now that the dawn had come, they were already circling in the sky, although no bird had yet found the courage to descend and start pecking at the corpse.

Iggy climbed into the driver's seat of the Hades. He cranked up the mill and brought the computer on line. All round him, other drivers were starting their engines, and the Jetboys' big old psychedelic Amex Commando was already moving out, with a clutch of bikes following the battle-scarred bus like evil chicks behind a grizzled old mother hen. Iggy let his engine idle until it was warm, and then he eased the Hades forward. The most pivotal day of his life had truly begun.

It took almost a half hour to maneuver the Horde into some semblance of battle order. Iggy knew that, with this bunch, there wasn't a prayer of doing anything fancy. The best he could hope for was a simple, if ragged, line-abreast assault. He reassured himself that, when you outnumbered the enemy more than two to one, elaborate tactical moves weren't needed. He had the power to sweep the defenders in front of him and smash them with his first assault, and that was good enough. If any were left with fight still in them after that first ordeal by fire, they could more than be taken care of by the raw killer instincts of groups like the Jetboys and the K-90s.

After a lot of yelling and cursing, Iggy had the Horde at least all pointing in the same direction. There was nothing to do but go. Iggy sat for a moment before letting the clutch out and rolling the Hades forward, the agreed signal for the whole army to move. A lesser man might have prayed or reflected on his mortality, but Iggy owed nothing to any God. He wasn't even sure if cloning had left him any mortality on which to reflect. So he was a clone. So what? He felt fine and functioned better. Ask Ilsa McCoy if she had any complaints. So he'd been rebuilt, and maybe even reprogrammed. It was better than being dead and he was certainly no one's puppet. The woman who believed that was right now hanging from his gallows. Smiling, he eased his foot off the clutch and the Hades moved forward.

"Okay, rock and roll."

"It was in the final days in Nashville. Me and six others were holed up in this basement, under fire for seven days. The whole force had been broken by then. Fragmented groups, all trying to survive and get out as best they could. The Companions of Blood were everywhere. Every day they'd overrun another of our positions. If there were any survivors, they'd take them out and crucify them. The Bloods always traveled with a truckload of wooden crosses."

Kurtz and Bambi looked at each other. Paladin never talked about his past, and for him to do so now, just as the battle was about to start, had an almost eerie quality.

"Like I said, we'd held out for seven days. We had

plenty of ammunition, but that was about all that we had. No food and precious little water. We were all getting kinda crazy. The explosions had disturbed the city's rat population and they were running everywhere. On the fourth day, we started eating the bastards. Drinking their blood. We swore we were going to survive. A major oath. Kinda crazy. You know what I mean?"

"We finally decided that the only way out was if we could dig through the floor and break into the sewer system. The digging took thirty-six hours, but we did it. We sent one guy down to scope out the sewers. Unfortunately, he came back an hour later with a squad of Blood storm troopers. He'd been captured by a patrol and he'd sold us and the oath out, to save his own stinking skin. With him leading them back through the sewers, we didn't know what had hit us. They took us alive.

"I was the last in line to be crucified and I had to watch as they did the others. And all the time, our former buddy is down on his knees, praying up a storm, loud as he can, to convince the Companions of Blood that he'd had a battlefield conversion to Jesus and he was one of them."

"So how did you get away?"

Paladin stared out into the distance. "Just as they were going to nail me to the lumber, Bear Hite launched a counter attack. A rocket landed right on the execution site, and I was able to escape in the confusion."

"And the one who betrayed you was Iggy Mengele?"

"He wasn't called that back then, but yeah, it was him. Treacherous, oath-breaking little shit. That's what makes all this kinda personal."

The dust thrown up by the Horde was a telegraph. The moment Paladin's people saw it swirl into the air, they went into action. Paladin himself was in the gunner's seat in Kurtz's Omega 60, one of the leading group of five ramcars that headed the right-hand column. He had control of the communications net, and he broke the long night's radio silence when he spoke into his helmet mike.

"Okay, here we go. Maintain your positions at all cost. Don't anybody get excited and break formation."

Kurtz put the hammer down and the Omega's speedometer eased toward sixty. Paladin leaned forward in his seat. "You take it easy too, Vito. This ain't no race. We don't want to get there first."

Vito Kurtz snarled good-naturedly back at him. "You just mind your guns, boy. I know what I'm doing."

The Horde had been rolling for less than a minute. Iggy had bikers in front of him. They turned in their saddles as they came past, waving, brandishing their weapons, and making obscene gestures to the drivers they had overtaken. Three Jetboys were performing a crazed motorized ballet as they raced along doing sixty plus over rough country. Although Iggy had started out leading the charge, the bikers had come burning through the ranks and were now outrunning everyone, going for death or glory. "Screw 'em" was Iggy's only thought. If they wanted to die early, that was their problem. He glanced left and right. The faster cars were keeping pace with him, each one throwing up its own bow wave of dust as it hurtled into combat. Iggy could imagine how the rear ranks must be driving on blind faith alone with dust cutting visibility to almost nothing.

Iggy looked into his rearview mirror and saw Billy Dalton's Security Seven with its chipped camouflage paint right behind him. The idiot probably thought he was being loyal, but Billy had become too inquisitive to live.

"Yeah, stick close, kid. I got plans for you."

At a half mile, the two armies could see each other clearly. Paladin spoke a single sentence into his helmet mike. "It's time, Mac."

The three-word go-code was all it took. Fire flashed along the walls of Pomona and a flight of short-range missiles screamed into the air. For a moment, they left straight vapor trails, then almost immediately dropped into the ranks of the charging outlaws. Bursts of orange flame erupted and rolling puffballs of black smoke rose to form miniature mushroom clouds. Airbursts blossomed into multiple star shells over the enemy, and away to Paladin's left, a white phosphorous warhead flared into a small blinding sun, leaving him awed, despite all his years on the road.

"Brace yourself! I figure we'll hit them in about thirty seconds!"

Iggy fought with the wheel as a rocket burst some thirty yards in front of him, throwing a pair of bikers and their machines high into the air. The Hades' suspension protested as he swung the car into a fast turn that almost brought him into collision with an armored pick-up. A second rocket burst beside him on his right and another farther back to the left. A Bastion rolled and burned, and when he flicked on his radio, he could hear men screaming. He cursed the gunners on the walls. Those sons of bitches were going to be trouble. He tried the radio again. He needed the heavy trucks with their rocket platforms to start doing something about those swine on the walls, but the radio was a cacophony of gibberish. As well as the screams of the burned and injured, some idiot was yelling "banzai" over and over again. No way was Iggy going to get any orders through. It hardly mattered though. Any moment the two charging armies were going to hit, locking together in car-to-car combat, and then they would truly enter the realm of chaos.

The sound of the two armies making first contact was like the crunch of doom, although no one who was in a position to hear it had any time to listen. The Omega jumped and bucked and there were strange metallic rattlings and bangings on the truck's armor as Kurtz plowed through the confusion of motorcycles that preceded the main body of outlaws. A rat-a-tat-tat of louder bangings followed as the Omega was hit by a burst from a machine gun. Paladin had no time, though, to think about his own safety as the Omega continued its headlong rush. He was pumping the gun controls and riding the recoils, tossing missiles as fast as the lasers could find targets, and then he was thrown hard against his safety harness as the ramtruck plowed into its first four-wheeler.

The victim was a Hudson Hammer that all but folded in half under the impact. It was carried along by the Omega's momentum for many yards, breaking up as it went until the truck was finally free of the wreckage. Paladin was hurled from side to side by near miss explosions, and the armor was being continuously pounded by bullets. He took a quick look through the gunner's view slit and saw little but smoke and flame. They were now right in the middle of the enemy ranks. On either side of him, the other ramcars from Pomona were inflicting the same damage and taking the same kind of punishment.

Kurtz yelled above the racket, "It's the goddamned Valley of Death, boy! I kid you not!"

* * *

Iggy was angry and confused. He had nothing in front of him to shoot at. All round him, a war was going on, but he personally had no target. He hadn't even fired his guns yet. In a sudden flash of insight, he realized what that bastard Paladin had done. He played it tricky. He'd only engaged the Horde at two points on the line, pushing through with his big rammers, intending to turn and take the Horde from the rear. In all probability, the bulk of the defenders were now already behind him.

"Son of a bitch!"

He would never have expected Paladin to be so smart. The trick had been around for a long time. As far as he knew, it had first been used by Alexander the Great against the armies of Darius III, but it still appeared to work. Iggy knew what he had to do, but he wasn't sure how to do it. A number of the vehicles around him were slowing down. The walls of Pomona were very close and the other outlaw drivers seemed to be experiencing the same confusion.

He yelled into the near useless radio. "Anyone who can hear me, regroup on me! Regroup on me! Regroup under the walls!"

They were turning, going back, into the pall of dust left by the outlaws, coming up behind them, from the direction that they'd least expect. Paladin scarcely dared hope, but it seemed as though his plan was working. Kurtz appeared to share the feeling. He laughed out loud. "This is going to be like shooting fish in a barrel."

The very next moment, though, it was as though the world exploded. The windshield blew inward and the Omega was filled with smoke, flame, and flying glass. Either it had been hit somewhere in front or it had driven through a very near miss. The truck was still running but bouncing and lurching wildly. Was Kurtz still driving? It felt like they were out of control.

He crawled forward to the driver's seat. "Vito! Yo Vito! Are you okay?"

Kurtz didn't answer. Paladin got up beside him and one look was all it took. Half of Kurtz's helmet had been blown away and half of Kurtz's head had gone right along with it.

Iggy brought the Hades to a stop. He was less than fifty yards from the walls of Pomona, far too close for the defenders above to angle down their rockets and do him any harm. Other cars were racing toward him. One or two were hit by micromissiles on the way in, but it seemed that inside some seventy yards out from the walls, nothing could hurt them. They were actually sheltered there. To a degree, the regrouping was starting to work. Outlaws were homing in on Iggy from every direction. It only remained to hang in until he had enough for a force and then he could go looking for whatever men and machines Paladin had left. Maybe the battle wasn't going as well as Iggy might have hoped, but they'd be inside Pomona before nightfall.

And, as he toyed with that piece of optimism, the skies suddenly began to rain liquid fire.

Paladin was trying to steer the Omega with one hand and lever Kurtz out of the driving seat with the other. He wasn't succeeding particularly well and he narrowly missed some large vehicle. The worst part was that he wasn't even able to tell whether it was a friend or a foe, just a big dark shape in the man-made dust storm. A loud knocking was coming from the engine, and Paladin's heart sank as it was followed by a very loud and terminal bang. The mill cut out and the steering instantly turned stiff and sluggish. No use staying with the truck. He didn't hesitate. He kicked the emergency release to the driver's door. The bolts blew and the door flew off. Paladin didn't even bother to look. He grabbed his shotgun and jumped blind, hoping for the best.

With a scream of rage, Iggy floored the Hades, gunning it from zero to sixty in a little over six seconds. Those bastards up on the wall had suckered them in, waiting until a bunch of them were thinking that they'd found some sort of shelter and then dropping the flame cloud on them. The rear of the car was covered with sticky adhesive fire, but with a little luck, he could perhaps blow it off with sheer speed. It was little consolation, but Dalton's Security Seven was nearby, also burning.

The rapid acceleration might have worked had not a sudden burst of 20mm cannon fire from the wall sent Iggy spinning sideways. He felt rather than heard the rear wheel go, and knew the Hades was of no further use. His final thought as he bailed out was that he still hadn't fired a shot in this battle.

Paladin crouched under the tilted side of a wrecked half-track. The Omega was some fifteen yards away, stalled and dead, another metal corpse on this now littered battlefield. Cars continued to roar through the dust and smoke and there was firing going on around him. He thought that he also heard the sound of falling rockets and prayed that it was Mac Connolly and his men up on the walls and not the outlaws storming the stadium. He ran through a quick mental checklist. He had weapons; both his sidearm and shotgun had come through the jump from the Omega. His suit was torn, he'd lost his helmet and suffered a few cuts and bruises, but otherwise he was unhurt. The real problem was knowing what to do next. While he lay under the halftrack, he was relatively safe, but if he made a move, it would only be a matter of minutes before he was either gunned down or run over. From his makeshift foxhole, he could see other men on foot stumbling around in the dust. He didn't feel inclined to join them in their exposed and suicidal two-step.

As though to reinforce the point, a biker, possibly a Jetboy from his hair and armor, charged past him screaming and pumping his guns as though he'd gone totally insane. Following a sudden flurry of firing, he heard another motorcycle coming toward him, but this one seemed to be slowing down. While the bike and biker were still only a shape in the dust, Paladin raised the shotgun and jacked as hell into the breech. If the voice hadn't come when it did, he would certainly have fired.

"Paladin! Get on the back! Get on fast!"

The voice of Bambi Starr was unmistakable.

Something was very wrong with Iggy's left ankle. It had twisted under him when he'd jumped from the Hades. Getting to his feet caused sheets of pain to flash up his leg, but he didn't stop. He had to get out of there. He had to find some means of transportation and get back to the camp. Instinct told him that things were going very wrong. He had to get back and stop the rot. Wreckage and fires were all around him, but he could see nothing that would be any use to him except a snapped-off aluminum spar that he picked up and used as a crutch. Surely a still-working motorcycle had to exist in all this mess. Somewhere a driver must have been killed but his bike left unharmed. Or maybe he could kill a rider himself. A bike was coming up behind him. He drew his pistol and turned as fast as he could, but he wasn't fast enough. He got a glimpse of a grinning Jetboy and then the bike was gone before he had time to snap off a shot.

While he was still cursing his hell-spawned luck and the pain in his ankle, he saw the second bike. This was the one. This was the machine that he was going to use to get him out of there and restore his fortunes. He could still turn the tide of battle.

Paladin didn't need any second urging. He swung himself onto the back of Bambi's trike and she gunned it away.

"How the hell did you find me?"

Bambi shouted back into the slipstream, "I was making the turn and I saw you get hit so I followed you."

"How's the battle going?"

"It ain't over yet but I think we're winning. The immediate problem is that I'm clean out of ammo. I had a run-in with a bunch of Jetboys that tapped me out."

"So where are you going now?"

"I want to get out of all this dust and smoke. I can't even tell who's who."

Paladin was the first to spot the figure up ahead. A small, long-haired man in a blackened poncho was leaning on a makeshift crutch. As they passed him, he raised a pistol and tried for a shot at them, taking his time and seeming unconcerned about his own safety. As the bullet screamed off the trike's rear fairing, something was jolted in Paladin's memory.

"That's him! Holy shit, that's him!"

Bambi Starr was confused. "What?"

"Turn around, it's him!"

"What are you talking about?"

"It's him! It's Iggy Mengele!"

Bambi hit the brakes so hard that Paladin was almost thrown off the back. "Are you sure?"

Paladin didn't answer; he was already gone and running. Iggy saw him coming and fired before he really had the range. Paladin ducked behind a piece of wreckage and yelled to the outlaw leader. "Give it up, Iggy, the battle's lost."

The only reply was a fusillade of shots that sent Paladin deeper into cover. A large tractor rumbled past, ignoring both of them, and Paladin used the cover of its bulk to move closer to Iggy. The device worked well up to the last minute when Iggy spotted him creeping along beside the truck and fired. A searing pain lanced through Paladin's shoulder, even though his body armor must have absorbed most of the impact. He fired the shotgun from the hip without even aiming. Iggy's right arm took most of the blast. With a look of stunned surprise, he sank to his knees. Paladin stumbled forward with blood pouring down his arm. When he spoke, his voice was a croak.

"Finally, you. Iggy Mengele."

"Paladin."

"Right, Paladin. It's a long way from Nashville. You still got religion?"

"This is a hell of a way to meet again."

Bambi brought the bike to a stop behind the two of them, then came and stood beside Paladin. She looked at his shoulder. "Are you okay?"

Paladin nodded. "It hurts like hell, but I'll live."

"Is that really him?"

Again Paladin nodded. "Yeah, it's him."

A great deal of blood was coming from Iggy's arm, and he looked up at Paladin and Bambi with the most intense expression of venomous hate that either of them could remember. "So why don't you just kill me?"

Paladin actually smiled. "I don't have any nails."

Bambi glared down at Iggy with equal loathing. "Go on, Paladin, kill him!"

But Paladin didn't make a move. Bambi was shocked. "So kill him."

"Maybe we should take him alive."

"What?"

"Maybe we should take him alive."

Bambi thought about this. "What? Sell him to a zoo? Or maybe to Vanna Kreig?"

A new voice came out of the smoke. "He hung Kreig last night. After the boys were through with her."

Paladin and Bambi both whirled. A figure tottered toward them, so messed up that it scarcely seemed human. The man had burns all down the side of his face and body and the tatters of his clothing still trailed smoke. Blood seeped from multiple wounds. "He hung Vanna Kreig last night because she told us all his secret. She told us all how she created him. How she had him cloned and programmed so he'd make all this happen. Just so she could make a fucking TV show."

Iggy had also looked round. "Billy Dalton. Where did you come from?"

Dalton staggered to where Iggy was still on his knees. "Where do you think I came from? I came from the wreckage of your army. Most of us are dead already. I'm dead. The Jetboys are dead, Ilsa's dead, Tod Slaughter's dead. The last of the best are all dead and you led us into this. You had the power and you threw it all away for nothing."

Other figures were coming out of the smoke, the

survivors of the battle, damaged and dirty, with the blank expressions of the living dead. No one made any attempt to intervene in the confrontation between Iggy and Paladin.

Iggy faced Dalton and his voice was very quiet. "You followed me."

"We didn't know you were some damned clone. You were probably conditioned to make all this happen. All this for a damned TV."

Bambi Starr couldn't believe what she was hearing. "He's a clone?"

Dalton painfully nodded. "A damned Skynet clone, who set us all to killing each other. How many of your people do you think are left?"

A strange quiet was settling over the field. Sporadic gunfire still sounded but the storm fury of the battle had passed. Dalton looked at Paladin with eyes that abandoned sanity to pain. "Or maybe he can't be killed. He's been dead once already. Maybe he's a thing brought back from hell. Maybe you shouldn't try to kill him, maybe you should put him somewhere on display. Put him in a fucking zoo and let the burgerbrains get their kicks by looking at him."

"Kill me, and get it over with, goddamn it!"

It was the closest that Iggy Mengele had ever come to pleading, and Paladin just nodded. He put down the shotgun, drew his pistol, and, almost lovingly, put a bullet through Iggy's forehead. The pistol shot seemed to snap something in Dalton. His body folded and crumpled, and his last words as he sagged to the ground were little more than a rattling gasp. "Do it right, okay?"

Bambi looked confused. "What did he mean, do it right?"

Paladin sighed. "He meant exactly what he said. Do it right. You may not want to watch this."

With his face as white as a ghost, Paladin fired five more shots into Iggy's head, until it was nothing more than a bloody pulp. "No brains. No memories. Nobody will ever clone him again."

Bambi choked back a sob as Paladin put his arm around her. "Is that it?"

Paladin nodded. "Yeah, that's it."

"So what happens now?"

Paladin sank to his knees and looked round at the ruin of the battlefield. "I don't think the Pomona Bowl will be back in action for a long time. You could say our careers are on hold."

"So where do we go?"

"I'm getting the hell out of here. Going out to the desert. I can't take no more of this freak show."

"What about all the others?"

Paladin smiled. "They'll all drift off. Lay low. There's going to be an aftermath to this shit. Without Kreig to keep the military out, they're gonna be all over this area like a cheap suit. Looking to round up the desperate outlaws."

Bambi started to protest. "They won't round us up. We were working for Skynet, goddamn it."

"You're saying we were the good guys?"

Bambi looked defensive. "Yeah, we were the good guys."

"I don't think anyone they send out here will be bothering to tell the difference. We're all outlaws now."

"And all we can do is lay low?"

Paladin sighed. The pain in his shoulder was getting bad. "Lay low. After a while gangs will start gathering again. This isn't the last battle. We'll be back."

"You're starting to sound like Iggy Mengele."

"That was the trouble with Iggy. He was doing the right thing for all the wrong reasons. I mean, he hung Vanna Kreig didn't he."

Paladin got to his feet and began to slowly walk away. Bambi called after him. "What about me?"

Paladin grinned wearily. "You want to come and help me lick my wounds?"

Bambi laughed. "Sounds like a plan."

She hurried to catch up with him.

# TOR
# BOOKS The Best in Science Fiction

**LIEGE-KILLER • Christopher Hinz**
"*Liege-Killer* is a genuine page-turner, beautifully written and exciting from start to finish....Don't miss it."—*Locus*

**HARVEST OF STARS • Poul Anderson**
"A true masterpiece. An important work—not just of science fiction but of contemporary literature. Visionary and beautifully written, elegiac and transcendent, *Harvest of Stars* is the brightest star in Poul Anderson's constellation."
—Keith Ferrell, editor, *Omni*

**FIREDANCE • Steven Barnes**
SF adventure in 21st century California—by the co-author of *Beowulf's Children*.

**ASH OCK • Christopher Hinz**
"A well-handled science fiction thriller."—*Kirkus Reviews*

**CALDÉ OF THE LONG SUN • Gene Wolfe**
The third volume in the critically-acclaimed Book of the Long Sun.
"Dazzling."—*The New York Times*

**OF TANGIBLE GHOSTS • L.E. Modesitt, Jr.**
Ingenious alternate universe SF from the author of the *Recluce* fantasy series.

**THE SHATTERED SPHERE • Roger MacBride Allen**
The second book of the Hunted Earth continues the thrilling story that began in *The Ring of Charon*, a daringly original hard science fiction novel.

**THE PRICE OF THE STARS • Debra Doyle and James D. Macdonald**
Book One of the Mageworlds—the breakneck SF epic of the most brawling family in the human galaxy!

Call toll-free 1-800-288-2131 to use your major credit card or clip and mail this form below to order by mail

**Send to:** Publishers Book and Audio Mailing Service
PO Box 120159, Staten Island, NY 10312-0004

| | | | | |
|---|---|---|---|---|
| ☐ 530756 | Liege-Killer ................$4.99/$5.99 | ☐ 534204 | Caldé of the Long Sun ..........$6.99/$7.99 |
| ☐ 519469 | Harvest of Stars ..........$5.99/$6.99 | ☐ 548221 | Of Tangible Ghosts................$5.99/$6.99 |
| ☐ 510240 | Firedance ....................$5.99/$6.99 | ☐ 530160 | The Shattered Sphere ...........$5.99/$6.99 |
| ☐ 530780 | Ash Ock ......................$5.99/$6.99 | ☐ 517040 | The Price of the Stars ...........$4.99/$5.99 |

Please send me the following books checked above. I am enclosing $_____. (Please add $1.50 for the first book, and 50¢ for each additional book to cover postage and handling. Send check or money order only—no CODs).

Name _____

Address _____ City _____ State _____ Zip_____

# If you enjoyed this book...
Come visit our website at

# www.sfbc.com

### and find hundreds more:
- science fiction ● fantasy
- the newest books
- the greatest classics

### THE SCIENCE FICTION BOOK CLUB
has been bringing the best of science fiction and fantasy to the doors of discriminating readers for over 50 years. For a look at currently available books and details on how to join, just visit us at the address above.

**"Readers will remember Trana Mae Simmons's historical romances long after the last page has been read."**
—Michalann Perry

# CAPTIVE LOVE

"Who is he? This man you're looking for and determined to marry."

"I won't tell you his name yet. You don't know my father. He's a very bitter, angry man. Even though my mother's dead, he's using Toby to get his revenge on her. Father's insane about the matter."

"Insane enough to have you arrested for kidnapping Toby?" Cody asked in a calmer voice as he studied her ravaged face.

"Kidnapping? Toby's my brother! My God, I could go to jail and then my father could do whatever he wanted with Toby! I have to get him away from here!"

Cody grabbed Shanna as she ran past him, capturing her hands when she struggled in his hold.

"Please, Shanna," Cody mumbled. "I'll let you go if you promise not to run. You've got my word. I'll do whatever it takes to see that you don't lose Toby!"

Other books by Trana Mae Simmons:
**MONTANA SURRENDER**